The

DON ROBERTSON

Three
Days

Prentice-Hall, Inc. ♣ Englewood Cliffs, New Jersey

92024

For the late James R. Trast

In September 1914 a relic hunter found human bones that had been overturned by a plowman. Later this same man unearthed the remains of three Union soldiers, easily identified by buttons and fragments of their uniforms. In one of the shoes were found two well-preserved five dollar gold pieces. The bodies were later buried in the National Cemetery.

LEROY E. SMITH, *Illustrated Gettysburg Battlefield Map and Story*

1

THE DUST-WHITE SUMMER

♣ That summer was a fine dry summer. The sun rolled from Heaven's lap and bounced down across the chinks and valleys and round warm places of the Commonwealth of Pennsylvania. There is a haze in the morning, a fine thin haze. Coolness and dampness rise from the land. The sun is thin in the east, seen through this delicate haze. And that June there was a special quality of youth and promise and optimism. Things were coming from the land; the land was fat and rested and fecund. You looked out across the fields toward the great gray mountains and everywhere you saw the freshness; you smelled it; its aliveness rose at you as part of the air. ♣

THE MORNING of the day two days before the day he died Lt Alf J. Castetter of the 9th New York Cavalry awoke greatly desirous of a drink of whisky. Lately Lt Castetter had been drinking a great deal of whisky. When he could get it. Lately Lt Castetter had been fed up.

He was a stocky man, squat, with no fat. He was thirty years old. Now he lay in his tent and he struggled to come awake and dimly he heard movements of horses, men clearing their throats and hawking thickly. He was chilled. He did not want to open his eyes. His mouth tasted like dirty old fuzz. He wanted whisky, good whisky, to clean it out. He opened his eyes, sat up and hugged his knees.

There was a movement outside his tent and then someone pulled open the flap.

"Well, glory glory," Lt Maxwell R. Gwinn said, grinning down at Castetter, "Lazarus has arisen. Here we was about to bury you for dead."

Castetter gave Gwinn a sour look. "I bet you've been standing there six hours waiting to say that, you goddam Baptist."

Gwinn laughed loudly. He was a great one for laughing, old Gwinn was. Before the war he had represented a rural district in the state legislature in Albany.

He was always the hail fellow, the good sport. He was thin and wiry and ascetic and he didn't drink and he made Castetter sick.

Castetter stood up and pushed open the tentflap and went outside. He blinked in the sunlight. "Ohhh," he said. He yawned and stretched and scratched himself. Coins jingled in his pocket. Coins. He frowned at Gwinn. "Did I just hear money?"

Gwinn laughed again. It was enough to wake up the goddam dead. "Don't you remember?"

Castetter reached into the pocket and felt the coins cool against his fingers. He took them from the pocket and stared down at his hand: two fivedollar goldpieces. "Now where the hell . . ."

"You really don't remember?"

"Sure," Castetter said. "Sure I remember. A beautiful girl with long blond hair came into this camp and walked up to me and said: 'Lt Castetter, I'll give you ten dollars if you let me keep my feet warm with you tonight in your tent.'"

Another blast of Gwinn's politician's laugh. "Ah, you! You're a comedian you are!"

Castetter rubbed his tongue across the roof of his fuzzy mouth. And he tried to concentrate, tried to remember what had happened last night: did it have something to do with Lightfoot Masterson? He couldn't remember. Finally he said to Gwinn: "I was drunk. That's all I know. I was drunk. What happened?"

"You got them off old Lightfoot Masterson."

"Masterson? I got them off Masterson? How?"

Gwinn grinned. His teeth gleamed behind his mustache. "You bet him ten dollars you could recite some poem. Something by somebody I think the name was Gray. And you sure did recite that poem, Alf—you handed him the book and he followed your words in the book and a bunch of other fellers were looking over his shoulder and reading along with him and you stood up and your voice went way up loud and you recited something about the death of Richard Somebody."

"*Sonnet on the Death of Richard West?* The one that goes *In vain to me the smiling mornings shine,/ And redd'ning Phoebus lifts his golden fire:/ The birds in vain their amorous descant—*"

"Yep. That one. Anyway, you went through it all without making no mistakes and he paid you and then he went off somewhere. He sure was mad about losing that ten dollars, I'll tell you—"

Castetter wheeled and went back inside his tent. He felt inside his knapsack. The book still was there.

He sighed and rejoined Gwinn. "So where did Masterson go?"

Gwinn shrugged. "Probably back to his own outfit. I don't know."

"How drunk was he?"

"Pretty drunk."

"He doesn't know what he's doing when he's drunk."

"That's no business of mine. All I know is he staggered out of here. He was cussing like the devil, tripping and falling and getting up and all the time cussing. He sure was mad at you."

"Oh God," Castetter said. "Which way did he go? Off toward the creek?"

"Yep. I don't see what you're getting so . . ."

Gwinn's voice trailed away. Castetter was striding quickly toward the lip of the gully that led down to the creek. He wished he had a cup of coffee to clean the brown taste from his mouth. His eyes were clouded with sleepiness and fear and worry. Damn Masterson anyway. Didn't he know enough to pass out in camp where he'd be safe?

(Enos Masterson was a captain. He commanded a quartermaster unit bivouacked just down the creek. He had been one of Castetter's instructors back at Harvard in '50 and '51. Masterson was a fat man, bald, about fifty. He had absolutely no military qualifications, and he knew it and Castetter knew it and just about everyone else knew it. He had commanded a company of Massachusetts infantry, German immigrants mostly, at Chancellorsville. The outfit's previous captain had been shot dead while leading a charge. That day at Chancellorsville Masterson was the first man in the company to retreat. He had seen a man get sliced in half by a cannonball. He had screamed, turned, run, even had vomited. His men followed his example. They panicked and scrambled to the rear. Masterson was relieved of his command and put in charge of this quartermaster unit. Gen O. O. Howard, the corps commander, had not pressed charges against Masterson. He simply had put him out of the way, since it was easier and took less time to transfer a man than to courtmartial him. So now Masterson was Lightfoot Masterson. He held the highest rank of any physical coward in the corps. His fat flesh hung from him in great flapping folds, and he drank a lot and he recited much poetry. Three nights ago he had been reunited with Castetter, his old pupil. They had been drunk most of the time since then— Masterson because of his remarkable cowardice that day at Chancellorsville, Castetter because he simply was tired and fed up.)

Castetter thrashed down the side of a ravine. High weeds

slapped at his thighs. Once he stumbled and fell, scraping his hands. He struggled to his feet and continued. His steps crackled through the underbrush. He passed by the company sink. The hot thick smell of it rose at him and he made a face.

Then he was at the edge of the creek. Masterson's outfit was bivouacked about a mile upstream. The creek rushed, gurgled, made private little sounds.

"Masterson!" Castetter called. "Enos Masterson!"

He headed upstream. He supposed maybe Masterson had made it back all right. He went about a quarter of a mile and then he saw Masterson, lying face down at the edge of the water. Masterson looked like a man in the act of getting a drink of water. Castetter ran to him. Masterson's head was submerged beneath about six inches of water. Castetter dragged the corpse back from the water, then rolled it over on its back. Masterson's fat face was beatific. His beard dripped on the front of his shirt. Castetter stared at him for a long time and finally spat. O you goddam fool, he told the corpse. You goddam stupid fat frightened fool. Didn't you know where you'd be safe and not go stumbling into a creek? Where was all your academic wisdom?

Presently Castetter went looking for a detail of men to remove the body.

♣   This was the month of June in the year 1863. This was the month of the invasion plan, the month the North would feel the war. It was a simple plan, but it had many goals. It involved the Army of Northern Virginia under Gen Robert E. Lee. The goals—to push into the North and split its defenses, to capture perhaps Philadelphia and even Washington, to pound into the enemy's awareness the knowledge that nothing ever would defeat the South. So a great movement began, north from Virginia, north and east across Maryland and into the warm green hills of the Commonwealth of Pennsylvania. Gen Lee rode with his men and they cheered him. They moved quickly, these thin wiry men; they knew how to move quickly, and they had to. They sought to enter Pennsylvania ahead of the enemy, to smash through the heart of the Commonwealth before the enemy's Army of the Potomac could arrive to do battle. This plan had been devised by President Davis and his aides in Richmond. The war for them, despite the victories at Bull Run, the victory at Fredericksburg, the victory at Chancellorsville, had been defensive, and President Davis and Gen Lee were both aware that defense never won wars. After two years of fighting the Army of the Potomac back and forth across Virginia, the president and the general were both aware of the necessity for a forward movement. Virginia was tired and scarred; the time had come to scar the enemy's lands, to burn his barns and seize his crops and livestock, to slash and hack him the way Virginia had been slashed and hacked. (To the South the war had been a presence; to the North it had been something somewhere else.) Meanwhile, Gen Joseph Hooker, commander of the Union Army of the Potomac, was not sure what Lee was up to. Lee's cavalry under Gen J. E. B. Stuart ranged far ahead of the main body, which marched through Hagerstown Maryland into Pennsylvania, through Carlisle and York and a little town called Gettysburg. Only scattered militia units were in the path of this great force. The Army of the Potomac was to the south near Washington. Units were scattered across parts of Maryland and Virginia. Lee's enormous army moved forward, rolling back small defensive forces, mostly inexperienced militiamen in natty uniforms who turned and ran at the first sight of the rebels. Not that anyone blamed these militiamen. They could not hope to stop the invaders. The only available force for this task was the Army of the Potomac—but the Army of the Potomac was spread flabbily around Washington, which President Lincoln and the chief of staff, Gen Henry W. (Old Brains) Halleck, had insisted be given priority in any defense plans. The governor of Pennsylvania issued a call for volunteers. They were chewed up by Stuart's cavalry. This was June in the Commonwealth of Pennsylvania, a time of green growing things, and Stuart's browned wiry yipping men rode howling through the dust and warmth of summer, and citizens crept into the basements of their homes and put out all the lamps and stared at each other and trembled, and the Army of the Potomac lay spread flabbily around Washington as a force of seventy thousand Confederate troops (the Army of Northern Virginia, which had never lost) marched across the Pennsylvania line. Smartly. Quickly. With high optimism. ♣

THESE MEN of the Army of Northern Virginia marched along a road that coughed up dust, thick dust, rising from beneath their feet in steady endless swirls.

Cum gum cumgum cumgum cum gum cum gum: thousands of feet.

Glok glok glok glok went the horses, slowly, and with their sounds came more dust. Horses. Horses and mules. Wagons. Cannon. Dust. There were no clouds. The sun was orange.

Pvt Rufus Patterson coughed. He worked some saliva around his mouth. He tried not to think of how tired he was. He did not want to be tired. He wanted to be strong. In a war you have to be strong. You have to go along with the others, to do what they do. You don't want them to carry you. No proud man wants that.

He coughed again. Goddam dust.

Pete Bell marched next to him. "Feather in your throat?" Pete said.

"Dust," Rufus said.

"Work a lot of spit in your throat. Make it wet. Dust'll go away."

Rufus did this. The dust went away.

"It ain't nothin catchin, is it?" Pete wanted to know. He was a thin middle-aged man with bad teeth. He and Rufus were from the same town. They had joined up the same day.

"I expect it's the clap," Rufus said.

"In the throat?" Pete said, grinning.

"Got it from a girl in a dream last night."

"Was she worth it?"

"I like to die she was worth it. Inside out. Sideways. Upside down. There wasn't a thing she didn't know."

"That's how come you got it in the throat?" said Pete, going hee hee hee with quiet high thin amusement.

Rufus smiled but didn't say anything. Feet scruffled through the dust and there was little talk. You saved your wind. You didn't waste it in a lot of talk. That was one of the first things they told you. That was one of the first things you'd have learned even if they hadn't told you. You just didn't waste your breath in a lot of talk.

There is a difference . . . a difference between what you think you will do and what you actually do do. When you thought of marching you thought of parades; you didn't think of *this*. When you thought of killing you never thought of no mess.

Huh.

Mess. An all the noise. An the way a man holds his breath without knowin it, holds his breath until his face gets red, until finally, *whuuuhhh*, it all bursts from him without him knowin it, without him realizin that he was about to bust.

You hold your breath like that when you're firin at someone or someone is firin at you or you think maybe you're goin to die.

Rufus did not want to die. He marched heavily, his feet and all the other feet scruffling through the dust, and he shook his head to clear it of thoughts of death, of all the flashing vivid memories of the deaths he had seen. Pete Bell was humming next to him.

Rufus could not make out the tune. He never had been able to make out the tunes that Pete hummed. Good old feller, that Pete. Good old feller. Closest friend Rufus had. Quiet old feller, never was mean to nobody, yet old Pete never took no bad time neither. The man was a soldier, did like he was told, but he took no bad time.

Rufus was nineteen, and old Pete more than once had helped him, shown him what to do. And old Pete more than once had made it so Rufus hadn't turned and run.

It's a good thing for me I got him, Rufus told himself fervently. Lot of times I like to run an hide. Ain't nothin wrong with that neither. A lot of men they like to run an hide; I know it. But they ain't got Pete Bell. Me, I got Pete Bell. I don't run an hide.

It had been two years now . . . two years of marching back and forth across the Commonwealth of Virginia. Now the army was someplace in Maryland. It was going someplace different. Pennsylvania, the men said. Yankee country. Goddammit, that was good. Yessir, take the war to Mr Yank an see how he likes it.

Sunlight shimmered off the hillsides. Rufus' pack dug at his shoulders. His feet were hot and they itched. Dust entered his nostrils and he sneezed.

"Same to you an many more," Pete Bell said.

Rufus used a thumb to dig the dust from his nostrils. His knees and calves ached.

"What ails you, boy?" a voice shouted.

Rufus paid no attention to the voice.

"You there Patterson!" the voice shouted again. "I'm talkin to you!"

"Nothin wrong!" Rufus shouted.

The voice belonged to Cpl Mabry. Rufus didn't like Cpl Mabry. No one did. The word for him was sonofabitch.

Cpl Mabry was a very large man. He had been marching alongside the platoon, a little to the rear of Rufus. Now he fell into step with Rufus. He was grinning. "Somethin wrong?" he said. "You been coughin an snortin an carryin on somethin awful."

"I'm all right," Rufus said. He did not look at Cpl Mabry.

Mabry slapped Rufus on the back, making him wince. "You a good man, Patterson, for a Virginian. A little bit weak like all them Virginians, but what the hell, you done come through a lot ain't you? You been in the army two year an you ain't dead yet."

"Leave the boy be," Pete Bell said quietly. He didn't look at Mabry either.

Mabry laughed. "I ain't doin nothin," he said, slapping Rufus on the back again. "I'm just tellin this boy he a good soldier." He paused, snuffling. "Yessir, this boy here, this Patterson, he a pretty good boy for a Virginian."

Still laughing, Mabry moved away. With every movement he made clanking sounds. Everybody knew why, too. His pack was full of watches and coins and gold teeth and pictureframes and other things of value that had been taken from dead men. Mabry had looted corpses ever since the beginning of the war.

Mabry was a South Carolinian. The men in his platoon were Virginians. He was stronger than any of them. Pete Bell was the only man in the platoon who stood up to him. No one knew how Pete got away with it. Perhaps, they thought, because he did stand up to the corporal. No one else had the nerve, not Rufus, not anybody.

Mabry wasn't only the strongest man in the platoon; he was the largest. He had arms and legs like sides of beef. Last winter there had been a brigade wrestling tournament. Mabry won it. In the last match he came up against a bearded private named Slocum. This Slocum must have weighed at least three hundred pounds. Mabry broke several of Slocum's ribs. When they carried Slocum away he was screaming.

Mabry liked to amuse himself with the younger ones. Rufus was one of the youngest. Several times Mabry had slapped and punched Rufus just for the amusement. Several of the men had suggested to Rufus that he go to the captain. He didn't. He didn't do anything. He didn't try to protect himself; he didn't do anything. He didn't want to do anything. He didn't even want to think about it. He was afraid of Mabry; he was more afraid of Mabry than any Yank. A lot more. The man grinned at you; he just dared you to do anything. He called you Virginia trash and just dared you to do anything.

No one did anything, not Rufus, not anyone. Pete Bell stood up to Mabry, but not even he did anything. The standing up to Mabry was as far as it went.

(Even though he hadn't wanted to think about it, even though he'd wanted to push it away, Rufus hadn't been able to, not entirely. Here I am, he had told himself, out here an them Yanks they want to kill me an sure they scare me, sure they do, an yet the thing is . . . Mabry: I'm more scared of him an he ain't even goin to kill me. He just grins most of the time an maybe once-inawhile he pushes someone around a little bit, but he ain't goin to kill nobody the way the Yanks is tryin. So why am I more scared of him?)

So now, as Mabry moved away clanking, Rufus was ashamed of himself again. He had faith in pride, or at least he always had thought he had. But now there was no pride. He was just plain relieved that Mabry had moved away.

He did not look at Bell. They marched. They did not speak. They saved their wind.

Rufus was tall, with a thin face and high cheekbones, a face that was almost girlish. His eyes were a thin blue and they were set far apart. They were wide and they gave his face a quality of innocent astonishment. It was the kind of face girls liked.

And Rufus liked girls, too.

He decided to think of girls.

Yes, girls. He liked girls a whole lot.

Forget Mabry.

Think of somethin nice.

Forget sonofabitchin Mabry.

Rufus was from Suffolk Virginia and he had worked as a clerk in his father's drygoods store and he was a virgin. In deed, if not in mind or design, he never had had a girl. Not that he hadn't wanted to. Ohh he had wanted to for a long time. Even now, with this here war going on, with all the talk and everything about all the whores and other kinds of girls that soldiers were supposed to be able to shake out of every tree, Rufus hadn't had a one. Not a one. But of course he'd never admitted this to anyone. Especially now that he was a soldier. Why, who ever heard of a soldier who'd never done it? Huh. Real funny all right. Oh if they knew, if the fellers he soldiered with knew, he'd never have a minute's rest. They'd call him the Virginia Virgin, that's what, and oh they'd just rag him to death. So Rufus talked about the clap as though he knew what it was.

Cum cum gum gum gum went all those feet. The column of troops extended down the road as far as you could see. Over it hung this canopy of dust.

Huh. Me gettin the clap. That'd be somethin. Me: old Rufus Patterson, Pvt Rufus Patterson to you. How you supposed to get the clap when you ain't never had the thing that's supposed to give you the clap?

Oh if they knew, if these fellers knew, my life wouldn't be my own. No sir, you bet you not.

(Rufus' primary interest in life for the last four or five years or so had been girls, but so far nothing had come of it. Even now, with this here war going on, with all the fighting and killing he had seen, he never for long stopped thinking of girls. Every night he talked with Pete Bell about girls, and Pete kept telling him: *You wait till you get home. You'll find plenty of gals. Just don't let them work at your mind while you're out here, that's all.* All right. Wait. You're supposed to wait. I can wait I guess. I ain't gonna get killed, no sir. If I was going to get killed I'd of been killed a long time ago. I'd of been killed at Chancellorsville or Fredericksburg. I'd of been killed a dozen times. My luck's been real good. I got old Pete with me an he knows what to do an how to stay out of trouble. All I got to do is stay with him an I'll be all right. Stay with him. Stay with old Pete.)

Cum gum cum gum rose around him as a background, heard and yet not heard because that was the way Rufus was. Now, on these long marches, when you were silent most of the time, he seldom really heard anything. He was too busy within himself, too lost thinking.

We goin north.

Where north? Pennsylvania?

That's what the boys say.

That mean we gonna cut right up through old Abe's territory?

What about the Yanks?

Where're all the Yanks?

Oh you sure can ask yourself a lot of questions and the answers they aren't there. So you march. It won't be long now, you know that. You'll find the Yanks in a few days. Then General Heth or somebody'll come riding up to you and the other men and wave his sword and yell at you to go out today and heap glory on the name of Virginia and the Confederacy.

Your army always was heaping glory on the name of Virginia and the Confederacy.

It didn't know no better.

So you marched, and you thought of all these things; you kept trying to find the whys, but there were no answers (no answers anyway for a feller who wanted to go home and do something about getting himself a girl), and so you marched.

One foot.

Tuther foot.

One.

Tuther.

Cum gum cum gum.

And always the voices, drifting to you from within that background that was heard and yet not heard. Voices, quiet voices ribald and soft, rising over the long snaking column of marching men, voices drifting, voices fading and then rising, fading:

"We gonna give ol Abe . . ."

"Shut up."

"Shut up yoself, prick."

"Prick's best part of a man."

"An you might as well hang it up in the smokehouse till this here war's over, sonny . . ."

One foot.

Tuther foot.

Forward beneath the dust.

(And Rufus, in hot embarrassed bewilderment, saw Elizabeth Strawn come flashing across his mind's eye. He didn't want to think about her. He tried not to. But there she was, and now there was no dust, no sun, no drifting voices, and he was back home and he was talking with Elizabeth and they were at a dance in the armory (the regular Saturday night dance, with all proceeds going to Confederate widows and orphans) and Elizabeth was laughing, laughing steadily under her breath, and her mouth was pursed and her eyes were crinkly at the corners and she was laughing at him he guessed, but he didn't care; all he wanted was to dance with her. He was real clumsy, but he didn't care. *Uh, dance?* he asked her. *Certainly, gracious SIR,* she said, and then she was in his arms and she was light and graceful and he was about as light and graceful as a plowhorse and he was half with the music and half not and he was all in a sweat and she was the prettiest girl he'd ever known and she wouldn't stop laughing in that silent shaking pursed crinkly way. And she was laughing at him too. He knew it. But he was in love with her. Let her laugh if she wanted to. He was in love with her. He'd been in love with her forever. Her family lived just across the street from his. Her father was an engineer on the Virginia & Atlantic, a thin quiet little man who liked to sit on his porch of an evening and smoke his pipe and swat idly at mosquitoes and lightning bugs. Elizabeth's mother was a fat old biddy whose only interest was Elizabeth. She kept an eye on Elizabeth real close, as though Elizabeth would break if a man was to get within ten feet of her. And here it was that Rufus, old Rufus Patterson who lived across the street and followed Elizabeth around like a damn old dog, was in love with her. Some day (maybe after the fighting was over and he had come home a hero and girls were everyplace, just for him to snap his fingers at), some day he would tell Elizabeth he loved her. Some day, yep. All the days in the world from now. She probably doesn't even know I'm alive. Her and that Ben Ferrell. Now *there's* a hero for you. A lieutenant with old J. E. B. Stuart an he's captured a Yankee colonel already an he's just about the town's biggest hero an there's talk that maybe she'll marry him. *Hero. Huh!* There sure are a lot of chances to be a hero in *this* outfit. Do all your fightin on foot an spend most of your time either runnin forward or runnin back or layin behind some damn old log an firin shots and usually not even seein what you're firin them shots *at.* Big chance to be a hero, I tell you.)

Now he had forgotten sonofabitchin Mabry.

The sun smacked down on the marching men. There was not much talk. The men were saving their wind.

Then . . . thinly, away up forward . . . the sound of a cheer.

Rufus squinted, looked forward. The sound came from around a bend in the road.

A man behind Rufus asked no one in particular what all the commotion was about.

Rufus glanced at Pete. Pete was grinning.

"What's goin on?" Rufus wanted to know. "We win the war?"

Pete grinned but didn't say anything.

The cheer became louder, closer. Now some of the men up ahead were waving their caps. He could see them now. They had come around the bend. The road had straightened.

The cheer came back through the ranks toward him.

"Ought to be somewhere around here," Pete said.

"What?" Rufus asked him.

"The marker."

"Marker?"

Up ahead was a great valley, green and warm.

The cheer was very loud. Men directly in front of Rufus were yelling and pointing at the side of the road.

"There it is!" Pete hollered, pointing at the side of the road.

Now Rufus saw the marker. All around him was the sound of cheering. The marker was gray, the size of a small tombstone. Men were waving their caps. Someone fired a shot in the air.

He stared at Pete and then slowly he permitted a grin to pull itself across his face. He gave a great whoop.

Rank after rank of them, yelling, waving their caps, these men of the Army of Northern Virginia marched across the Mason-Dixon Line. Now they were in Pennsylvania. They yelled until they were hoarse. Now they were in Pennsylvania. Now, for the first time, they were in Yankee territory. They yelled and yelled. Rank after rank of them, marching heavily, yelling, moving down the long road into the valley so green and so warm, these men of the Army of Northern Virginia entered the Commonwealth of Pennsylvania. One man even did a little quickstep.

♣ The dispatches came back to President Davis in Richmond, and they were good, but he did not smile. His flunkies and sycophants smiled, but President Davis did not. And he knew Gen Lee was not smiling either. You saved smiles for victory. The invasion of the North was an accomplishment, but it was not victory. Besides, few things in this life, no matter what they were, made Jeff Davis smile. He left smiling to people who didn't have his responsibilities. The flunkies, the sycophants, people like that. He considered the political implications of this campaign. He knew his army was outnumbered and needed equipment. But now he could not help but be aroused with hope. Here was a stroke at once so daring and intelligent it must succeed. Hooker (and his superior, that pussyfooting old fool, Brains Halleck) were no match for Robert E. Lee, most men believed. Why, you can go on and take all of them . . . McClellan, Pope, Burnside, Hooker (and Brains Halleck, too, back in Washington hiding behind Abe Lincoln's skirts) . . . why, a hundred of them would be no match for Robert E. Lee. Now the North would relent, now—because of one great speeding crashing instant of movement—it would sue for peace, or at least receive a blow from which it would not recover. And furthermore, the man in Richmond reasoned, the campaign would aid in bringing assistance from Great Britain. The English had been sitting on their neutrality during the conflict, and the tendency there had been to view it as a kind of formalized insurrection. Now, if the plan to carry the war to the North were a success, the English would know the South had a superior fighting force and could be counted on to survive.

Thus, by showing the world a victorious campaign of aggression, the Confederacy would receive aid from abroad. The North's material advantage would be erased. So the Army of Northern Virginia, those thin gray wiry yipping men, moved north. There were seventy thousand of them that June of 1863. Within just a little more than six months they had soundly whipped the Yankees twice, first at Fredericksburg when the Union troops came storming up to the stone wall at Marye's Heights and were cut down like so much wheat under a great reaper (their commander, Gen Burnside, nearly annihilated his army in this great bloody failure), and then at Chancellorsville, where the new Union commander, Gen Hooker, was holding his own but thought he had lost and therefore retreated from a field he might have won had he not been clutched by indecisiveness and confusion. This same Gen Hooker (they called him Fighting Joe; his record had been good in the days when he was a corps commander and not charged with the responsibility of directing an entire army) still was in command of the Army of the Potomac here in late June of 1863. His men liked him. Chancellorsville had not erased much of their admiration for him. He was detested by many of the generals who were his subordinates (they considered him a rakehell, a scoundrel and a drunkard who had used political influence in assuming command after Burnside's crashing failure at Fredericksburg— and there was a great deal of truth in this), but still had the respect of his men—the footsoldiers, the great inarticulate mass of men who quite obviously held the destinies of ALL the generals. But Robert E. Lee, who fought the entire war predicating his strategy on the soft spots of the generals who opposed him, sensed Hooker's weakness and indecision. This did not bode well for Fighting Joe Hooker. The disaster at Chancellorsville had made him doubtful about a fight, as doubtful about a fight as about Joe Hooker. It took no great intelligence to see what the Confederates were up to, that they were invading the North in considerable force, and Joe Hooker probably wished he was anything in this world except commander of the Army of the Potomac, which would have to go out and contest the issue with Lee. But Hooker, confused as he was, went ahead, going through the motions anyway. His cavalry kept an eye on Lee's movements and reported that the main body of the Confederates was marching through Hagerstown Maryland north across the Pennsylvania line. Other reports told of J. E. B. Stuart's cavalry, which was ranging to the east and north—almost as far north as Harrisburg, the Pennsylvania capital. Now most of Hooker's troops were still in Virginia, far south of the Confederate invaders. Hooker gave this some thought, then wired to Washington for permission to attack Richmond, the Confederate capital, since that city was unprotected during the Southerners' march on Pennsylvania. But old Brains Halleck, acting with President Lincoln's approval, refused permission. Halleck ordered Hooker to stay with the Confederates and thereby protect Washington. Halleck and Lincoln were convinced that Washington must be protected no matter what. And so Joe Hooker, tired and bitter, moved his army from its camp in Falmouth Virginia. It marched parallel with the Army of Northern Virginia, about fifty miles or so to the east, on the other side of a narrow range of mountains. It was a forced march, north now, north to find the enemy and engage him. The Union troops were told to hurry, boys, hurry; the rebs are ahead of us. Meanwhile, Lee's men marched into Pennsylvania, turned east and tramped in the general direction of Harrisburg. Stuart's cavalry was out ahead someplace, roaming the country and chewing up the small units of natty militia. The roads were open and the weather was fine. ♣

PVT WHITFIELD JOHNSON did not mind that other men called him Wheatfield. He was an Illinois boy and proud of it.

His eyes were narrow and dark. Now, as he sat on old Gingerbread and looked out across the Pennsylvania hills, those eyes
were squinted in concentration. Beyond those hills there rose a
big cloud of something that looked an awful lot like dust.

Gingerbread neighed softly, sneezed, and chomped on some
grass.

Dust.

A marching army makes dust.

There ain't no *Union* army over there.

Well now Wheatfield, you know what *that* means.

He rode forward, gently jabbing his spurs into the horse's flanks.
Gingerbread broke into a gallop. Wheatfield rode easily. They
went down the side of a hill to a dirt road, turned west on the
road. The huge column of dust was off to the west.

This was what they called the Cashtown Pike. Cashtown was
to the west and a place called Gettysburg was to the east, near
where Wheatfield's outfit was bivouacked.

Gingerbread's hooves sent up great swirls of dust. Wheatfield
kept peering to the west.

You ain't supposed to do this when you're on picket, but I
reckon maybe Lt Castetter would be pleased to know that Robert
E. Lee's coming right at us.

Hah. I reckon he *would.*

(Gingerbread was a good old horse. Really moved. He was a
brown gelding, with only one spot of white on him anyplace—a
streak on his nose. The streak was shaped like a J. And now, with
just a little pressure from your spurs, he really moved. It sure was
warm. Nicelooking country too after spending more than a year
in Virginia. When this war ends, Wheatfield told himself, I ain't
ever gonna go no farther south than St Louis. I ain't fooling. Falmouth Virginia, the camp there where the army had wintered, and
had spent the spring too, Jesus that had been a cold place. The

ground always was damp, and the wind came up off that river cold enough like to freeze your ass off. Men were getting pneumonia and dying; a lot of dysentery was going around; more and more deserters were taking off every day, and every day too the Provost Guard came galloping in with prisoners (not rebs mind you, but Union men who had run away) and now and then one of the deserters was shot as an example to anyone else who had any ideas. Just went to show you. This war was changing, and a man was pretty thick if he didn't see the change. Back in '61, when the drums was drumming and the bands was playing and all the girls ran out in the street and kissed you and threw flowers in your path, why, in those days the war was almost like a church supper or something. Hell, remember when you was a boy and you saw pictures in books and in them pictures the troops always was lined up all nice and even and everything, and they went forward with their lines dressed, all in perfect order, and no man was afraid, and men died, yes, but they always was brave and their wounds was clean? But this now was 1863, and Wheatfield's army had lost more times than it had won, many more times, and nobody marched in perfect order, and you always was dirty, and your camp likely as not was cold as hell and smelled like an old outhouse, and when there was a battle you saw men sliced in half or beheaded, with legs and arms and feet and hands and other things shot off, and you didn't remember seeing Falmouth Virginia or Fredericksburg or Chancellorsville, or the things that happened there, in them old pictures. It had been a long time since any old girl had thrown flowers in your path. A long time since any old girl had kissed you.)

Wheatfield ran these things through his mind now, as he sat astride Gingerbread galloping toward that pillar of dust. And Wheatfield was smart enough to know there wasn't anything you could do to change them.

Girls throwing flowers in your path.

Things sure do change.

So now maybe Wheatfield had grown up. Now he did his job, but he did it because he wanted his army to win. He figured it this way: if you do your job and your army wins, the war will end and you can go home. With all of you still all there.

His horse galloped forward, and Wheatfield kept watching the pillar of dust, which was getting larger now.

Now Wheatfield considered himself a pretty hard feller. (At nineteen, a hard man who knew certain rules and would conduct himself according to those rules.)

Nineteen goddam years of age. (Cuss: Jesus Christ, every other word is a cussword. Back home his daddy would have whipped him good if he'd ever heard Wheatfield use all them dirty words. But in the army everybody, or almost everybody, cussed. Even generals and preachers. At Fredericksburg Wheatfield had heard a chaplain cuss like a crazy man. The chaplain was a great big feller. He had a black beard and deep eyes and looked like Jesus Christ, only bigger. He was standing at the top of a little ridge. He was watching the boys charge up toward Marye's Heights and the stone wall. And the rebs was mowing them down, fast as the brigades got there, fast as Burnside sent them up there to get chopped into slivers. And finally that chaplain began talking to himself. God, he kept saying. God. *That god damn nogood Burnside. God.*)

A chaplain cussing like that. Well, so now you know things that are different.

Wheatfield's life had expanded all right, expanded away from southern Illinois and his father's farm and the hot stifling summers, and his girl, Jane, plump Jane, the girl he had courted before the war.

No, Whit.

No, now you stop that.
Whit!
Hear me?
Now you STOP that!
Ohhh . . .
Whit . . .

Whitfield and Jane would wrestle; he would feel her and kiss her; she was always giggling and saying no now, no Whit, now you stop that Whit, and all, and by God when he got home he was going to take that old Jane and—

Yes sir. You bet you.

Things sure is different. This war's taught me a lot, a whole lot. (Back home people always were saying how Whit Johnson was a boy who always had his wits about him. Quiet. Steady. Dependable. Firm as a rock. Smart too, but not one to be going around showing it off. Maybe he'll never set the world on fire, people said, but he'll get by all right—and better than a lot of people who are noisier about their lives . . .)

The pillar of dust was larger now. Gingerbread was really moving. The road wound up into some hills. Wheatfield guided Gingerbread off into a clump of woods. He pulled up on the reins. Gingerbread moved forward cautiously. Steady, feller. Nice and quiet now. Underbrush crackled. Wheatfield patted his horse's neck.

Shhh now. Quiet.

Then, suddenly, horse and rider were out of the woods and in a clear place, a rounded knob of ground—pasture or something, he guessed—that overlooked a little valley.

And down in that valley, sure as hell, was old Johnny Reb.

Five thousand, at least. Maybe closer to ten.

It was a huge column, moving east along the Cashtown Pike, moving east toward Wheatfield's cavalry outfit, which was bivouacked just this side of that little town, Gettysburg. A hell of a lot of Johnny Rebs, kicking up all that dust, moving like they didn't much care who saw them.

An enormous wagon train rolled behind the troops. Dimly Wheatfield heard the sounds of the march, condensed into a low rumble, faint and fuzzy, as though he were hearing them through a wall of wool.

Well, Lt Castetter like as not would want to know.

He dismounted and scrambled to the edge of the knob.

Let's see: maybe eight thousand?

Yep. Eight thousand. That's a good guess.

He turned and ran back toward his horse.

"Whoa, Yank," someone said.

Wheatfield stopped and looked around.

Three Confederate soldiers came from behind some trees. They walked slowly toward Wheatfield. One of the men—he was tall and wore corporal's stripes—was laughing softly. "We kinda got you with your horse down didn't we?" he said.

Wheatfield put his hands in the air.

The corporal whooped and slapped his thigh.

They took Wheatfield to the rear. The corporal rode Gingerbread. "This is a good old horse," he told Wheatfield. "Yep, sure is a good old horse." He kept sniggering.

♣ This was a time of great movements. It also was a time of great confusions. Little bits and pieces of trouble nicked at the Army of Northern Virginia. Chips began to fly off its plan. There were hesitations, errors. Nobody knew exactly what would happen next. In all previous battles the Confederates had functioned primarily as a defensive force, acting on the enemy's movements AFTER he had committed himself. But now these Confederates were the aggressors; they took more risks (aggressors always do), and their plan was therefore open to delays and flaws. The first flaw, it turned out, was the splendid raiding cavalry of Gen J. E. B. Stuart. And of course the use of this cavalry was supposed to be one of Lee's strongest advantages. These men, these raiders, this quick mobile force, were the eyes—the scouts, the intelligence—of the Army of Northern Virginia. But the trouble was: they were ranging too far, riding too hard. Now, as June ended, they were too far ahead of the main body of the invaders. They were somewhere near Harrisburg, galloping through small towns, routing the scattered bands of militia. They were most of the time at least fifty miles east of the infantry, too far away for effective contact, too far away certainly to be used as the eyes of the Army of Northern Virginia. Stuart's expedition had, in point of fact, made the body of the Confederate force sightless. So, because it was forced to grope, the Army of Northern Virginia was slowed. It marched and it countermarched, roughly east now toward Harrisburg, but slowly . . . very slowly. And so, as this warm yellow June ended, Joe Hooker's Union army was beginning to catch up. It had its cavalry; it therefore had its eyes—it knew the location and disposition of its enemy. Its movements were decisive. One of the features of the Southern plan—SURPRISE —had been erased. Hooker—the man who failed at Chancellorsville and would live in raw bitterness with that failure all his days—put his army of the Potomac on the move in smart order. His corps poured into Maryland, faced north and west toward the enemy. Hurry, boys; hurry, the officers urged. The men responded. Joe Hooker—rake, military politician, schemer —still was able to make them respond. They moved smartly. The Confederates were groping now, but Joe Hooker's men were moving smartly. Two armies, clogging the roads with enormous eruptions of dust. Into Maryland now, and Pennsylvania, through all that lushness, into a countryside ripe and firm and green.   ♣

THE MORNING of the day one day before the day he died
Lt Alf J. Castetter lay in his tent sick from whisky. There was no
light yet. It must have been about four or so.

He kept thinking about what had happened to Masterson. Poor
old Lightfoot.

It's all a grotesque joke: that's what it is.

The whole corps was talking about it. The medical officer had
listed the cause as a heart seizure. But the men in the corps knew
better. An enlisted man always does. He knows his officers. He
knows the ones who drink: he knows the ones who are pious;
he knows the ones who are cowards, the ones who are bitter, the
ones who are tired, the ones who are discouraged, even the ones
who are completely fed up. An enlisted man may be the world's
most stupid unwashed illiterate, but he knows—by instinct—those
officers who are worth a damn and those who are not. You can't
fool an enlisted man.

(Yesterday, after finding Masterson, Castetter had heard the
talk. *That's the man who ran so fast at Chancellorsville, ain't it?
Didn't folks call him Lightfoot?* The men, standing around, talking and spitting. *Yep. That's the one.* Coffee hissing in a can. *Poor
feller. I guess he kinda got drunk to forget.* Men squatting in the
shade of a tree. *Man like you or me, he can run. Officer, he's supposed to stay and fight. Lot of times that ain't so easy. Me, I'm
glad I ain't no officer.*)

They have no contempt. They understand. They are quiet about
it and they can squat drinking coffee and discuss it sanely and
come to some kind of a conclusion about it and then talk about
something else.

But Castetter hadn't been able to let it go. The whole business
was silly. It was stupid and it was pointless and it was ridiculous.
Masterson flopped there with his head under the water. Castetter
had almost giggled.

Oh stop thinking so much.

It came from being a minister's son. Came from reading too much. Castetter always had thought of himself as some kind of intellectual, a man attuned to matters of profundity and meaning. But where was the lesson in old Masterson's death? The man had been an absolute military misfit, a flabby pedant. He had been commissioned because he had a so-called intelligence. The army had needed intelligent men. So Masterson had tried to lead a charge and had seen the pain and terror and death and had collapsed.

Masterson, why were lives put in your hands?

You were from Cambridge Massachusetts and what in Cambridge Massachusetts had prepared you for this war?

Castetter sat up. He rubbed his eyes.

Goddam.

(Before Sumter Castetter had been a reporter for the New York *Call*. A reporter: *i.e.*, a greasy hack sitting back and reporting the venal acts of venal men. And all the time smirking and feeling superior . . .)

I need a drink.

Get up, Castetter.

Arise, ye sainted dead.

Castetter, do you hear the trump of doom?

O how loud it is.

He crawled from his tent. He stood up and again rubbed his eyes. There was a faint grayness in the east, but otherwise everything was dark. Yesterday Castetter and his men had ridden hard all day. Now they were bivouacked just west of a town in Pennsylvania. Place called Gettysville. No. Gettysburg. Pretty little place, with a college.

He put his head in his hands and squeezed his temples. Last night he had drunk alone, emptying the last pint he had had in his knapsack. Masterson had supplied him with the stuff. But now there wasn't any left.

Good morning, o brave Republic.

What's good about it?

In vain to Castetter the smiling mornings shine.

Horses snorted, pawed the ground. He heard men moving around. A new detail was getting ready to go out on picket. There had been talk of a large Confederate force somewhere to the west of this place. The pickets had been doubled and had been ordered to keep a sharp eye.

Castetter commanded this company now. He had been junior lieutenant at the start of the war. So far seven company commanders (four dead, three wounded) had left the outfit and now Castetter, by virtue of his seniority, was in charge. He and good old Max Gwinn were the outfit's only remaining officers. Castetter ranked Gwinn by a few days' seniority. Gwinn, who had fought out west for a time, had been with this unit for only about a year now.

And he's just waiting for me to get shot, the sonofabitch.

Castetter walked to an open place at the edge of the camp. He walked slowly. He weaved just a bit.

Then there was the sound of hoofbeats and a dozen men or so rode to where he was standing. They reined up around him.

"That you lieutenant?" a voice wanted to know.

"No. I'm Jenny Lind. Anyone care to hear me sing?"

Several men laughed. Castetter wondered if they liked him. Oh for God's sake.

One of the men saluted. "Sergeant Hall, sir," he said.

"Detail your men in a wide arc across that road. On foot," Castetter said, pointing through the shadows in the direction of a pike that led west. "And, uh—stay alert. I understand there's a war being fought around here someplace. A man named Robert E. Lee just might come riding up that road."

"I wouldn't be surprised, sir," Sgt Hall said. Several of the men snickered. They rode away.

Castetter stood alone again. He waited for the night pickets to return. The dawn was brighter now, and he could make out things around him.

The men liked him, he guessed. He was no spitandpolish martinet like Max Gwinn. The men perhaps sensed that Castetter didn't give a damn any more, but they didn't care too much. They were able to take care of themselves. Castetter knew beyond any doubt that his death would do nothing to impair the outfit's efficiency, but he was glad the men liked him. A man who doesn't give a damn is easy to get along with. He isn't snapping at you all the time.

The night pickets came in, riding leisurely. Sgt Hogan was in charge. He reined his horse in front of Castetter and saluted.

"See anything?" Castetter asked him.

Sgt Hogan was an enormous redbearded bear of a man. "Naw," he said, rolling a hunk of tobacco in his mouth, spitting thickly. Sgt Hogan was a good man, but he didn't give a whoop for military courtesies and Castetter never had heard him say sir. But Castetter never had pressed the point. Hogan was a good sergeant, and good sergeants are too scarce for you to worry about whether or not they say sir.

"How about Johnson?" Castetter wanted to know. "Any sign of him?"

"Naw. Just like I told you, the rebs probably got him."

Castetter said nothing. He stared at the ground. Johnson: the men called him Wheatfield. A nice fellow. Redfaced. From Illinois.

"We dismissed?" Hogan asked him.

"What?"

"We dismissed?"

"Oh. Oh yes."

Men and mounts entered the bivouac. Then somewhere a bugle sounded. Groans. Sleepthick oaths. Sighing, whispery, annoyed sounds.

Castetter walked back to the camp. He still was thinking about that Johnson boy. Sergeants and corporals were shouting at the men, rousing them. Castetter didn't hear.

Gwinn was waiting for him at his tent. "How you doing?"

Castetter coughed, cleared his throat. "I feel like hell," he said. "What do you care?"

"You're the commanding officer."

"Just what do you mean by that?"

Gwinn shrugged. "Now don't get in a state. I'm just worried about you, that's all. You know—with yesterday and everything, you finding your old friend Masterson like that—well, I thought . . ."

"You're always thinking."

"I'm here as your friend."

"Friend," Castetter said.

Gwinn scruffed his feet in the dust. "What don't you like about me?"

"Christ's sake. You're not running for office out here. What the hell difference does it make what I like or don't like about you? I'm tired. I want to take a nap. Are you here on official business or what?"

Gwinn didn't say anything.

"Can't you wait until I die?" Castetter asked him. "Then you can have the goddam company."

"I didn't mean it that way . . ."

Castetter said nothing. He entered his tent and lay down. He closed his eyes. His head hurt. He heard Gwinn's feet still scruffing outside. Then an abrupt sound, as though Gwinn were about to enter the tent. Then a hesitation, then the slow sound of his steps fading away.

Thank God.

Now wait a minute, Castetter. Are you being fair? Why did you have to go and say those things? So Gwinn *is* an oaf. You didn't have to treat him like *that*.

What's so wonderful about *me* that I can say those things? What prize did *I* ever win?

Oh, stop *thinking* so goddam much . . .

(Gwinn wasn't a bad officer, once you stopped to consider everything. He certainly was a good horseman. Better than Castetter. And he was brave enough too.)

He knows how to ride a horse. That's more than I can say for me.

(Castetter had fallen off his horse at Chancellorsville. The horse was a contrary animal and had reared when a shell went off about twenty feet away or so. Reared away up, sending Castetter plummeting to the ground.)

Oh, to be an officer and to be *dignified*.

(Chancellorsville: the Confederates' charge through Howard's XI Corps, all those Germans—Preacher O. O. Howard's German immigrants—running back, screaming and fainting and falling, with the rebs yipping and whooping behind them, clubbing them with their rifles, chasing them right through their camp and out onto the road, shooting them down as though it were some enormous wild unlimited squirrel hunt. *Whap whap whap*—Dutchmen falling everywhere, screaming, drowning in a swamp of their own blood. Dutchmen torn to pieces, torn to rout. Dutchmen giving way, collapsing, funking out, the whole goddam XI Corps.)

So we lose another battle.

Hooker funks out too and we lose another battle.

Whap whap whap—the rebs kill us and Hooker does nothing.

Hooker falls apart. The army falls apart.

Oh well. We should be inured to defeat by now.

Masterson, my fine distinguished scholarly friend, you had the right idea.

You threw up.

And you ran.

Me, too.

I want to throw up.

I want to run.

Castetter felt in his pocket and jingled the two coins he had won from Masterson. The sun was up now. He could feel its warmth now here in his tent.

Shine, smiling morning.

He jingled the coins and absently wondered what had happened to that Johnson boy, the one they called Wheatfield.

♣ His army was moving smartly and his cavalry was doing a good job of keeping track of Lee's movements, but Joe Hooker was through and he must have known it. He called for reinforcements. Lincoln told him he had more than enough men now. Hooker raged. Lincoln! What did HE know about how it was to do battle with this man Lee? How can you win when you get no cooperation? And so Joe Hooker (whose rage was a terrible thing) resigned. Some say he was very anxious to resign. Some say the last thing he wanted was to fight Lee again; Chancellorsville was a wound from which he hadn't recovered and the argument with Lincoln was a good excuse for resigning with some honor. But this is not known for sure. At any rate, he did resign, and George Gordon Meade, one of his corps commanders (skinny bearded fierce crabby unloved

George Gordon Meade, who was considered by most of the men to be too pious, too much the regulationbook martinet, the prim academician), was named to take his place. Hooker (oh the men had waved their hats and had cheered for him the day he had assumed command; they had known him as a fighter) grumped away from the Army of the Potomac . . . Fighting Joe, the rakehell, the clever finagler, the drinker and gambler, the ambitious angler, the brave man who lost bravery and decisiveness that day at Chancellorsville when wounded men burned to death screaming at the crossroads in the wilderness, when Gen Oliver Otis Howard's XI Corps (mostly German immigrant men) fled in panic . . . Fighting Joe, who lost courage and decisiveness on a day when events had demanded nothing else, who thereafter lost the will to contest Lee's gray legions, grumped away to the west to fight in Tennessee under Grant and Thomas, to fight smartly too, with great courage at Lookout Mountain, but always to be known as The Man Who Lost Chancellorsville, to live with it, to die with it. And who was this man Meade who took his place? Where would this pious martinet succeed where cautious McClellan, stupid Pope, misguided Burnside and indecisive Hooker had failed? What was Meade against that old wizard Lee? What was the Army of the Potomac now as it moved toward what might be the great battle of the war? How would this change in command, coming so soon before this battle, affect its morale and leadership? No one really knew. The men marched, and for the most part they kept their thoughts to themselves. Maybe Meade was an old woman and all that, but they were willing to give him a chance. They had given little Mac McClellan his chance. They had given Pope and Burnside and Hooker their chances. All had failed—and Pope and Burnside and Hooker had failed disastrously. So, the men reasoned, how much worse can this new feller be? And they came to the conclusion that he couldn't be much worse, that he might even be better. And besides, they told each other, what the hell choice do we have? Might as well make the best of it. Give him a chance. See what he does. He was no coward; the men who had served in his corps knew that. And sometimes courage meant something. It hadn't meant anything in the case of Hooker, but—well, there always was the chance this new feller would be different. It didn't hurt to hope so.   ♣

CPL LEW MABRY of the Army of Northern Virginia walked through the bivouac. He cursed and he spat and he kicked sleeping men. The kicks were swift and hard. Several of the men, younger ones, groaned or whimpered.

Mabry was a large young man with an innocent face. He was very strong. He walked briskly among the men. "Get up you goddam privates!" he shouted. "We going out for some Yanks today! Get you lazy asses up!"

The men moved slowly.

"Come awn!" Mabry shouted. He pounced on some of the slower ones, grabbed them by their shirts, pulled them upright. "Get up you bastards! Directly I'm goin to stick a poker up you asses!"

Now the men were getting up. There were grunts and mutters and flatulent sounds.

Mabry rubbed his hands together. He grinned. Man I feel mean today, he said to himself. "Rise up, soldiers of the South!" he shouted. "Rise up! Rise up!"

Man they sure stuck me with one dragass platoon . . .

Mabry went to a tree, sat down beneath it and watched his men. Now and then he yelled at them just to keep them hoppin.

Mabry's uniform was fairly new. He scratched himself. The wool felt real good against his armpit. Ain't every man can get a wool uniform.

(He'd had to lick an old sergeant to get it. He and the sergeant had come across it on the body of a dead major on the battlefield at Chancellorsville. Mabry and the old sarge had been out looting corpses. They grabbed for the major's coat simultaneously. Mabry pushed the sergeant. The fight began. About a hundred men came to watch. The sergeant was bigger and heavier, but Mabry had this strongness and a darting quickness. The fight lasted about ten minutes, and ended when Mabry brought his knee smartly into the sergeant's groin. The sergeant gave a weak yelp, then passed out. Four men carried him away. Mabry watched the men carry the sergeant away and he laughed and laughed and danced a little jig. Then he stripped the corpse, put on the uniform and then ripped off its insignia of rank. He didn't want anyone to mistake him for a major. He had a great respect for rank and always honored it—provided it meant a man was an officer. He didn't have much use for old sergeants.)

He opened his knapsack, then glared up at the men. "You want the whole goddam war to pass you by? Come awn!"

He brought a large jar from the knapsack. Carefully he set it on the ground. Then he stood up. "Line up column of twos!" he yelled.

The men formed an uneven double row. Mabry stood in front of them and called the roll:

"Allen!"

"Uh."

"Bell!"

"Yep."

"Dalton!"

"Here."

"Edwards!"

"Yep."

"Emery Franklin!"

"Right here, corp."

"Franklin Franklin!"

"Me too, corp."

"Hodges!"

"Ho."

"Incastle!"

"Yep."

"Manwell!"

"Here."

"Patterson!"

No answer.

"Private Rufus Patterson!" Mabry hollered.

"He'll be back in a minute, I reckon," Bell said.

"What's he doin?"

"He's in the woods."

Patterson came running up and took his place in ranks.

"Patterson?"

"Here."

Mabry walked to where Patterson was standing. "You goddam nogood Virginia sonofabitch, you ever do that again when I'm callin roll I'm goin to fry your ass an feed it to my horse." He grabbed one of Patterson's wrists. He twisted it. Patterson screamed. Mabry released the wrist and went back to his position in front of the platoon. None of the men had moved. Patterson whimpered.

"Ruggles!" Mabry yelled.

"Here."

"Stevenson!"

"Here."

"Thomas!"

"Here."

"Wynn!"

"Yep."

They hadn't had their breakfasts yet. He dismissed them. They fell out and huddled around their campfires.

Mabry returned to his tree and sat down again. Watching the men, he unscrewed the top of the jar of preserves.

Goddam Patterson. He think just because he from Virginia he somethin special. He an all of them. Well they all just a bunch of trash.

Well, don't let that worry you none there Lew Mabry.

You just keep an eye on them.

You got you a horse now. It's real easy to keep an eye on them.

He reached inside the jar and gathered some of the jam in his hand. It was cherry jam. He'd taken the preserves from a farm woman yesterday. She'd called him a filthy rebel traitor. Hell with you you old bitch, Mabry had said. Yep, hell with all you Yanks.

Slobber and jam ran down Mabry's chin. He licked his lips and watched the men. His eyes glittered.

(Mabry was large, but his face was young and soft and guileless. He was twentytwo years old, a South Carolinian. Back home he had made a living running down niggers. He had the best damn set of niggersmellin hounds in the whole state, he bet. He was good with his hounds old Mabry was. They loved him. He took good care of them, was gentle and generous with them. He would cry when one died. He nursed them when they were sick. He would not shoot a dog when it broke a leg. Instead he would make a splint for it and then sit up all night with that dog, all day, all night again, sit up with that dog and think nothing of it. And so the great hounds whined and sucked around him like kittens. Oh they howled and roared after the niggers, but they were gentle and affectionate with Mabry, timid and deferential, and stared at him with love in their great bloody eyes. And the best days of Mabry's life had been spent with his hounds, going out with them, taking after some nigger, the dogs baying and groaning and yipping, feet padding and crackling and splashing through woods and brush and swamps. And finally catching up with the nigger. His frightened cries: *No massa no please massa take em offa me I be good!* Oh them niggers . . . big black bucks, eyes rollin, crouched down, pleadin with you: *No massa please massa I go back I don't run away no mo!*)

Mabry smiled. He sucked jam off his fingers.

He capped the jar very tightly, then returned it to his knapsack. The knapsack was heavy with various things he had picked up since the beginning of the war. He never let it out of his sight.

He had had to slap that farm woman to get her to be still.

He stood up and yelled at the men to form a column of twos. Up and down the line came the call to fall in. The division moved out on the road and marched east into the sunrise toward a place called Gettysburg. Gen Henry Heth, who commanded the division, was said to be looking for shoes. The men needed shoes.

Mabry ordered his men forward. Then he walked off to a clearing and climbed up on his horse, the one that Yank prisoner had called Gingerbread. It was a good horse. Mabry was fond of all animals. He rode out to the road and held the horse down to a walk. The men in his platoon glared up at him. He yelled at them to keep moving along. It sure was good not to have to march.

♣ The date of Gen George Gordon Meade's assumption of command of the Army of the Potomac was June 28, 1863. There have been few times in history when a man has had the need for decisiveness thrust upon him with such suddenness. The position of Meade's army—and the position of the Union— was perilous, to say the least. An invader was loose in Pennsylvania and Maryland. To defeat him was imperative. But at first Meade's actions were not decisive. Caution always had ruled his life, always would. He was fully aware of the gravity of the situation, and therefore made an attempt to get his bearings, to probe, to get things organized. The first rule of decisiveness, Meade felt, was to organize your forces. Thus Meade's decisiveness those first few days of his command was an outright deliberateness. All his movements were draped in caution. The main body of his army was in Maryland, strung around Emmittsburg, which was just south across the state line from the little college town of Gettysburg Pennsylvania. Meade was of the opinion that the battle to decide the fate of the Union would be fought somewhere near Emmittsburg. Here in Maryland, he felt, the two great armies would converge. But, nevertheless, the I Corps (under Gen John F. Reynolds) and the XI Corps (under Gen Oliver O. Howard) of Meade's army had crossed into Pennsylvania and were near Gettysburg. They were on the lookout for a force of Confederates said to be to the west someplace. Cavalry under Gen John Buford was aiding the venture. The night of June 30 this cavalry force was spread out across the western approaches to the town. Reynolds and Howard were bivouacked nearby. To the west (not far away that night) was a Confederate infantry division commanded by Gen Henry Heth. In the morning it intended to enter Gettysburg and try to obtain shoes. Neither side had any idea that this would be the site of the battle. A skirmish perhaps was expected, but hardly much more. As a matter of fact, the Confederates thought the town was defended only by militia. ♣

LEORA BAGLEY stood by the gate (she was slender and white in her prettiest dress) and waved at the men—all those dirty strong *wonderful* men—as they marched by, tramp, tramp, tramp.

They waved at her too. Some of them hollered things at her, words and phrases she didn't understand. She was sixteen.

First the cavalry had come, and now all these marching men. Oh it was all so nice. Now the rebs wouldn't come back. Leora and everybody else had been afraid back a couple of nights ago when the rebs had spent the night in town. She and her mother and Johnny, her brother, had stayed up all night. They hadn't slept a wink. Goodness. They had huddled down cellar and they had stared at each other and their eyes had been bright with fear. Outside, the rebels had scruffed through the streets, along the road past Leora's house, which was on the edge of town not far from the seminary.

Everybody had been so frightened.

But that was all different now, and so Leora smiled and waved and some of the men shouted words and phrases she didn't understand. But they were smiling, too, and many of them waved.

Oh this sure was a wonderful evening. Now just let the rebs try to come back here.

Look at them. They look so strong. Tramp, tramp, tramp, boys: "Hi!"

Officers smiling on their horses. Grimy artillerymen marching beside the huge guns.

"Hurrah! Hurrah! We're glad to see you, boys!"

Leora wished her father were here to see all this. But he'd gone to Harrisburg to join the militia. The governor had issued a call for all ablebodied men to join in the defense of their homes. Oh well, there wasn't anything to worry about anymore. He'd be home in a day or two now that the army was here and everything.

Tramp, tramp, tramp they went, smiling and laughing and waving at her, calling out to her, hollering things she didn't understand (but in a friendly way, so she guessed the things they were hollering were all right) and smiling at her in such a way that she just knew they were pleased to see her looking so friendly and soft and slender in that pretty white dress. Tramp, tramp, tramp: dust swirling from beneath their feet, wagons rolling, great straining horses puffing and snorting, pulling artillery pieces. Tramp, tramp, tramp: men waving their caps at her.

"Hurrah!" Leora shouted. She smiled brightly at the men.

They had been marching and riding past her all afternoon. It was evening now and getting dark, and finally she went back into the house. The lamps were on in the parlor. There was no need to sit in the dark anymore.

She went into the kitchen. Her mother sat there. Mamma was drinking tea. Johnny was out back someplace.

Mamma looked up and smiled. "You have a nice time?"

"Yes! All that marching! Our boys! It's wonderful!"

"There, there. Catch your breath."

Leora sat down across from her mother. Leora's face was flushed. She was a pale girl, and her face already was burned from the wind and the sun. Her eyes were gray. She was very slim. Her figure was filled out well, like a woman's. (This frightened her, this filling out, this changing—and so she tried not to think about it. She didn't like frightening thoughts.) Now she rattled on gaily, breathlessly. She told her mother of the galloping cavalry, the grinning shouting men, the enormous pieces of artillery all black and dusty, the officers on their fine horses, the steady tramp, tramp, tramp. Mamma had worked in the kitchen all day, hadn't gone out to see the excitement. Leora couldn't understand this, couldn't understand how Mamma could be just content to sit here in the kitchen and not go look. How can you not want to go look? Oh, Leora felt much older than sixteen, yes yes yes. There was a ringing within her that she had never felt before, a ringing and buzzing and banging that made her forget she was only sixteen. Instead she was wise and older and knew many things: she was standing on the periphery of a great war; today she had seen a part of that war (or at least a movement within it); today she had seen a part of history (something to be recorded, a time, an event, something of importance), and she was unable to distill these feelings into a real coherency but she knew they were there and she understood them.

But Mamma. Well, Mamma didn't want to know.

Johnny yanked open the door and exploded into the room from the back yard. "The rebs are coming!" he hollered.

Leora stared at her brother.

There was an urgency in Johnny's voice. It told you to pay attention. "Willie Frazer's daddy was over by Cashtown today. He saw a big long column of rebs. He got back here fast as he could and he went and told General Buford."

"Who's General Buford?" Mamma wanted to know.

Johnny's face clouded full of scorn. "He's the cavalry commander."

"I shouldn't have let you go out," Mamma said weakly.

"What's that got to do with anything?"

"Don't be snippy, young man."

Johnny was twelve. His hair was dark. He was slender like his sister. Now he stared at Leora. "What'd I do?" he asked her.

He says they're coming back, Leora told herself. She rose and walked to the door that led to the back yard and the barn. She said nothing to Johnny. She thought of her father all nervous and excited who had rushed out—how long ago?—five days ago, rushed out of the house. *Everything'll be all right*, he had said. *I'll be home in a week.*

(A week. It's been almost a week now. And Johnny says the rebs are over by Cashtown. They'll come here and they'll fight with our boys. I know that.)

Daddy ran a hardware store in town. He was fiftytwo. What did he know about fighting and wars and all that? Besides, he was too old. Fiftytwo and going off to join the militia! Who ever heard of such a thing? Mamma had argued with him, but Daddy had said *no. This is one time they need everybody they can get.* Then Mamma had wept. *I need you,* she had wailed. But Daddy had insisted, had listened to no arguments. He'd always been quite a bit stubborn. Once he got an idea in his head he wasn't likely to change his mind. So he took the train to Harrisburg and now he was off goodness knows where and . . .

Leora stared out the kitchen window at the barn. From behind her came the marching sounds. "You and your big talk," she said to Johnny.

Johnny shook his head. "No mam, I ain't just talking," he said. His voice was high and squeaky, his eyes wide and defiant. "You wait; you'll see."

"You little snip!" Leora said, turning to face Johnny.

"Shhh," Mamma said.

"He's lying! He's trying to get us scared!"

"I ain't lying!"

"Children, now you keep quiet. Both of you," Mamma said. She faced Leora. "Now maybe he did hear something . . ."

"Don't believe him!"

"Now maybe he did hear something. He's got no reason to fib."

"I got no reason to fib," Johnny said.

Mamma sat down heavily. She was blinking. She was a large woman, with drooping breasts and a red face. She was twice Daddy's size, but he had always been boss—never mind her size. She relied on him; she always wept the times he wasn't with her; she would sort of drag around the house. These last five days she had been sniffling an awful lot. Leora didn't like it when Mamma sniffled. It made Leora feel funny. She hadn't ever been able to get used to seeing her mother weep.

"Your father . . ." Mamma said. She sniffled and her voice faded away.

"He'll come home now," Leora said. "Our boys are here. Everything'll be all right. No rebs'll come here now."

"They'll come here to fight," Johnny said.

"Be still!" Leora said.

"This talk . . ." Mamma said. Her sniffles were louder now.

"That's all it is: just talk," Leora said. "He just wants to scare us."

Mamma stared hopefully at Johnny. "You just trying to scare us? That's all you trying to do?"

Doggedly Johnny shook his head from side to side. "No. If you don't believe me, you just go out and ask Willie Frazer's daddy. He was over by Cashtown today. He'll tell you."

Leora moved toward Johnny. She raised an arm. Johnny backed away.

"You got no right lying to us," Leora said.

Johnny stomped his foot angrily. The sound was like a shot. "I ain't lying!" he shouted. He was near tears now himself. "What reason I got to lie? I'm only telling you what I know!"

"Oh please stop," Mamma said. "Don't argue. It makes me feel sick." She rose and left the room. Leora and Johnny watched her. They heard her clump upstairs.

Leora moved toward Johnny again. "You mean little snip."

He backed away. "I'm just telling—"

"Our boys are outside."

"That don't make no difference to Robert E. Lee."

"Don't talk like a Copperhead."

"I ain't no Copperhead!" Johnny yelled. He was crying now. He sprang at Leora and punched her in the chest.

"You!" Leora screamed, slapping him.

Johnny moved back. The right side of his face was streaked where her hand had hit. "I ain't no Copperhead!" he wailed. He put his hands over his face.

Leora stared at the floor. "Well now, I—" she began.

She went to Johnny and put a hand on his head and mussed his hair. He looked up at her bleakly. Then they hugged each other.

That night Leora lay awake for a long time. Oh this war, she said to herself. This war. She heard Mamma crying in her bedroom. This war. Leora stared at the ceiling and thought of the rattle de dattle de of drums and the ta ta too ta ta too of trumpets and the sounds of marching and horses and—thinly—outside her window thousands of men made sleepy martial sounds and the whole thing made her breathe thickly and feel excited down away low in herself where she never had felt excited before. Now she knew she shouldn't have fought with Johnny. She didn't mean to think oh this war. No. What she really was thinking was oh this excitement. She knew this now. A battle maybe here! You couldn't help but be excited. Gettysburg: the war right here. I am a young woman, she said to herself. Maybe I will be some kind of a heroine. A nurse or something. Me, a heroine! And those boys out there tonight they are defending me.

Me.

I hope Daddy is all right.

Now I lay me down to sleep. I pray the Lord my soul to keep. If I should die before I wake, I pray the Lord my soul to take. Bless Mamma and Daddy and Johnny and the army out there and make it so that Mamma doesn't bawl too much. Amen.

She closed her eyes.

Those men smiled at me. Maybe they think I am pretty. Those funny things that been happening to me down there lately. Mamma says they're signs that I'm growing up. I guess maybe I am pretty.

rattle de dattle de

ta ta too ta ta too

oh we'll rally round the flag boys, we'll rally once again, shouting the battle cry of freeeeedommmmmm: ohhh go to sleep now: a b c d e f g / hijk lmnop / q r s / t u v / w / and x y z and how does it go? Tomorrow will be some day yes.

♣ This last day of June was a day of caution, slow movements and alertness. The armies were wary. Neither side knew exactly what the other was up to. George Gordon Meade was of the opinion that the battle would be fought near a stream called Pipe Creek, which was back down in Maryland. And Lee, lacking much cavalry for scouting and intelligence reports, thought it would be fought closer to Harrisburg. Certainly neither side thought of Gettysburg. It was a minor geographical pinpoint. Confederate skirmishers near the little town withdrew when Buford's Union cavalry entered. But it was only cavalry, and Henry Heth's advancing shoehunters, when apprised of this, did not expect much of a fight. As a matter of fact, many of the men under Heth still believed the town to be defended only by militia. The battle was several days away. Or so they thought. They did not know of Reynolds' and Howard's infantry corps waiting there in Gettysburg. ♣

PVT RUFUS PATTERSON of the Army of Northern Virginia chewed unenthusiastically on what you'd have had to call a real hard piece of hardtack. He and Pete Bell and several other men were sprawled at the edge of a creek. They had been marching all day and they were tired. Rufus could feel calluses on his calluses. His shoes were pretty near all gone. He reached down and rubbed his feet.

His wrist still hurt from where that Mabry had grabbed it this morning.

"Tomorrow they say we get some shoes," Pete Bell said.

Rufus rubbed his ankles. "Who's they?" he wanted to know.

Pete grinned. Most of his teeth were missing. "They is God, boy. They is the people who tell us what to do an where to go."

"You mean like Mabry?"

Pete didn't say anything.

"Sonofabitch ought to be shot," someone said.

Pete stared at the man. "You want to do it?"

"I didn't say that," the man said. His name was Wynn. He was from the Tidewater.

"Shoot him," Pete said. "Sure somebody ought to shoot him. Sure. Bing—right when there's a fight goin on . . ."

"Easier to say than do," another man said. "He's on our side."

Pete Bell cleared his throat and cackled thinly.

"Bing," Rufus said. He pointed a finger at a clump of trees across the creek. He swallowed some more hardtack, washed it down with coffee. "We're all ascared of old Mabry."

Pete smiled. "That's the God's truth. I'm ascared of him. I don't know a man in this platoon who ain't. Why is it a man has to be ascared of meanness?"

"It's somethin that's strong," Wynn said.

"Ain't we strong?'

"Not like Mabry," Wynn said.

Pete made a rasping sound, cleared his throat again. "Yep," he said. He swallowed some coffee.

Nobody said anything for a long time. Somewhere all the crickets in the world were going ching ching ching. Rufus lay back and cradled his knapsack under his head. He whistled softly and stared up at the stars. "I sure would like to be home," he said.

"Don't say," Pete murmured dryly.

". . . have me a girl, a nice warm girl, right layin here with me instead of goddam old Pete Bell."

Pete laughed softly. Wynn, who lay a few feet away, snickered.

". . . a girl who knows just one word," Rufus went on, "an

that one word is yes. A girl maybe just a little bit fat. You know, fat where fat means somethin. Ahuggin away. Ahuggin me an akissin me and knowin just that one word: yes."

"Jesus Christ," someone said.

Wynn laughed. "Don't nobody go sleepin on his belly."

Rufus closed his eyes and concentrated on the image of a girl. Just any girl right now. Any girl who all she knew how to say was yes. Any girl, even Elizabeth.

But slowly the image drifted from his mind. A man never thought for long about anything but the war. He wondered when they'd find some Yanks. Tomorrow maybe. Well, so what does that mean? Me an Pete Bell, we ain't run yet. I been ascared, yes sir you bet you, an old Pete I bet he been ascared too, but we ain't run yet. Me an Pete, all we do is stay. I'm scared an I know it but I stay. I ain't no hero like Ben Farrell (them fellers with J. E. B. Stuart is all heroes, to hear people talk, an get the girls too), but I always done what I been called on to do. I'm scared of Mabry too. I'm scared all the time. But I ain't run off yet. Fredericksburg an Chancellorsville an all them other big an little fights: sure I always thought of runnin. But I ain't run yet. That don't mean I ain't never *gonna*. It just mean I ain't yet.

General Lee sir, I like to have the livin Jesus Christ scared out of me every time we get into a fight.

General Lee sir, I want to go home and get me a nice girl.

General Lee sir, why is it I'm ascared all the time even ascared of Mabry?

(She's probly at some dance or somethin right now, probly agrinnin at some feller with her eyes all scrootched up, tossin back her head with them nice curls aflyin. AT CHANCELLORS-VILLE WE CHASED THEM GERMANS AN LORD SAVE US JESUS CHRIST ALMIGHTY HOW THEY RAN! ATRIPPIN OVER EACH OTHER. AYELLIN AN ACAR-

RYIN ON. WE CHASED THEM AN I REMEMBER HOW
WE ALL WAS LAUGHIN. LAUGHIN. LORD SAVE US
JESUS CHRIST ALMIGHTY. And sometimes she gets all
mixed up in your mind so you can't see her clear at all and you
wonder what is the matter with you. I don't hold with thinkin
too much about this war. It ain't like bein in school or marchin
in a parade an singin an all that. I don't hear much singin no
more. I oughta stop thinkin about girls till we get home, Pete
says. He says I got plenty of time for them later. Old Pete, I guess
he's right. I guess maybe I should do like he says. There ain't
nothin to be ascared of. I got Pete with me an he knows what to
do an all I have to do is stay with him. Now if that Mabry could
only go and get himself killed. Now I lay me. So this is Pennsylvania. Sure is warm. WE CHASED THEM GERMANS
UNTIL IT GOT TOO DARK AND WE COULDN'T SEE
NOTHIN.)

I ain't gonna run. Elizabeth, I love you.

♣ Dismounted pickets from Gen Buford's Union cavalry force
were spread across the western and northern approaches to
Gettysburg. The western line ran roughly parallel with a quiet
tiny trickling stream, Willoughby's Run. Skirmishers, lying
prone, dotted its banks. Now it was dark; trees and men and
horses and equipment were indistinct. Everybody was nervous
and alert. A man coughed or cleared his throat and you
jumped. This Robert E. Lee, you never quite knew what he was
up to. There were reports that he was coming in this direction.
You kept your rifle right close nearby. ♣

PVT WHEATFIELD JOHNSON and about a
dozen other Union prisoners were quartered in a barn. There was
a sentry inside the barn, two others outside. Three men watching
twelve or so. The guards were young. Wheatfield was amused by

them. They sure were nervous. Huh, old Robert E. Lee probably had sent these fellers back with the prisoners because he'd known they'd run back first time a shot was fired anyway. This way, old Lee probably had figured, he'd get some use out of them.

Wheatfield and another prisoner, a lank stragglebearded man named Caleb Bushnell, sat propped against a wall at the rear of the barn. Wheatfield had taken off his boots and was rubbing his ankles and the blisters on his feet. Whoo, he kept saying to himself. Whoo. This marching ain't for me. No sir. I guess I sure did find a home in the cavalry. Whoo.

The rebs had been marching the prisoners two days. Last night they'd had to sleep out in the open, guards and all. There had been a lot of marching, a whole lot. And countermarching too. Wheatfield guessed the rebs didn't have any safe passage to the rear and didn't quite know how to get the prisoners out of the area. He grinned, thinking: Wellsir, I guess we're more trouble than we're worth. Twelve prisoners, three guards. Don't hardly seem worth the trouble. Don't hardly seem.

And he guessed maybe tonight would be as good a time as any to cease being a prisoner.

Caleb Bushnell, the man next to him, was asleep. His head was back against the wallboards and his mouth was open and he was snoring.

The prisoners, sprawled on the barn floor, were silent. Most of them were asleep. A man in the army, prisoner or not, all he has to do is stop marching and he's asleep. Sitting up or lying down. Sometimes even standing, if there's something to lean against.

Wheatfield sniffed. The smell of hay and feed and manure was thick. It made him homesick. Back home the barns weren't so big and prosperous, but they smelled the same. Haw haw. I guess I never thought I'd ever get homesick over the smell of a barn.

Well, goddamit . . .

I *do* want to go home, sure.

If I keep on being a prisoner and they send me down to Belle Isle or someplace like that, hell, there's no telling how long it'll be before I get home. Maybe never. They say things ain't so good down there. If I ain't a prisoner there's always a chance I might get a furlough. A furlough huh? What's that?

He glanced at Caleb, snoring away there next to him.

He took a deep, slow, sighing breath of barnsmell and thought of Caleb.

Bushnell was a straggler. The reason he was a straggler was kind of peculiar. He was from New Jersey, had been brought up by an older sister who had moved to Hagerstown just before the war. When the Army of the Potomac began its northward pursuit of Lee's army, Bushnell saw a chance to visit her. Things were moving so fast that he thought well, it won't make any difference for a day or two or so; I'll go see Annie and then hurry right back and nobody'll miss me. So he left his regiment at Frederick and walked northwest to Hagerstown, keeping to the woods at the edge of a road. Annie was pleased to see him. He was the baby of the family and always had been her favorite. She went out to the barn and killed a chicken and they had a great feast. Her life was lonely (her husband was serving with Thomas in Tennessee) and she didn't have any children, so she'd been kind of rattling around the house. But that all changed with Caleb's arrival. He talked a lot, boasted a lot, and sitting there listening to him brought the war a lot closer to her than all her husband's letters put together. For two days she stuffed him with enormous meals and listened to his talk. (He was a rifleman with Hancock's corps and had seen action at Fredericksburg and the crossroads at Chancellorsville. *That was where the wounded men were fried like that chicken you got there in the stove, he told her. I mean—well, you want to hear this?* She nodded, so he went on: *Everything was burning. All the shells and everything, they'd set the trees and brush afire and some of the men were hurt too bad to crawl away so the fires caught them and you kept hearing them scream. Oh listen to me. This is no thing to be telling a woman. I don't know what got into me.*) They exchanged bits of news about their brothers and sisters; Caleb took his first good bath in more than a year; he cleaned the lice from his beard. (*That sure is some beard, she told him. Sort of makes you look like the Christ Jesus.* Then they both laughed, and he stroked his beard profoundly.) But this all ended when the Confederates marched into Hagerstown. Caleb—who had no intention at all of becoming a deserter—still considered himself a part of the Army of the Potomac and thus made preparations to leave Hagerstown. But he did not reckon with the woman who lived next door to his sister. This woman's husband was fighting with the rebel Pemberton at Vicksburg. (That was the way things were in Hagerstown and all Maryland for that matter.) Anyway, this neighbor woman told a rebel officer of the federal deserter who was staying at the house next door. The troops arrived about twenty minutes after Caleb's departure. They caught him before he had gone two miles. He was wearing his uniform and so they did not shoot him as a spy. That had all been two weeks ago. Since then they had been marching him in great widening circles. For four or five days he had been attached to Gen Longstreet's mess as an orderly and had been worked carrying slops fourteen hours a day. But at least he had eaten well. Then the rebs had decided they could carry their own slops and Caleb had been thrown in with this tiny group of prisoners. He and Wheatfield had got to talking with each other yesterday. He had been sympathetic when Wheatfield had told him of the loss of Gingerbread. He had stroked his beard profoundly, with sadness.

Wheatfield picked at his teeth with a piece of straw. Yep, he said to himself, tonight's as good a night as any. I sure don't see no future in this.

He nudged Caleb.

Caleb blinked his eyes open. "What's the matter?"

"Not so loud."

"Well?"

"You like being a prisoner?"

"Finest thing in the world," Caleb said.

"Yep. They tell me Belle Isle's the finest place in the world."

Caleb dug his fists into his eyes and pinched the bridge of his nose. "You want to stop being a guest of the Confederacy?"

"Kind of thought so," Wheatfield said, spitting out some wet straw. "Wouldn't be hard."

"How?"

"Crawl out."

"In the dark?"

"We'll bellycrawl for a little ways, then we'll keep to the woods. These here guards, we can get away from them."

Caleb didn't say anything.

"Far as I can tell," Wheatfield said, "we're only about twenty miles from this place Gettysburg. That's where my outfit is."

Caleb grunted. "How do we know it's still there?"

"There's gonna be a fight there."

"Hum."

"I can always go by myself."

"Now. I didn't say I wasn't going."

"It's better when you have company," Wheatfield said.

"Yep. Two can do better than one I guess."

"There's always a chance we'll get shot."

"You ain't making this sound like Baptist choir practice."

"It ain't gonna be," Wheatfield said. "We're gonna have to do a lot of walking. I ain't looking forward to that. I'm in the cavalry, remember?"

Caleb chuckled.

"Well?"

"Uh. Well. Let me think about it. It ain't quite dark yet."

"All right," Wheatfield said. He lay back and spat out the piece of straw. He closed his eyes. He wondered how old Gingerbread was doing. That reb corporal sure had been a mean man. And you could tell his men didn't like him. But they were afraid of him. Poor dumb rebs, you wonder why they kept on going. Half of them didn't even have no shoes to speak of. And they were so thin and all. (He sure did think it was funny that I was walking and he was riding. I bet he won't treat Gingerbread so good. He sure did think it was funny. I hope I see him again. I'll funny him I ever see him again.)

Wheatfield opened his eyes and stared out toward the front door. He stared at the guard standing there.

Now looky here, look at him.

Such a little feller.

The guard was small and thin, very young, no more than fifteen. His hair was blond. He kept wetting his lips and blinking and taking long deep gulping breaths. He stood perhaps forty feet from Wheatfield.

Look at him.

Poor little feller.

Dumb too I bet.

He turn his back once. That's all. Just once. Just as soon as it gets nice and dark.

Then—real quick—me and Bushnell can crawl out the back window.

Ever since his capture Wheatfield had been working this problem over in his mind. (Find me a nice safe way to get away. I don't want to get killed, that's for sure. I just want to get back to my outfit. And all of a piece. That's all. So maybe tonight huh? With Bushnell. Yep. I just might be needing help. He seems steady. A man you can trust.)

Wheatfield smiled thinly. He thought of the little window at the rear of the barn. Soon as everything was dark they could do it. The other two guards were outside, marching around and around the barn, but a man, or two men, if they were careful enough, probably would be able to crawl away.

Sure. All you have to do is be quiet.

Beats going to Belle Isle.

The little guard's tongue was pink. He kept rubbing it across his lower lip. He was sitting on a milking stool, his rifle cradled across his knees. The barn was becoming quite dark now. Another guard entered with a lamp. He hung it over the place where the little guard was sitting.

Some of the prisoners were asleep. Wheatfield could hear their snores. The guard who had brought in the lamp said something to the little guard. Wheatfield couldn't catch what it was. The little guard nodded quickly and then the other went outside again. The little guard pulled the stool against the door and leaned back.

Poor little feller, Wheatfield said to himself. He thought of the ragging the prisoners had given the little guard today, telling him to go home before his mamma gave him a whipping, advising him to skedaddle before the fighting began because—sure as hell— some Union colonel would catch him and roast him on a spit because he looked like he had the makings of real tender and juicy meat. The little guard had been on the verge of tears. But he was the one with the gun, and the prisoners knew enough not to go too far with a scared little boy who'd fire for any reason he was so scared.

But if he can't see you and don't know you're sneaking away, he ain't going to fire.

Now things were quite dark. Wheatfield and Caleb were off in shadows. Wheatfield very carefully put on his boots again. They hurt against his blisters, but that couldn't be helped. He nudged Caleb. "Well?"

"I been thinking."

"Well?"

"All right."

"Might as well start."

Caleb nodded. They crawled toward the rear of the barn. The straw made snicking little sounds. They sounded like gunfire to Wheatfield. He held his breath. So did Caleb. They crawled behind a horse stall and now they were out of the little guard's sight. They straightened up and darted on tiptoe to the rear window. They could hear one of the guards whistling outside. For some reason Wheatfield was very thirsty. He wished he had a glass of milk. Caleb was first out the window. Wheatfield heard him drop softly to the ground. Going out the window, Wheatfield caught his britches on a nail. There was a slight soft ripping sound. He froze, listened. There was no break in the whistling. Carefully he disengaged his britches from the nail. There was a slight scratch on his rear end. He could feel a stinging sensation. He wanted to giggle, but swallowed it. He finished climbing out the window and dropped down beside Caleb. They crawled forward very slowly. They couldn't see a thing. Sweat stung Wheatfield's eyes. He closed them. It didn't make any difference. He couldn't see anything anyway. He heard the guards' footsteps in the weeds and on the road out in front of the barn. The whistler had stopped. Wheatfield had no idea whether Caleb was still with him or not, but he wasn't of a mind to ask. Once one of the guards passed within about three feet of him. He could have reached out and grabbed the guard's legs. Wheatfield and Caleb crawled perhaps two hundred yards, then slid down a ravine and lay exhausted at the edge of a creek. The whistling had resumed, but now it was quite faint. They rested at the edge of the creek for perhaps half an hour, then struck off east through a thick woods. It was the direction of Gettysburg, Wheatfield hoped.

2

THE FIRST DAY

♣ This battle was no neat formalized test of arms, mainly because neither side suspected that the other would want to fight at Gettysburg. Meade thought in terms of Pipe Creek, down in Maryland near Frederick. Lee thought in terms of a site near Harrisburg. And so, because both sides were confused and because neither had an exact idea of what the other was up to, the two armies almost literally blundered upon each other at Gettysburg. Many men would die at Gettysburg, but their deaths would have no meaning in the longrange and truly planned strategic sense. Henry Heth's Confederates were hunting shoes. Buford's Union cavalry and the Union corps of Reynolds and Howard were camped in Gettysburg, but most of the shoehunters thought this was a small band of militia. And no damn militia in the world would give any trouble to the Army of Northern Virginia. ♣

THE MORNING of the day he died Lt Alf J. Castetter of the 9th New York Cavalry sat astride his horse, facing west. He peered out across Willoughby's Run. He saw dust rising behind some trees and he heard shots coming pop pop pop through the warm wet air. The time was about eight o'clock, and the sun was up full now, full and yellow and bright, quite hot.

Most of the morning dew had vanished, and there was only this
light dampness in the air. Pop pop pop came the shots, very
faintly, blurred. Maybe somebody's gone out hunting, Castetter
said to himself.

Castetter's men were dismounted. They lay behind trees and
stumps and bits of brush. Nobody said anything. (Castetter had
been up since three, getting the men ready, deploying them. Infantry was hurrying up from the rear, but it might be several hours
before its presence would be felt.)

Castetter fumbled in his pockets and finally came up with a
cigar. It was bent. He smoothed it between his hands, then lit it,
using a huge sulphur match. He struck the match against the stock
of his pistol. His horse shied just a bit. "Ho," he said to the horse.
He sucked very deeply on the cigar.

No horses this time boys.

You're supposed to delay Mr Johnny Reb.

I'm supposed to see that you do.

Hah.

Delay them boys. Give the army time. Give Reynolds and Howard time to move into position.

Napoleon said an army moves on its stomach.

Well no wonder it moves so slowly.

Until now, Castetter had been too busy to think. But now there
was nothing to do but wait and so his mind wandered:

There aren't a hell of a lot of skirmishers between us and them.
How long are we expected to hold this position? Well now, isn't
that a question? Yes sir. Oh yes SIR. And nobody bothers to give
you the answer. No indeed. That leaves it up to me. So all my ex-
periences, all the twistings and wanderings of my life, everything,
all of it, breathing, making love, eating, getting drunk, writing that
slop for the Call, listening to Father and his sublimely dull sten-
torian appeals to the Great Lord Jehovah and watching motes of

dust dance in the sunshine from his church's windows all those endless Sabbaths, everything, everything, every breath of air, every pulsebeat and footstep and even the times I visited whorehouses and played poker—everything has led to this present reality: *now.*

Oh for God's sake *stop* it.

Stop impressing yourself with your own cliches.

Even when you try to think of something meaningful all you can come up with are cliches.

Were you weaned on them or something?

Ha ha ha. The Tit of Banality.

. . . but I remember the day when I was fifteen and found Charlotte Anne Barton (ah, Charlotte Anne Barton—she was fifteen too, with such a thin light delicate skin) and she was picking wildflowers in the woods out back of Billy Wharton's father's place . . .

Ah, stop this.

. . . and her arms were full of some yellow flowers the names of which I do not remember. If I ever did know them. And she was so shy. And her smile—I remember that smile. Great God yes I do. I don't know what it was she was afraid of but I guess it must have been me. And wasn't she doing something with her mouth too? Working it ever so slightly with her tongue moving out over her lips? Yes, that was it. And I remember I was carrying a stick. I remember saying hello and walking to her and prodding her belly (very gently) with an end of the stick. I do not remember why I was carrying that stick. Maybe just to be carrying something, to hit at trees or drag in the dirt . . .

No goddamit!

I will *not* see this *now.*

. . . and only a week before Billy Wharton had told me that he'd heard from a friend of Charlotte's that Charlotte was sweet on me. Charlotte had told the friend she was in LOVE with me. I remember wanting very much to laugh at Billy but not being able to and that puzzled me greatly. Prior to that time I had laughed at thoughts of love . . .

Castetter leaned forward and closed his eyes so he could see this more clearly. Pop pop pop went the shots, but now he did not hear them.

. . . and so I had this information about Charlotte Anne Barton and instead of laughing I was embarrassed. I stood there in the woods out behind Billy Wharton's father's place and I grinned at her (still holding that stick at her stomach) and after a time she giggled and said something which I do not remember now. I think it had something to do with how silly I looked, what with that stick and the way I was grinning at her e&c e&c . . .

He opened his eyes and stared blankly out across Willoughby's Run. There was no evidence of fighting except the sound of the shots. He felt in a pocket and jingled the coins he had won from Masterson.

. . . I remember we held hands, Charlotte Anne and I . . .

We will retreat slowly.

. . . hers was warm. Now why would I remember *that?* . . .

We will give the infantry time.

. . . quite small and soft too . . .

We will do as we are told. Military discipline, you know.

. . . I am at a loss to explain why she suddenly wasn't shy any more, why she suddenly had giggled and then had taken my hand. She walked with me quite willingly, and she laughed easily, and she chattered, and her hand was warm and soft in mine, warm and soft and moist, and the warmth and the softness and the moistness coursed from her to me and made me tingle, and she had an advantage over me, and I was of course completely inarticulate . . .

Castetter's horse let out a great blasting flatulence.

Several men guffawed.

"That the reb artillery lieutenant?" someone wanted to know. More guffaws.

Castetter grinned. He leaned over and patted his horse's neck. The horse exhaled and pawed the ground.

Castetter surveyed the men. Some had dug themselves behind little piles of dirt. The mounds had been dug out with bayonets, bare hands, anything. The bayonets were something new. They'd only been issued last night. Most of the men didn't know how to use them. A cavalryman usually doesn't have much use for a bayonet. But the men had seen enough infantry units and had observed how the infantrymen always had dug in before a fight and so most of them had done the same. First thing right off this morning.

. . . and after a time we sat under a tree and rested, I remember. She sat very close to me. She smelled like the flowers she was holding. Her hair was very soft and rubbed against my neck. She was quiet again. Her eyes were wide and light and wet. I wanted to do something but I didn't exactly know what it was. I had no words ready, nothing ready. She smiled and laid the flowers aside. There was nothing shy in her face now. She leaned forward and put a hand on the back of my neck. She scratched me there, very gently. I was having trouble getting my breath. I felt thick and heavy, thick and heavy all over. *Alf, I love you,* she said. She kissed me on the mouth, very hard. Great God . . .

The sound of shots was louder now. Castetter did not notice. He jingled the coins.

. . . that afternoon was very long and not long at all. We spent it sitting there against that tree. She kept making tiny mewing sounds, and I did not know what to do. I remember that after a time *I* was kissing *her* too. I remember fumbling at the front of her dress (I could feel her heartbeat), and I remember her hand over my wrist and her hand was strong and she shook her head no. *We—we have to be nice,* she whispered. There was just a suggestion of roundness to her chest. I never had felt a girl there before, never had wanted to and now *did* want to, and at the time it was almost more than I could bear. There were many kisses. Sweet kisses. Who dares say they were not sweet? I told her I loved her too, and then she wept just a bit. Just a bit mind you. Just a bit. But I guess maybe there was a lot more that never came out. She would not tell me why she wept. I kissed her many many times and finally her weeping stopped. She kept scratching my neck, fondling me. There were many things I could not understand. It was nearly dark when I walked with her to her home. She would not let me within sight of the house. We kissed behind the barn I think it was. She wept again. Again I asked her why. She would not say. Finally she broke away from me and ran inside the house. I never saw her again. Her family packed up and left for Illinois three weeks later. I tried to see her several times, but her father (a big man, with a red face and a very soft voice that always surprised people) told me: *No sonny, you stay away from here.* And (smiling): *You'll get over it. I know about it. These things pass.* He didn't even let her go to school those last three weeks. The other fellows joshed me about it and finally I got into a fight with I think it was Sam Potts and I whipped him and then they stopped joshing me. You'll get over it, her father had said. Well, I never did. No. I never did. Maybe the reason she wept that day with me was because she knew her family was moving away. I like to think so. So anyway, now I am astride a horse and I am awaiting the enemy and what I am experiencing is that great catastrophe they call war, and I think about a girl I remember only as a kind of thin sad shadow . . .

Why don't I think about something that *means* something?
You and your silly adolescent . . .
A lot *that* meant.
Maybe it did.
Anger: Certainly. Go ahead. Talk to yourself with anger. Look around at everything, and everything is clouded with this anger, sourness. Somewhere whatever that thing was dropped into a vacuum.
College. Remember?
. . . I remember sitting in Masterson's office. It was a dusty little cubbyhole. It smelled of breadcrusts and old books. Masterson was smiling. The great pile of my manuscript lay mounded on the desk in front of him. He'd obviously read the whole thing. But I didn't like the way he was smiling. There are ways of smiling and ways of smiling. The way he was smiling was too soft, timid, frightened, not wanting to offend. He took a great deal of care in choosing his words. *Castetter, he said, uh, you have an enormous vocabulary. Your command of the language is superb. Quite astonishing. I was, uh, quite yes quite impressed. However, there is more to writing than one's command of the language. So I think you might as well know the truth, or, uh, at least the truth as I see it. I'm not asking you to believe me. Just hear me out. After all, remember YOU came to ME. Anyway, what I'm getting at is this: you don't, uh, well, you don't seem to KNOW too much. You hold life off at arm's length, and because you do your command of the language defeats you. I hate to say these things. I know how hard you must have worked. But YOU brought the book to ME, remember* . . .
   e&c e&c e&c
   Off at arm's length.
   Far, far off.
   All my life.

Yes.

Empty.

. . . I had worked a year on that book. Masterson probably thought he had done me a favor. So now I am a sneering reptilian literary hack nothing cipher enormous clear empty zero with nothing to say and a fine command of the English language in order that I might say nothing: idiot, full of sound and fury: idiot idiot idiot . . .

The cigar had gone out. Castetter threw it to the ground.

His horse gave a quick snort. Castetter blinked and leaned forward. The shots were much louder now. There was quite a bit of smoke.

"Hey, lieutenant, you better get off that horse," one of the men said.

Castetter made a chucking sound to his horse. He reined it around. "Who wants to take this thing to the rear?" he yelled.

Perhaps thirty men—Castetter's half of what was left of the company—were within earshot of him. The other men, commanded by Max Gwinn, were off to the north.

Castetter looked around at his men. All were on the ground now, hugging it, gripping their rifles and carbines. Now everybody could hear shouts and screams over the shots. A breeze caught the odor of burnt powder. There was more smoke. It came from the other side of the stream.

Castetter was high in the saddle, a good target. He dismounted. "Well?" he shouted. "Who's it going to be?"

No one said anything.

He held the horse's reins loosely and waited for someone to speak up.

No one said anything.

He waited. No volunteers.

Finally he grinned at the men. "Give an officer credit for some brains, will you? I'm going to get down in the dirt with everybody else. Now—who's going to take my horse to the rear?"

"Just let him go, lieutenant," someone said. "He'll be all right."

Castetter shook his head from side to side. "No. I don't want my horse getting shot."

Nobody said anything. The shots and shouts and screams were quite loud now.

Castetter looked across the stream. No sign of anyone yet, but it wouldn't be long now.

He turned back to the men. "Frear!" he called.

Silence from the men.

"Where's Frear?"

There was a thrashing sound in the underbrush. Frear stood up. He was fat, sixteen. His face was very soft and pink. He came forward.

"You take my horse to the rear," Castetter told him.

"Lieutenant, I—"

"That's an order," Castetter said. He grinned at the boy. Frear was the youngest. It was only right that he be sent back. Castetter had brought the horse here in the first place because of Frear.

"Can't you—" Frear began, but Castetter held up a hand.

Castetter pointed at the other men. "Any of you men think Frear is a coward?"

"No!" came in chorus.

"There," Castetter said to Frear. He handed him the reins. "Now you skedaddle," Castetter said.

Frear rode a horse quite well for a fat boy. He got into the saddle gracefully. He saluted. He was sweating heavily. He gave the other men one quick wounded glance. "Cha," he said to the horse. He reined it around and headed east.

Castetter walked to a fallen log, then crouched behind it with a corporal named Young. He had entrusted his carbine to Young.

All the sounds were very near now.

"Ought to be seeing our skirmishers any minute now, sir," Young said.

"Any minute," Castetter said.

Nobody said anything.

Smoke coming from the woods across the stream rolled down on Castetter and his men.

Young coughed violently. "Jesus Christ," he said.

"Here they come," Castetter said. "Give me my carbine."

Union men came crashing out of the woods across the creek. They were running, but they weren't running very fast. Occasionally one would turn and fire into the woods. They splashed across the stream. Three, five, six, nine, ten—eleven men who had been sent ahead under Sgt. Hogan. Eleven men out of twenty were returning.

Hogan was the last man out of the woods. He loped unhurriedly, grunted heavily as he crossed the stream, then joined Castetter and Young behind the log. "They're coming right along!" he hollered.

Castetter expelled his breath through his nose. "Let's stop them!" he shouted to the men. He stood up and waved his carbine, then ducked behind the log again. Doing such a thing always had made him feel like a fool, but it was expected of him. In a fight you were supposed to do what was expected of you.

Then the Confederates came, maybe a hundred of them, bursting out of the smoky woods. All yelling. The sound of their yelling was high and whiny and yipping—a jerky yet continual yeeeeeaaaaahhhhhhooooo!

The Confederates ran forward, crouched, fired. Ran. Crouched and fired. Ran. Dodged. Castetter's men and Gwinn's up the line returned a smart fire. The Confederates wavered, then scattered. The yipping yell died away and was replaced by shouts and scattered screams of pain.

Castetter fired through an opening in the log, carefully, deliberately. He saw a rebel lift up his head to take a look around. He fired. The rebel pitched forward. Bullets spattered off trees and dug up little puffs of dirt. Castetter hoped Gwinn's men were doing all right.

Next to him, Young grunted, fired, loaded, grunted, fired. The line was holding. The rebels banged away, but the line was holding. The rebels crawled in high weeds at the other side of the stream. Castetter counted eight dead men bobbing in the stream. The firing now made all other sounds impossible. Castetter hoped Frear would make it safely to the rear. Some of the shots were very close. Castetter fired at anything that looked as though it might move.

♣ The Union defensive line extended from south of the Cashtown Pike parallel with Willoughby's Run to a rounded place called Oak Hill, which was north of the rightofway of an unfinished railroad. The line then proceeded east across the road that led north to Carlisle. Roughly then, the line took the shape of a great inverted letter L. Buford's dismounted cavalry was at the forefront of the line along Willoughby's Run. That is where Henry Heth's Confederates attacked, thus beginning the battle. Heth's men were a division of Gen A. P. Hill's Confederate corps, and the rest of the command was not far behind it. It did not take these Confederates long to learn this was no militia they were facing. Word rolled back through the ranks. This was at about nine in the morning of July 1, 1863. ♣

"EEEEEYAAAAAHHHHHOOOOO!" Pvt Rufus Patterson screamed as he and the others ran whooping and dodging

forward through the brush toward the little stream. The Yanks
were putting up a smart fire from the other side and the sun was
as hot as anything and he was sweating like hell and occasionally
he stumbled and pitched forward on the ground but he kept
going, he kept going and he didn't think much about it. Other
men—including Pete Bell—were running forward with him. Everybody was yelling. Smoke was sour in his nostrils and made him
cough, put tears in his eyes.

Rufus ran right alongside Pete Bell. They both were hunched
over. The fire from the Yanks was very thick now. Shots rico-
cheted all around them, against trees, off rocks. Rufus and the
others yipped and whooped and fired, but finally they all had to
drop to the ground and bang away at the Yanks from prone positions, crawling forward slowly as they fired. The Yanks had a
good position at the other side of the stream.

Rufus wiped the tears from his eyes and crawled forward very
slowly. Pete grunted along beside him. Weeds and grass scratched
at their faces. Most of the yelling had died away now. "That ain't
no militia!" Rufus yelled.

He didn't hear Pete's answer because just then the Yanks began
an artillery barrage. The great thick sound of the barrage mingled
with the riflefire, and now Rufus knew that was no militia up
ahead. He heard the faint sound of the Yanks cheering.

Bwohmmm, bwohmm, bwohmmm! came the barrage, and the
earth trembled from many explosions. Rufus stopped crawling
forward. So did Pete Bell and the others. Rufus did not even dare
look up now. A steady sheet of fire poured over their heads. We're
pinned, by God, he said to himself. Pinned.

The realization came to him in a sick shocking wave. It wasn't
the first time his outfit had been pinned; it probably wouldn't be
the last—but you never got used to it. Eventually you either went
forward or back, but either way was mighty dangerous. And you

couldn't even get a good bead on the Yanks. You weren't able to lift yourself high enough to see what you were firing at.

A man lay in the weeds, and the weeds were all around him, blocking his vision. About all he could do was prop his rifle in front of him and fire blind. This was stupid. No telling who you'd hit. Chances were it would be one of your own men. So Rufus did not fire. He lay in the weeds and trembled. He didn't know whether he was afraid or not. Sometimes maybe he was. Other times he guessed he wasn't. You never really knew. You lay in heat or wetness or sudden cold, you lay there and trembled, you rubbed your face in the dirt and thought not at all of your dignity, you trembled and gasped and held your breath—and yet you did not quite know whether you were afraid.

With, now, rumbling over your consciousness and enveloping it, the Yanks' heavy endless cannonfire, explosions and screams and flying dirt.

Pete Bell lay face down about ten feet from Rufus. Not lifting his body at all, Rufus crawled to his friend. It made things better if he was with old Pete. Old Pete knew how to get by. The riflefire was endless now; it seemed to come from everywhere. The artillery barrage echoed way far to the north, and Rufus guessed the Yanks were letting them have it all up and down the line. Somewhere somebody gurgled. The sound carried clearly, over all other sounds. Rufus' eyes widened for a moment. "Must be the whole damn Yank army!" he shouted to Pete.

He didn't hear Pete's answer. His eyes smarted from all the smoke. He closed his eyes, then grinned for a moment. He was thinking of what had happened to old Mabry. Haw haw. About an hour ago Capt Hawk had ordered Mabry down from that horse Mabry had taken from the Yank cavalryman. *You march right along with the others!* Capt Hawk had shouted at Mabry. He'd given old Mabry real hell. *If you want that horse you can LEAD it!* he'd told Mabry. He'd been madder than seventeen chickens in a bathtub. Seventeen chickens in a bathtub. Mabry had been mad too, but hadn't said anything. Mabry was afraid of Capt Hawk. Everybody knew that. He'd led his horse along and hadn't said a word. Haw. Here Rufus opened his eyes and nudged Pete Bell, who had had a big laugh out of it too. Pete didn't move. He nudged Pete again. Still no movement. Rufus grabbed Pete by the shoulders. Pete rolled over on his back. His face had been shot away. There wasn't anything there except a mashed red pulp. Rufus gave a high bleat. He threw himself over the corpse. Old Pete must have looked up at something, old Pete must have looked up at something, old Pete, he—ohhh. Blood still flowed from Pete's face. Rufus got blood all over his hands and arms. He held Pete's head in his arms and he cooed. He hugged Pete and shook him. Tears ran down Rufus' cheeks and carried saltiness to his mouth. He was very frightened now; it was a wet wild fright. He wanted to run away. But running away meant standing up. He couldn't do that. He slapped the corpse, kicked at it. "You got no right!" he yelled. Then he giggled—weakly, with tears dribbling down his cheeks, making dirty streaks. The giggles turned to laughter. He crawled away from his friend's body, crawled to a cool spot under a tree, heard nothing now, saw nothing now, crawled to that spot under the tree and laughed until he passed out.

♣ In support of Buford's cavalry the morning of the first day of the battle were two Union infantry corps. Gen Reynolds' men of the I Corps of the Army of the Potomac were tested and hard. They were veterans. They could be counted on. But Gen Howard's men of the XI Corps were those immigrant Germans who had fled in such a panic at Chancellorsville only two months before. By noon of July 1, 1863 there would be concentrated against these three units nearly all of the Army of Northern Virginia. Led by Robert E. Lee. This Confederate force numbered three infantry corps (in this war the Confederacy had few corps, but they usually contained more than twice as many men as any single federal corps). They were commanded by Generals Hill, Longstreet and Ewell. They never had lost a battle—unless one considered Antietam's confused stalemate a defeat. And now, with such an enormous numerical advantage, it appeared quite likely they would move to another quick and decisive (and not even particularly bloody) victory. After all, most of the Union forces were some distance away, spread out down in Maryland. And the Army of the Potomac was under a new leader who hadn't had much time to get things organized. The skinny and illtempered George Gordon Meade never had been noted for any particular speed in moving troops. Certainly neither Lee nor Hill nor Longstreet nor Ewell had any reason to suspect that Meade would be able to bring up quick aid for Gettysburg's outnumbered defenders. So the Southerners pushed forward, suffered a few minor defeats (one Confederate brigade, under Gen Archer, was wiped out; Archer himself was taken prisoner by a burly Irish private from the I Corps; the private was killed that afternoon), but inflicted heavy casualties. A hot little fight took place in a cut made by the rightofway of the unfinished railroad. The Confederates swept in, were pushed out, swept in again. Reynolds' men resisted bravely here, but finally had to withdraw. At the same time, Buford's dismounted cavalrymen slowly retreated from their position by Willoughby's Run. Howard's Germans (fighting to the north, at Oak Hill) weren't budging, however. This day they did a great deal to erase the disgrace of what had happened at Chancellorsville. But the battle was not going well for the federals. They simply did not have enough men. They were making the Confederates pay, but for how long? The fight was a lot bloodier than the Confederates had expected, but how long could these federals be expected to hold out? How long, in other words, before they collapsed? ♣

CPL LEW MABRY ran whooping down the side of the railroad cut. He stumbled over bodies and equipment and groaning wounded men, then started climbing up the other side. A Yank captain stood up there. The Yank captain kept pulling the trigger of an empty carbine. His eyes were wild and frightened. Mabry's whoops changed to great rolling belts of laughter. (Oh look out Mister!) Mabry reached the top. The captain brought the carbine up like a club. Mabry very calmly walked to within about ten feet of the captain. The captain hesitated, then dropped the carbine and started to raise his hands. Mabry shot the captain through the neck. The captain smiled. Blood spurted from his neck. He fell forward and began to roll down the side of the embankment. Mabry stepped aside and let him pass. The captain's body went over the edge of the embankment—toward more Confederate troops who were scrambling upward. It hit one man broadside and sent him sprawling.

Mabry ran across the top of the embankment. He was laughing so hard he had to hold his side. Men streamed past him. He watched the Yanks retreat across a field. He laughed and laughed.

O glory an a blessin!

The Yanks were in full retreat all right. The field was dotted with running dodging blue uniforms. Screaming Confederates poured after them. They let loose blast after blast of riflefire. Yanks crumpled and fell all over the field.

The pain in Mabry's side was sharp. His wind was all gone. Still laughing, he fell to his hands and knees. Then he fell back and held his side.

That captain had been the last Yank left standing at the top of the embankment.

An *I* got him!

Me!

Old Lew Mabry.

Now ain't that somethin? They ain't nobody can say . . .

(This had been just one hell of a morning, the kind of morning you wish you had more of, yas sir. Mabry wondered what had happened to his platoon. He'd lost it somewhere. Half the time when there was a fight you got separated from the others. So much smoke and firing and men running and everything. And of course Mabry had been leading that horse. It had been a good old horse, yas sir. But just before the fight began the horse had stepped into a hole in the road and had broken a leg. Mabry had had to shoot it in the head. He remembered the puffing sound it made just before it died. He'd sure hated to shoot that old horse. Gingerbread—the Yank scout had called it Gingerbread. Funny name for a horse, but yet there was no getting around it: it *had* been the color of gingerbread. And Mabry had felt bad about shooting it. He'd never killed an animal before. But Capt Hawk had come up to him and had said: *Mabry, the Yanks are right behind them trees there* (pointing); *that's where we're goin* (frowning at the horse, which had just stepped into the hole and was lying on its side); *nicelookin horse. Go on. Shoot it.* Mabry had turned his head just before pulling the trigger. The puffing sound had seemed almost as loud as the shot. For a few minutes there Mabry almost had been sick. Then he had gathered his men together and they had advanced through the woods. They hadn't been able to cross the stream for quite some time. Stevenson had been killed trying to get across. A sharpshooter had shot Bell through the face. The Yanks had let loose with artillery and the whole company had had to hug the ground. Reinforcements finally moved in and they managed to get across the creek. Mabry lost touch with his men somewhere on the other side of the creek. He didn't know what outfit he was with now. He had wandered around for an hour or two, stumbling through smoke and a great deal of shouting milling confusion, and then—after climbing a hill and looking around—he saw the fighting at the railroad cut. Like an idler out for a Sunday stroll and looking for something interesting to watch, he was drawn to the fight. Good thing, too. He'd had a chance to kill a Yank officer. He'd never killed one before, so far as he knew. And the feeling afterwards was just fine, yas sir.)

Still laughing and spluttering and holding his side, he watched the artillery move in. Men yelled and cursed. Horses were covered with sweat. Infantrymen ran past the artillery pieces and poured down after the Yanks. The artillery fired, deafeningly, into the ranks of the retreating federals. Mabry took his hand away from his side and held his ears. Men cheered and waved their hats. Mabry kept laughing, more quietly now, but intensely. The cannoneers were bare to their waists, and most of them were as black as niggers. The air was filled now with the tight sour smell of shot.

Finally Mabry stood up. He made his way through the howling screaming yipping mass of troops running across the field where the Yanks had retreated. He went to the edge of the cut and stared down. He saw the dead Yank captain, sprawled red and limp in the position of the crucified Jesus. Many other dead men were down there too. Mabry climbed down the embankment and walked among the corpses. Cheers and shouts and laughter rolled down to him. The cannons kept up their mighty BWOHMMM! BWOHMM! BWOHMMM! He stared at the dead men. Most of the dead men were federals. Now and then a wounded man would groan or sob. A Union corporal with an enormous hole in his chest asked Mabry for a drink of water. Mabry grinned at him. An endless stream of men ran past him. They pushed at each other, ran down the side of the cut, across it, then up again and into the field where the Yanks had fled. The smell of shot made Mabry sneeze several times. His eyes watered. His pack was heavy on his back but he did not notice. He examined the corpses very closely. No one paid any attention to him. The advancing Confederates were a great disorganized mob. He kept out of their way. Officers and privates ran together. Everybody was shouting. A general whom Mabry didn't recognize galloped past on a fine black horse. He was waving his sword and shouting: "Hurrah! Hurrah! Go get them, boys!" Mabry watched the general. He wanted to tell the general how he'd killed that Yank captain, but the general rode on, shouting and laughing and waving his sword.

The dead men were everywhere. Mabry was interested in the expressions on their faces. No two dead men had the same expressions. It was hard to walk down there, the dead men were so numerous. He took their watches, rings off their fingers. He stuffed his pockets. He'd been doing this ever since the beginning of the war. He had walked six miles to enlist. He would have walked a hundred. He pushed and tugged at the corpses. His exertions made him give out squealing little gasps. He came to a dead Yank sergeant spreadeagled over a stump. The sergeant's stomach and intestines protruded. In his shirt pocket was seven hundred dollars in paper U. S. currency. Mabry snorted and threw it away. He never had saved any kind of money except coin. The sergeant's stomach and intestines fell out after Mabry's exertions. Mabry did not notice. He forced open the sergeant's mouth and examined it for gold teeth. There were several fillings. Mabry took a rock and smashed them out. Blood came flying from the corpse's mouth and spattered Mabry's cheek. He did not notice this either. He washed the fillings in water from the dead man's canteen.

♣ If any one man could claim heroic dimensions during the wild and confused and sometimes even aimless fighting on the first day, that one man was the Union officer, Gen John F. Reynolds, commander of the I Corps of the Army of the Potomac. His troops were outnumbered; they were spread too thinly, over far too long a line—yet during this first day they fought as men do when they feel the future and survival of a cause in their hands. And, in point of fact, the future and survival of the American republic just about WAS in their hands. A breakthrough then, a rout, would have given Lee free passage to Harrisburg. There was no doubt of this in Reynolds' mind. He was in over-all command of the Union forces on the field—his corps, Howard's corps and Buford's cavalry. Nothing else. These men, these few men, these men who were being chopped and whacked and slaughtered by the Confederates, had to hold out until the remainder—and greater part—of the Army of the Potomac arrived. If they didn't, the door would be opened to catastrophe. Gen John F. Reynolds was shot dead at eleven that morning. ♣

LEORA BAGLEY stood on the front porch of her home. She was wearing the white dress. Her eyes were red and her hair hung lank, with no curl. She was bent forward with her shoulders hunched. Everything she saw was blurred. She gasped and choked on her sobs.

Last night, oh last night she had felt such an excitement, such a great happy anticipation. There would be a great battle. The Union troops would defeat the secessionists. All her life she would be able to tell people how she had seen a great battle won by the army of Courage and Right and Freedom. She had put on the white dress because, after all, it was going to be an occasion.

But nothing was working out.

Things should work out. They shouldn't be like this.

Why was I so happy last night?

Her vision blurred and cloudy from her tears, she looked out to the road. Horses and wagons and guns trundled past, loud, heavy. Off to the west came the sound of cannonfire, the steady endless roaring, punctuated by the snapping clatter of rifles, and out there on the road the walking wounded were moving past, heading east to safety: all those men (she must have seen a thousand) walking as fast as they were able, some of them stumbling and falling and then very deliberately and painfully getting to their feet, all those men, some holding their wounds, some moaning or howling or screaming, all those men, in procession out there, moving east, moving to the rear, moving to safety. Earlier Leora had gone out there and had tried to help some of them. They had pushed her away. Some of them had cursed her. She had run weeping back onto the porch but she hadn't been able to go inside. She stood there and watched them, watched the notwounded march past toward where the fighting was, watched the great whorls of smoke come up from the hills and fields there to the west, felt the vibration and loudness and heaviness of the cannon and wagons that rolled and clattered down the road, heard the snorts and high whinnies of horses, saw the mounted officers waving their swords and shouting orders: she saw and heard all these things, she felt the sun pound down from above, and she was without the feeling of excitement: she simply wept, and dust from the road got into her eyes.

She wished Daddy was home.

She wondered why she kept standing there. Mamma and her brother Johnny were inside. Mamma was in bed, with a sheet pulled over her head, and all morning long she had trembled and whimpered. Johnny was with her. He held her hand. She had insisted he hold her hand. She wouldn't let him go. He had wanted to go outside to watch the fighting; he had screamed and had stomped his foot and had stormed like a wild boy, but Mamma hadn't let him go anywhere. So he was sitting up there with her now, and he was as mad as anything.

If Daddy was home, he'd know what to do.

What's there to do?

What are you supposed to do?

Anything?

I hope he's all right.

Maybe he was shot . . .

NO!

He is my Daddy and he wasn't shot.

The sound—all that roaring and blasting, the trundling noises, the shouts, the snorts and whinnies, the screams and moans— blotted the sound of Leora's weeping. She put her hands over her ears and closed her eyes. She wanted to run. She wanted to jump off this porch and run away from all this noise and confusion, run and run until the running and the distance erased memory, until she would not see those wounded men holding the red places where they had been hit, those men who clutched themselves and cursed her.

They said dirty things to me.

Why here?

Why can't they go fight their dirty old battle someplace else?

This is nice country.

We never wanted any battle.

Those men, so many, so many hurt.

I don't want to look any more.

I'll open my eyes and take my hands away from my ears and they'll all be gone.

Not today. They're here today and you'll see them all the time.

You'll hear them too.

You'll hear this always.

Get away from me, sis. I'm all RIGHT:

. . . was what one of the wounded men had said to her. Why? She'd just been trying to help. She shook her head, then opened her eyes and took her hands away from her ears.

The wounded men staggered out there. She watched them and could not move. Off to the west the smoke was very thick. It kept rising, rising. Wagons and cannon kept rolling past. We're losing, Leora said to herself. We're losing and pretty soon now the men who aren't wounded will come by. I know it. I just do too know it.

The sun was bright and white high in the sky. It was about noon. Leora felt sweat on her upper lip, in her armpits. She wailed very loudly but could not even hear herself for all the noise. The men out there did not wave at her.

Nothing was like yesterday.

An officer, tall and straight on a big brown horse, reined to a halt in front of some of the wounded men. The horse's coat was flecked white with sweat. It panted and snorted.

The officer's uniform was as clean and neat as anything. "How's it going up there?" he asked the wounded men. He had to shout to make them hear over the din.

"Better not go up too far," said a man who was holding his head.

"You'll get your butt shot off, Cap," said a man whose hands were over his buttocks.

The officer didn't say anything. He galloped off toward the west. The wounded men continued their slow stumbling shuffle to the rear.

Leora looked to the west, watched the officer disappear. Now all she could see were dust and smoke. The steady sound of explosions did not diminish. Neither did it rise. And then, running up the road, came men who were not wounded. It was the advance wave of the retreat. Leora swallowed a huge dismal lump. Officers came galloping after these men and tried to turn them around. But there were too many men running now. They streamed down the

road, across fields, even on the lawn there in front of Leora's
home. They did not look at her. They kicked up much dust. They
kept moving. They did not look back. Leora didn't want to watch,
but she couldn't help it. The dismal lump was lodged somewhere
in her stomach.

These men were moving quickly but they did not seem to be
in any particular panic. Most of them still carried their equipment.
But they simply would not pay any attention to the officers who
were trying to rally them. The enormous sounds from the west
were coming closer now. The men streamed past Leora's home,
and after a time horses and equipment and heavy cannon also
went by. Everything now, moving to the east. (The Bagley home
was by itself at the west end of town. Five hundred yards farther
were the first houses of Gettysburg. Leora's position on the porch
commanded a view overlooking a hill that slanted down a mile to
the farm of their neighbors, the Luke Brandts. Leora could make
out Luke and his wife standing in their barnyard watching the
troops go by.)

The road now was jammed. Dust and shouts and the sound of
many horses rose from the confusion. The wind blew much dust
in Leora's face. She did not notice. She kept wiping her nose and
rubbing her eyes but really she did not notice. All her concentration was focused on the retreat and her own dismal lump.

Several officers galloped past her. One saw her there and reined
to a halt. He turned his horse around and rode up to her. He was
very young. He tipped his hat and smiled. "Better get inside,
miss!" he shouted, still smiling. His voice barely carried over the
rumble of the wagons and the rumble of the firing and the low
deadly monotonous rumble of the feet of all those men who were
moving to the rear.

Leora stared at him.

"Did you hear me?" he shouted.

She didn't say anything.

"Miss?"

She nodded. Her nose was running.

"Get inside! For God's sake bolt your door!" The young officer wasn't smiling now. His face was very red. Dribbling streams of sweat ran down his face.

She nodded again.

(Noise. Noise everywhere.)

He tipped his hat again, then jammed his spurs into the flanks of his horse. Back to the road. More dust.

Leora did not move from the porch.

Her head hurt.

She guessed she should go inside. But she just couldn't. It seemed she had to stand out here and watch all this. She had to see what was happening; it made no difference if a million rebels came along. She tried to remember how excited and expectant she had felt last night. And now, as she watched the retreat, as she watched all these men moving to the rear, she noticed how more and more of them were running. And some now were dropping their packs. The road was littered with discarded equipment. Wagons and guns rolled over the discarded equipment, crushing some of it, sending some of it spinning off the road. Wagons and cannon kept rolling by. Drivers wielded great whips and shouted at their horses. Leora felt sorry for the poor horses. They were doing their best weren't they? Poor horses: they had heavy loads to pull.

Nobody was going west now. The entire army seemed to be in retreat. Officers. Everybody. Faster and faster. With the noise louder now behind them. (Noise. Noise everywhere.)

Three horses pulling a cannon stopped in front of Leora's home. An officer shouted orders to four men. The men were halfnaked, soaked in sweat. Slowly, very slowly, heavily, they went to work on the cannon. It roared, bucked, settled back in dust. Again, quickly, on an order from the officer: the roaring, the bucking.

Leora jumped back. (Noise. Noise everywhere.) She scrunched her eyes closed tightly. Very clearly came to her the sound of her mother's screams upstairs. She put her hands over her ears. She nearly swallowed her tongue. The sun was very warm. She felt it on her face. The sweat grew sticky in her armpits. The officer gave more orders. Then the sound of horses, the rumbling of the gun's wheels. She opened her eyes.

Now more men were hollering. A detachment of cavalry galloped by. The men were firing back over their shoulders.

And just then, for the first time, she heard that yell.

Eeeeeyaaaaahhhooooooo! it came, clearly and piercingly over all other sounds—followed by short rhythmic sounds, as though from a thousand dogs.

She stared to the west. Smoke rose everywhere. She screamed. She screamed again.

They were ragged and gray. Most of them were so thin.

Men in gray, ragged men, thin men, men yipping and waving their arms, came running along the road. They jogged easily, yelling and slapping each other on the back.

Leora ran into the house. She slammed the front door and bolted it. She ran into the kitchen and bolted the door there too. She ran upstairs. (Noise. Noise everywhere.) Mamma and Johnny were huddled in the bed. The sheet was pulled over both their heads. For an instant Leora wondered if Johnny wanted to go look now. She crawled into bed with them. They all wept with great force and loudness. The bed creaked from their hysteria. The room was very stuffy. They did not notice. They wept until finally there was nothing left. Outside the rebels whooped and yipped and whistled and sang. The sound of explosions was to the east now. Leora and her mother and her brother lay beneath that sheet for a very long time. (Noise. Noise everywhere, even after their weeping had ceased.) Finally Leora got up and opened the window.

   ♣   Smoke and dust and a dry-and-wet sick choking miasma of human smells rose swirling heavily from the earth that first day. It was a day of great noisy whirling running galloping movements. The Confederates advanced. The federals retreated. Everywhere there was bravery. There always is. Men (most men) are afraid before they go into a battle—but once they are there, with the immediacy of death and terror and pain pounding pounding pounding at them in the whines and roars and cracklings of combat, they (most men) become almost calm, yes, and sometimes even thoughtful. Nothing is so bad, they think, when it is endured with others. Endurance when it is lonely is much worse. The man in battle looks at other men, sees them fighting, holding firm. He knows he is not the only one in this fix. This knowledge gives him courage. He supports his comrades; he also holds firm. Of course this is not true undiluted courage. But it is courage with a raw pragmatic meaning beyond the cardboard heroics of storybooks. In this courage there are no ideals; you think not of the flag. You do not even think of survival. Rather you EXPERIENCE the DESIRE to survive. To THINK of the anatomical structure of courage and its reasons is patently ridiculous. Say now you there bubber, you there from the State of Maine (tall trees in thickness against the sides of hills, clear clean cold creeks with yellow and gray and black and brown rocks and stones and pebbles rounded from the rush of water, humpbacked rolling sprawling mountains rising in their arrogant and timeless chilly snow-streaked grandeur), you there bubber, you lie in dirt and your eyes narrow (eyebrows scrunching together) as you sight your rifle and you fire, cawhack, and maybe a reb screams or topples or grabs himself or something, and this (this thing you are doing, this sniping, this cawhacking, this narrowing of your eyes, this deadly and dispassionate slight and very accurate pressure of the finger against the trigger), this is courage, this is courage in whatever its ultimate meaning may be, and it makes no difference that this morning you were afraid. You are not afraid now; others are with you; that makes a difference. You lie there with your feet hurting and your arms and shoulders aching and your rifle is very heavy indeed and your heart is rumblebumping in your throat and your throat is dry and sometimes your hands tremble and you keep wiping them against your britches to get rid of the sweat and more sweat is dribbling down the back of your neck and then down your spine where you cannot reach: you lie there and feel all those things and you keep sniping and you do as you are told, and this is courage. You care for yourself very much; you now know what a precious thing you are, what a miraculous gasping straining logical purposeful organism you are. So bubber you are brave; you are brave because it would not do to be cowardly; you are brave because the others, most of them, are doing the same as you. And, most important, you are brave because you know a brave man is more alert and thus has a better chance to save himself for the next time, when it will all happen again. ♣

CALEB BUSHNELL had a very bad limp.

He had turned his ankle or something about two hours ago when he and Wheatfield jumped into a ditch. A reb cavalry patrol had almost surprised them walking along this road. Now Caleb leaned heavily against Wheatfield as they slowly headed east. They hadn't come too far since their escape last night. They'd been lost for a time, thrashing around blindly in some woods. Finally, after the sun had come up, they had climbed a hill, had got their bearings and had headed east.

They had seen this road from the hill. It was a narrow and

dusty old road, but at least it was straight. It headed east through a succession of low round hills.

They saw several farmhouses. Wheatfield told Caleb they'd probably be able to get some food at one of them. After all, these were *Union* people in this part of the country. They'd be glad to help.

But since Caleb's accident they hadn't seen a farmhouse. He groaned and moaned and slobbered; his weight against Wheatfield was becoming heavier and heavier. That goddam patrol: Caleb and Wheatfield had been very careful. They had walked along very quietly. Listening for every little sound. A bird would twit and they'd both jump. They walked kind of hunched over, ready to run, to dive into the ditch—as they did, tumbling, when the reb patrol came galloping past. That was when Caleb turned his ankle, his right ankle. It was swollen now.

Wheatfield grunted under the weight of his friend. Wouldn't you just know it? he kept saying to himself. They didn't see us. Fine. Just fine. But look what happened instead. Do some people (me, for instance) have no damn luck at all?

Aw, stop that.

You got enough to worry about without feeling sorry for yourself.

Wheatfield was very tired. The sun was hot and steady in a sky that was cloudless. The air he breathed was dry, yet he kept sweating and sweating. The blisters on his feet, his sore ankles, all that marching he had done—oh, Wheatfield was tired all right, and now Caleb had twisted his ankle or whatever and the two of them now were slowed down almost to a crawl. They staggered forward from side to side of the road. Silently Wheatfield kept cursing and cursing that goddam reb patrol.

Then, following the road up and over one of the low rounded hills, they saw the farmhouse. It was white, large, neatlooking.

These people in Pennsylvania sure did know how to keep up a place. Behind the house was an enormous red barn decorated with squiggly lines, circles, crosses, arrows. Somebody had told Wheatfield these were hex signs, guaranteed to keep trouble away. He had seen these great barns everyplace for the past week or so. They certainly did give a farm a presence.

My God look at that, he said to himself. Enviously. There certainly wasn't anything like that back home in Illinois. Huh—some folks got it pretty good. Ah well, they'll probably give us something to eat and let Caleb rest a little.

"You hungry?" he asked Caleb.

Caleb made a weak groaning sound. He was considerably taller than Wheatfield; his weight was quite heavy; he kind of dragged his bad foot or leg or whatever it was.

Wheatfield rubbed his lips together. He tugged at Caleb, dragged him. Caleb was getting heavier and heavier. "What'd you say?"

Caleb grunted over the words. "Yep. I'm—yep, I'm hungry."

"You can lay down for a bit when we get there," Wheatfield said.

Wheatfield's back and legs hurt. Now and then Caleb gave little shrieks.

Wheatfield lurched, gulped air: We'll never get there. It's not there at all. No. I'm pulling and tugging but it don't make no difference. We ain't never going to get there. This sure was a fine idea. Escape, yes sir. Nothing like escaping from the rebs. Yes sir. Look at Caleb. Ain't he glad he escaped? Maybe he broke his foot or something. That's just fine. Oh just fine. Well what was we supposed to do? Stay there and let them rebs send us off to Belle Isle or whatever? Well goddamit I'm tired. What kind of a way to fight a war is this anyway? Rebs are all over the place. I can see them now just coming over that hill yonder and coming down on us and shooting us because we snuck away. All night long we thrash around them woods like a couple of blind dogs. Why? Yep—fine question. If we'd of stayed we'd of gone to Belle Isle or someplace. So we get away. And now look. Oh this is real fine. Yes sir. Now look at that house and barn up yonder. Maybe Robert E. Lee is setting in there with his whole staff. Ha ha ha, now wouldn't that be something? I hurt goddamit. Dragging this feller along. He's a lot bigger than me. Him and his groaning. We'll never get there. Never get there. How do we know what's there when we do get there? Fine house and barn. Farmer. Must be about dinnertime. I don't see nobody out in the yard. They sure do keep their places up. Belle Isle. Tired. He I bet he is hurt bad just my luck I can't leave him out here what in the name of God am I going to do?

Then they were in front of the farmhouse.

Flies brushed at Wheatfield's face. He used his free hand to shoo them off. "There'll be a place now where you can lay down," he said to Caleb.

They entered the yard. Wheatfield shook his head admiringly. He stared at the barn. A farmer always looked first at a stranger's barn. Not the stranger's house. His barn. A man can live almost anywhere, but any farmer who thinks of himself as anything has to have a warm dry place for his stock. And these people in Pennsylvania sure did keep good barns.

Wheatfield helped Caleb across the front yard. They didn't see a soul. "Just a little bit more now," Wheatfield said. "Little bit."

Slowly, heavily, Wheatfield dragged Caleb up the steps and onto the front stoop. There were no sounds but their breathing.

Wheatfield pounded on the front door.

They waited. Caleb leaned against the house. Wheatfield's arm that had been supporting Caleb hurt.

No answer. Wheatfield pounded again, loudly.

More waiting. Still no answer. "Hey!" Wheatfield hollered. His voice carried far.

No answer. Nothing. He looked around. The house was very clean. It was an old house, but whoever lived in it apparently took pride in keeping it scrubbed. The outside walls were made of oak and painted white. The front door was a dark brown, wood color.

But no one came to the door. Wheatfield strained his ears but didn't hear anything.

He tried the door. It opened easily, swinging away from his hand with a small weak creak.

Wheatfield blinked. He peered inside. The room was thick with darkness. It smelled cool and it made the sweat itch on his face.

He left Caleb leaning against the front of the house and took a step inside. "Anybody home?" he said softly.

Not a sound.

He went back to Caleb and helped him inside. They took a few steps, then stumbled and nearly fell. Wheatfield tightened his grip on Caleb just in time to keep him from hitting the floor. They staggered forward, lurching, trying to keep their balance.

"Don't move, rebs," someone said. Loudly. In an old voice.

Wheatfield swallowed some kind of a thickness. He felt Caleb stiffen.

"Just stand right there quiet," the old voice said.

There was a thumping sound, as though someone were pounding a heavy stick on the floor. Then a swishing sound, and off at a side window the curtains parted. Light tumbled into the room.

The old man grinned at them.

He was at least eighty, tall and straight and bald. The wrinkles in his face were heavy and deep. His shoulders and chest and arms and hands were thick. His fingers were long, and now they were wrapped around the stock of an old musket that must have been at least six feet long. The musket did not waver.

These are blue suits we're wearing, old man, Wheatfield wanted to tell him, but he couldn't find the words. He was having a hard time keeping down the thickness.

Then he noticed that the old man had a wooden leg. It was what had made the thumping sound.

The old man grinned, spreading wide the great wild disorganized pattern of wrinkles and sags on his face, and he laughed a high cackle of a laugh. He thumped a few paces closer to the two intruders. Caleb moaned. The old man's finger tapped tit tittittit tit tittittit on the trigger of the musket. It was ever such a light and soft sound, but it was very distinct.

Wheatfield coughed. "We ain't—" he began.

"Shhh," the old man said. "I told you shhh."

Wheatfield sighed and spread his hands. "Ah," he said. He wished Caleb would say something.

Caleb fell against Wheatfield.

Wheatfield braced him. He stared pleadingly at the old man.

The old man moved forward a few more steps. He frowned at Wheatfield.

"We're Union men," Wheatfield blurted out, the words ending in a kind of sigh.

"I'll kill the both of you, you stinking rebels."

"No!" Wheatfield shouted desperately. "Look at our uniforms!"

A few more steps forward. Another frown. "You're spies," the old man said. "Spies trying to fool an old man. Trying to fool an old fool. There's no fool to fool like an old fool. I'll show you who's the fool." He opened his mouth and laughed very loudly. His teeth were helterskelter and yellow. The laugh was a woman's laugh, not deep at all.

Caleb began to tremble. His eyeballs rolled up. "NO!" he bel-

lowed. He pulled free from Wheatfield and fell into a chair. There
he closed his eyes and passed out. Tit tittittit, the old man's
musket followed Caleb.

"Brave soldiers," the old man said, snuffling down his laughter.

"We're Union men," Wheatfield said.

"Would you spit on the Confederate flag if there was one
here?"

"Yes."

"What do you think of old fools?"

"What?"

"Answer my question."

"My friend is hurt, mister. I'm a Union man. So's he. All you
got to do is look at our uniforms. We just came here to rest—
that's all. I don't know nothing about old fools."

"You'd spit on the Confederate flag?"

"Yes," Wheatfield said.

"I wouldn't. I tell you why. Spitting's too good."

Wheatfield didn't say anything. The old feller's crazy, he told
himself. Crazy as crazy can be.

"Answer my question about old fools," the old man said.

Wheatfield stared at the floor and considered diving at the old
man's feet.

The old man dropped the musket on the floor. "Union men,"
he said.

Wheatfield leaped forward for the musket.

"Don't bother," the old man said. "It ain't been fired since
Eighteen and Twelve."

Wheatfield grabbed the musket and lifted it. He opened the
breech. It was empty. "Jesus Christ," he said. Then he expelled a
great deal of breath. Caleb groaned weakly in his chair.

Wheatfield straightened up. He wanted to embrace the old
man. Funny, somebody threatens you, says he might kill you, and

then he removes the threat and you want to hug him. When you make up with your worst enemy he's more than a friend; he's your best friend.

The old man wasn't smiling now. He shook his head from side to side. "I know you're Union. Escaped prisoners maybe? I saw you come up the road. I guess I just wanted to play."

"Escaped prisoners," Wheatfield said. "We got away from them last night. We been walking and walking. This feller with me hurt himself jumping into a ditch."

"Oh," the old man said. He waved an arm. "Have a seat." He hobbled over to a rocker by a window.

Wheatfield leaned the musket against a wall. He sat down on a wooden bench by the door.

"New Orleans. Eighteen and Twelve," the old man said.

"Uh?" Wheatfield said.

"Last time I fired that thing," the old man said, nodding toward the musket.

"Oh," Wheatfield said, thinking: What are you supposed to say?

The rocker creaked. "There's something to eat in the kitchen."

"We are kind of hungry."

"You can go get it yourself. I'm the only one here."

Wheatfield thought of the size and neatness of the place. "You live here all by yourself?"

The old man snorted.

"Where's everybody else?"

"That any of your business?"

"No. Just talk. I didn't mean to pry into your business."

"Sure you did. You did too. That's all right. I don't mind."

Wheatfield grinned. He still was breathing in and out very deeply. He stretched his legs out in front of him and massaged his calves.

"I live here with my two boys," the old man said. He snickered. "If boys is what you want to call them. One's fiftytwo. Other's fifty. They went off last week with their wives and their kids. War was coming here and they was afraid so they went away. Scared. Yes sir. Real good and scared. So everybody went away. Everybody except me. Ain't nobody scares me. No man on this earth. Not you, not nobody. You just try and scare me sonny."

"I don't want to," Wheatfield said. "I'm just tired."

"What about the other feller?"

Wheatfield glanced at Caleb, who was asleep. "He's hurt. He don't want to scare nobody either."

"I lost a leg on account of I wasn't scared."

"Eighteen and Twelve?"

"Yep. Under Andy Jackson. You ever hear of Andy Jackson?"

"The president?"

"Yep. You don't hear so much about him any more. Gangrene. They had to cut it off and they got me drunk on whisky and I passed out and when I woke up it felt like I still had a leg down there but I didn't. No leg. I don't know what happened to it. I sure was drunk that night. They put that bottle to my mouth and it was like I was sucking high tit. I floated. Let me tell you. You don't hear so much about Andy Jackson these days. Eighteen and Twelve is a long time ago. New Orleans. Lot of niggers with French names in New Orleans. You ever been to New Orleans?"

"No."

"You like fighting for the niggers?"

"Never thought much about it."

"You know I built my own wooden leg? Took a long time to learn to walk on it. Tell me something: do you ever think?"

"I don't . . ."

"What I mean is: you ever just sit and think? I mean about anything at all. Any old thing at all."

"I guess so," Wheatfield said. He stood up. He was hungry. He didn't want to talk with this old man anymore. Old men they talk and talk, and nothing follows the way it should. They keep repeating themselves and they never keep on any one thing for any length of time. Back and forth their minds go. Back and forth. Wheatfield had known plenty of them back home. Old men sitting shooing flies in front of Luden's general store back in Mattoon. Starting off talking about the weather and going on from there into any fancy, any vagrant flick of intellect. And always their eyes were clouded over with something you couldn't get through to no matter what.

Wheatfield pointed toward a door. "The kitchen in there?"

The old man nodded, rose and stumped after him. "You going to leave your friend in the parlor?"

"Let him sleep."

The old man followed Wheatfield toward the kitchen. They went along a hall. Everything was clean. Wheatfield glanced into a couple of side rooms. It was a big place all right. The walls, the floors, the furnishings (most everything was thick and heavy and of oak), all looked as though someone—or maybe two or three people—had spent a great deal of time taking care of them. This was one thing Wheatfield had noticed about the people who lived in this part of the country. They seemed to enjoy the things that were theirs; they seemed to enjoy neatness, the clean thing, the good thing kept good, fashioning here from God's bounty a way of living that was neat and comfortable and stolid and clean and predictable. (Wheatfield believed in God, in a straight and heavy pattern devised by Him, and such a place as this made him feel good.) But now there was this war and the good people who had lived in this house, the neat and clean and stolid people, had fled, leaving only this fuzzyheaded hobbling old man. The good people who had lived here had known that war was neither neat nor clean, that the sights and smells and sounds of war were not predictable, that war was not a good thing you could improve, or scrub, or preserve. But the fuzzyheaded old man had stayed. And had wielded an empty musket. And had talked. Old man's talk. Old man's courage too, and Wheatfield understood.

The kitchen was large and light and airy. Its walls were whitewashed. An enormous castiron stove dominated the room. A loaf of bread lay on a large whitewashed oak table. Wheatfield twisted off a hunk of the bread. The bread was some stale, but it was good—thick and chewy.

"Things are kind of old and stale," the old man said. "I'm old and stale myself and don't do much cooking." He took a knife from a cupboard and went to the stove. He opened the oven door and pulled out a large platter of cold lamb. He sliced off some pieces and ripped off a shank. He brought the meat to Wheatfield on a plate.

Wheatfield grunted and took the meat in his bare hands. His jaws worked noisily. Juices ran down his chin, down onto his shirt, but he did not notice.

The old man brought him a tincupful of water from a jug. "I ain't got nothing for you to drink except water. My sons they took the cows and all the stock to a neighbor up the road about two three miles. Me being old and stale and all, I wouldn't have been able to milk the cows. You know, I been thinking about something. My sons, I bet they didn't like taking the stock to George Gunstadder's place. George and his family stayed. Like me, they stayed. It's their home and they stayed. I bet my sons were ashamed. But ashamed or not, they did it. They were ashamed I bet, but they were scared too, and they were more scared than ashamed. You think maybe that's so?"

"Um."

The old man sat down across the table from Wheatfield. "I'm eightyone years old and I'm six feet two inches tall, wooden leg and all, and when I was seventytwo I could still get my pecker up. Woke up one night. There the thing was. Stiff as anything. But that was nine years ago. It ain't happened since. Sure did make me feel good at the time though. Nine years ago. Huh. But now I can't even milk the cows. We keep eleven cows. I couldn't no more milk eleven cows now than I could fly to the moon. It works at your shoulders and arms, makes them sore. Milking cows that is. Not flying to the moon. Hard work for man when he's old I tell you . . ."

The words rattled, rushing, on and on. Wheatfield did not look up from his plate.

"Your friend he don't look so good," the old man said. "You think maybe his ankle's broke?"

"Um?"

The old man repeated his question.

"Don't know," Wheatfield said.

The old man made a sucking noise through his teeth. "I had an ankle broke once. Tripped on the steps coming up on the stoop right out there in front. The ankle of the leg that ain't wooden I mean. I'm eightyone. Lived here all my life. A man's life all spent in one place. Except for Eighteen and Twelve. The recruiters came around and a little redheaded feller I remember beat a drum. Dlum dlum dlum, real fast, dlum dlum dlum, and people gathered around and some feller made a speech and I was carried away I guess and I was the first one to join from around here. First one. Carried away. They carried me away all right. At New Orleans. Leaving a leg of me behind. I don't even know what they did with it. You ever think about what it means to be old? I got this farm here. I got more than two hundred acres. I built this place in Eighteen and Twentynine. The old place, my father's place, was back behind a barn. I built this house because my wife —she died in 'Fortysix—because my wife she always was complaining about the draughts in the old place, how you couldn't ever keep it warm. She was right too. I was born and raised in that old house and I never was warm. So I built this place. I like it. It's warm. And by God I built it and it's mine. This whole damn place is mine. One of these days it won't be mine. Soon now I suppose I'll go. Just an old man who talks too much. Might as well go. What's the difference anyway? You don't want to be old sonny. No sir. Don't let nobody tell you different. I'm old. Nobody ever pays any mind to me. Nobody listens. I talk and talk. Nobody listens. I guess that's all right. Probably I ain't got nothing to listen to. Old men they feel sorry for themselves. Hell, boy —you take my advice and see that you die when you're fifty. Then you won't have to go through thirty years of being something no one gives a whoop for. John—he's my oldest son, the one who's fiftytwo—he says he swears he never knew a soul who talked as much as me. Himself, he don't talk so much. He got a big fat wife and he got six kids. One of John's boys—Eustace: he's nineteen— is in the army out west in Tennessee I think it is. My other son, the one who's fifty, his name is Frank. He got a big fat wife too. Six kids, seventh on the way—and two that died. Let me tell you there's been a lot of kidmaking in this house. And you know what? I think John's jealous. Yes sir—jealous. Frank's got just about seven any day now and John he's only got six. They never have talked much to each other John and Frank, but I never saw any aggravation between them. Now I think there is. John's jealous because his brother's about to pass him up. Wonder if John got anything left. Wonder if he can catch up. Ah huh huh ah. Anyway, the whole troop of them—John's family and Frank's family—live here. All except Eustace that is. Or did. Until the rebs came. They didn't want no part of the rebs. Maybe you think I don't like them. You're right. I don't. What'd you say your name was?"

Wheatfield gnawed away at the meat. He didn't hear the old man's question.

The old man's face tightened in its profusion of wrinkles and sags. He wet his lips with a grayish tongue. "*THE REBELS ARE COMING!*" he shouted.

Wheatfield dropped his food and vaulted from his chair. The old man sniggered. "*Where?*" Wheatfield hollered, panic rising in his throat.

"Everywhere," the old man said.

"What?"

"Sit down. I just wanted to bring you to."

Wheatfield sat down. "Why'd you do that?"

"You weren't paying no attention."

"To what?"

"Me," the old man said. "I been talking."

Wheatfield put his hands, palms down, on the table to stop the trembling. "God," he said.

"Nobody pays no attention. You a reb spy?"

"Old man, I told you once. You shouldn't ought to have scared me like that."

"I told you, you goddam reb. I told you I ain't afraid of nobody."

"Don't call me a reb," Wheatfield said angrily.

"Then you listen to me," the old man said. "A man takes you in, gives you something to eat and tries to be friendly and you ain't got the courtesy to listen to what he's saying. You been taught manners?"

"I been eating."

"You want more?"

"I'd be obliged."

"Get it yourself."

Wheatfield went to the stove and sliced some more meat. The knife was unsteady in his hand and the slices he cut were uneven. He took several more deep breaths, then returned to the table.

"I wouldn't hit you on the head if you thanked me," the old man said.

Wheatfield looked up and what the hell anyway, he laughed. "I thank you very much," he said, lingering over the words with formal gravity.

"All right. All right. Go on. Eat. You're hungry. Anyway, I probably shouldn't of scared you like that," the old man said, but the tone of his words made it clear he had been hurt.

Wheatfield sensed it. He looked up quickly from his plate and put the meat aside. "My name's Johnson. Whitfield Johnson."

"Johnson? You say *Johnson*?"

"Yes."

The old man reached across the table and seized Wheatfield's hand. "Johnson. That's my name too. Johnson. Walter Johnson."

"Pleased to meet you," Wheatfield said, grinning.

"What part of the country you from? Maybe we're kin."

"Illinois. There's a lot of Johnsons in the world."

The old man scratched his chin. "I got a cousin living in Chicago. No—no, her name ain't Johnson. It's Fitch."

"Hmmm," Wheatfield said profoundly, nodding. After he did it, he laughed at himself. What do I care he has a cousin named Fitch and not Johnson?

The old man opened his mouth to say something.

The hoofbeats carried very clearly.

Wheatfield stared for an instant at the old man, then jumped up and dashed into the parlor. He peeked out a front window. A squad of secesh cavalry was galloping up the road. Jesus. He turned from the window and went to Caleb, who was still asleep in the chair. He shook Caleb viciously.

Caleb blinked and made a face.

"Come on," Wheatfield said, keeping his voice low. He pulled Caleb upright and dragged him into the kitchen. Caleb, floundering, was so much dead weight.

Walter Johnson, erect, his eyes wide, stood waiting for them. He stumped across the room and opened the back door. "Cellar door's around the side of the house. Go down there and keep still."

Caleb drooled. Wheatfield dragged him out the door. He heard shouts, orders. The rebels' horses neighed and snuffled at the front of the house. Wheatfield dragged Caleb down the cellar steps and then went back up and softly closed the door.

Everything was damp and cool and dark. Caleb had collapsed on the floor. Wheatfield pulled him to a corner, propped him upright and held a hand over his mouth.

The old man was thumping around upstairs.

Then there was the sound of boots, some shouts, a loud deep laugh.

Water was dripping somewhere in the cellar. Drip. Long pause. Drip. Long pause. Drip. It made Wheatfield thirsty. He wished he had some more of that water the old man had given him in the tincup. He kept his hand over Caleb's mouth and they sat in the corner of that cellar, down there in all that darkness, all that dampness and coolness that made Wheatfield itch where the sweat was, and the rebels' voices carried down clearly. So did the loud high voice of the old man who called himself Walter Johnson.

". . . no, damn you," Walter Johnson was saying, voice rasping, "I ain't seen no one. And anyway, you think I'd be about to be telling you?"

"Easy sir," a soft rebel voice said. "Don't take on so."

"There ain't nothing scares me," said the voice of Walter Johnson.

"I just bet that's true," the rebel voice said. Courteously.

"Goddam old fool," another rebel voice said. "We won't get nothin out of him. He just wants to act big. Be a big Yank hero."

"Be quiet," the first rebel voice, the courteous one, said.

"We ain't got time to be—"

"Be quiet I said."

"Go on and go," Walter Johnson said. "I ain't seen nothing. There ain't been none of our boys around here three four days —and you know it too. What're you here for? You going to shoot me? You think I been spying?"

"We heard of some Yank cavalry," the courteous voice said.

"What you been drinking?" Walter Johnson wanted to know.

Several of the rebels laughed.

"Goddam insurgents," Walter Johnson said.

More laughter. "Full of piss and vinegar, ain't he?" one of the rebels said. Boots clomped as they walked around the kitchen. There was a jabber of talk and a steady wump, wump, wump of boots. (All this came very clearly to Wheatfield. He smiled. He guessed the old man was all right. Then the smile faded away. He didn't like to think of what would happen if one of those rebs came down cellar.)

". . . eightyone years old," Walter Johnson was saying, his voice shrill. "I'm eightyone years old. My family, all the younger people, they skedaddled when they heard you fellers was coming. Not me. This is my place and you fellers is on my property. It was my daddy's and his daddy's too. I don't know nothing about no cavalry. I wish I did, then I could lie to you and I'd get a lot of satisfaction out of it."

"Now, sir," the courteous voice said.

"You going to shoot me?"

"Sir?"

"You going to shoot me? I'm eightyone. I'm just about your match ain't I?"

The courteous voice laughed. "*Too much,*" it said.

"God bless Abe Lincoln!" Walter Johnson said fervently.

The rebels whooped with laughter. The boots moved through the house . . . toward the front door, Wheatfield hoped. He heard the old man stump after them.

"You can go back to your dinner now," the courteous voice said.

"Dinner?"

"On the table in the kitchen."

"Oh. Dinner. Yes."

(Wheatfield closed his eyes and bit his tongue.)

"God bless Robert E. Lee," the courteous voice said, laughing.

(Wheatfield opened his eyes and released his tongue.)

"Say a prayer for him grampa," another rebel voice said.

"In a pig's—"

"Now, now," the courteous voice said. "We have a pretty fair idea of your sympathies, sir."

"Get the hell out of here!"

The rebels laughed and left. There were whinnying and snorting sounds. Then the sound of hooves. Then no sound at all except the clump of the old man's wooden leg.

Then a shout from Walter Johnson: "Come on out! You fellers planning to spend the winter down there?"

Wheatfield sighed, then laughed, loudly and easily.

♣ But they didn't kill Reynolds soon enough. He had seen the danger and had acted upon it. It was Reynolds, tall Reynolds, strong and calm, great heart, who examined the situation, fused heart and intellect and did the things that were necessary to keep his army on the field, to keep it from fleeing—and it was Reynolds who called for the rest of the Army of the Potomac, the bulk of Meade's troops still in Maryland. In time to do some good. Before time drained into defeat. Climbing up the belltower of a Lutheran seminary just west of Gettysburg, Reynolds and his staff surveyed the fighting. It was not going well at all. His own corps and Buford's dismounted cavalrymen were off to the west, outnumbered and retreating, fighting with enormous spirit but falling back. And all roads now were flooded with advancing rebel troops, converging from the north and west and southwest. Confederates and Confederates and Confederates. Reynolds and the men quietly watched the on-rush of the invaders. After a time he turned and surveyed the country behind them and to the south. The seminary and its belltower were located on a ridge running north and south, commanding a fine view for about five miles in any direction. So Reynolds looked around. And saw something. South of Gettysburg. He probably smiled. For there, to the rear, east a bit but mostly south of the town, he saw another and higher ridge, much longer, but also running north and south, the north end crowned by a cemetery, the south end disappearing into two large hills named Round Top and Little Round Top. "Now there," Reynolds said, "there is a good position." He immediately sent a message to Meade, informing the federal commander of the skirmish that was becoming a battle, asking him that the rest of the Army of the Potomac hurry forward, hurry, hurry, and telling him of the fine defensive position that ran south from the cemetery to the Round Tops. The message caught Meade at breakfast. The crabby old commander lost no time. He ordered all units forward and sent his ablest corps commander, Gen Winfield Scott Hancock, to the scene immediately, telling Hancock not to wait for his troops but to go to Gettysburg and see what could be done with the forces that already were there. Winfield Scott Hancock: for whom the term "ablest" is lame indeed. And he was many other things too. He was a man of great bluster and stalwartness and profanity. He was tireless; he was a splendid disciplinarian. And, above all, he was a realist. He knew the courage and capabilities and resources and intelligence of the enemy. His own men, the men of the II Corps, worshiped him. His nickname then (and always) was The Superb. Abraham Lincoln is said to have valued him above all generals save possibly Grant. He was a career soldier and a student of the law and government. He believed in Duty and Obedience and Fidelity and Integrity. Stern of face, with a high brow and a long thin sour mouth partly hidden behind a stringy beard, Hancock thought of the enemy, Lee's army, as he rode forward that day. And he thought of the Army of the Potomac. And he knew, he saw in the clarity of his good mind, that the strength—the raw heavy developing power—of the Army of the Potomac some day would prevail, if not today then tomorrow or next year or the year after. But it WOULD prevail: that Winfield Hancock knew as a certainty. And he knew that even a defeat here would not alter the certainty of his side's triumph. So he galloped forward to see what he could do. And Gen John F. Reynolds rode among the men through the thickest of the fighting west of the seminary. And a Confederate sharpshooter shot John F. Reynolds right through the face. Killed him instantly. But the bullet was too late. Reynolds had found the defensive position (the ridge they called Cemetery Ridge) and he had sent the word. His troops were in retreat and there was a great deal of disorganization but at least there was a plan. So, according to the plan, the federal forces withdrew back through Gettysburg. They consisted of what was left of Buford's cavalry, the I Corps and the XI Corps. Their losses were heavy, but they inflicted heavy losses too and in so doing kept the retreat from being a rout. The bruised Confederates did not dare pursue too quickly. (The XI Corps, those Chancellorsville-stained Germans, were brilliant in their defense of Oak Hill and kept the Union army from being flanked from the north.) The retreat took all day.

The scattered troops were regrouped as they arrived on Cemetery Ridge. Rearguard units resisted stiffly. The Confederates had won for the time being, but (even though they took many prisoners and killed many men, especially at the railroad cut) the time being is not forever. ♣

AT NOON of the day he died Lt Alf J. Castetter led what was left of his company in a retreat. He helped carry a litter on which Max Gwinn lay.

They were off on a side road someplace. Castetter didn't know exactly where they were. They had held their position at Willoughby's Run as long as possible. Longer perhaps. Only fourteen men still were on their feet. The company had gone out this morning with fiftyseven. Fourteen out of fiftyseven. Hold out as long as possible. Yes. Hold out as long as possible.

"My daddy has a dog for me," Max Gwinn said from the litter.

"Be quiet, Max," Castetter said. "Just please be quiet."

"He said he would bring me a pup," Max Gwinn said.

Castetter did not look down at the litter. There was a bullet in Max Gwinn's skull. He was blind. There was a great hole in his left leg.

Castetter and his men shuffled along this side road and there was no panic. They were too tired. The sun beat down like a great banging yellow drum. Sounds of battle were all around them but here, along this road, they were in an eddy. They could hear the fighting but they couldn't see it.

Castetter hadn't realized how heavy Gwinn was. The pain of carrying the litter reached up into Castetter's arm, his shoulder, his back. He kept grunting. He neither saw nor heard things clearly. Even the sound of the fighting was indistinct.

(This one had been the worst, he knew. Maybe it was just that the last one was always the worst. But why would that be? Each time all the manifestations, all the big events, all the little events, are scorched right into your brain. You never forget them. You get sicker and sicker and sicker. You get more fed up and more fed up and more fed up. Why then should the last one always be the worst? All morning, or almost all morning, they had fought along that line by Willoughby's Run. For a long time their fire had kept the rebels pretty well pinned down. They would come charging out of the woods and across that short grassy space—only they wouldn't come charging too far. All up and down the line rifles would crack and rebels would fall. There were screams from the rebels as they fell like soft dolls flicked over by a tired child. But they kept yelling that goddam yell each time they made one of those senseless charges. That goddam yell surging from their throats. Then dying, dying with dying men, dying as dying men fell, dying buried under the thunderous fire. But the rebels kept coming. Hundreds of them—yipping and whooping and running and crawling and dodging. Ragged men, messy, scraggly, but hard men, brave men, men you killed because that was what was expected of you. You took no joy from it. Ah great God no; you took no joy from it. That is the most obvious fact in all man's experience. But you had to kill them. Why? Because what is a man, yes, what is a reasonable man if he will not stand up with his fellows and do something for the social structure? Pompous thought? Perhaps. But where else is the justification? Superficial? Quite likely. But where else is the answer? You spend a quiet morning in the country by a little stream and you kill, and you are yourself only externally, only in your flesh and pain and terror. In reality you are a part of a great faceless THING—an army. An army that represents a government, which of course is a greater faceless THING. And you cannot exist without these THINGS; your life has no basis in any other reality. So you kill, you kill and kill and kill. You bite cartridges and you squint and fire and watch the rebs fall; you do these things again and again. There is a chance you too will be killed. You know that only too well. You try not to think about it. Not to think about something is to deny its existence, isn't it? *Isn't it?* Ragged Southerners, running forward, charging and dying, so many hundreds of them, and Castetter had known that he and his men wouldn't be able to keep them back forever. Young, the corporal lying next to him behind that log, had been shot through one ear and nearly out the other while reloading his rifle. He had collapsed soundlessly, or at least as soundlessly as Castetter had been able to tell, what with the din. The Confederates had brought up artillery, lining the pieces on a rise overlooking the little stream. First the rebel cannon had knocked out the Union batteries, such as they were. Then the Confederates swung their sights down and let loose a shaking booming roar of fire directly into Castetter's company. Cannonballs tore into trees, landed in the dirt and sent it flying wildly in thick gritty sprays. The heat overwhelmed you. Trees were afire. Men groaned and Castetter kept firing, biting, loading, firing, biting, loading, and men screamed and Castetter kept firing, biting, loading, firing, biting, loading, and the cannonballs made curious whirring sounds as they sailed over his head and ripped into the trees, and finally he ordered a retreat. Ordered a retreat. Hah! That was no retreat. He and his men, those who were left, were simply overrun. There never are enough men when you need them. They're always getting themselves killed. And so finally the time came when the rebels came out of the woods and did *not* fall. It was a time of bayonets, of men milling and thrashing in the dust, of men wielding their rifles in the manner of clubs, of screams and protruding guts and shots fired at close range. Each man was on his own. This was the greatest cataclysm of them all. It always was. The time of the bayonets was the time you were the closest to being an animal. Castetter, a cavalryman, never had gone through it before, but he learned its rules quite quickly. So did the others. Those who lived. One man, a middleaged private named Sloan, a skinny fellow with thin whitish skin and knobby wrists, did not learn the rules. He died quickly and stupidly. When the Confederates crossed the stream in their final and victorious rush, Sloan did a preposterous thing, a thing that was unbelievable. He STOOD UP and began shouting at the rebels. He faced them squarely and called them probably every dirty name he knew. He didn't last long. One rebel cracked him across the head with the stock of a rifle. The blow knocked old Sloan down. He tried to get up but another rebel bayoneted him through his cheek and up into his brain. Sloan gave one high yelp that certainly, Castetter thought, must have come after he was dead. That was how the cataclysm went. Sloan had been something of a griper, not very good on a horse either. How did he ever get into the army, let alone the cavalry, in the first place? He had no business being there to die; he didn't even have that much dignity. And then for a time, perhaps a minute, perhaps five, perhaps an hour, Castetter had no clear idea—correct that: make it no idea at all—of what he was doing. The world was a kaleidoscope of sound and heat and wild frantic swinging movements. Men milled around and thought of nothing except themselves. (Where then was the concept of the social structure, Castetter old genius?) Milling men, running men, vague in outline within the dust and smoke. Castetter, taking Young's rifle and bayonet (such a thing as a bayonet did not fit on an officer's carbine), killed several Confederates. The ease of the blade's entry gave him a slight start the first time. (This rebel was very young, with dark thick uncut hair, and he screamed that goddam yell and charged straight at Castetter, forgetting to protect himself. Castetter thrust the bayonet in the young rebel's belly all the way to the hilt. The rebel looked at the bayonet and began to weep. Castetter twisted the bayonet and withdrew it and the rebel collapsed and Castetter glanced at the bayonet and there was not as much blood as he had expected and he threw up and started running and killed several other rebels, but quickly and did not remember their faces. Somewhere he stumbled across the men who were carrying Max Gwinn. Old Max had been trying to rally them, the men told Castetter. They didn't know how he had been shot. They'd simply found him lying on the ground. And he was alive. That was the peculiar thing. He had been shot in the skull but he was still alive. He stank, however. The wound in his head somehow had brought on a bowel passage. Castetter helped the men carry him.)

Castetter's mouth was dry. It felt as though someone had rubbed sand in it. He reached for his canteen with his free hand. He drank deeply, then spat out the water. It tasted like warm mud.

His shirt was torn. He had no cap. He had lost his forage cap somewhere back along the little stream. His feet hurt. God damn the cavalry anyway, he said to himself. My ass is callused like a suitcase but my feet are as soft as a wetnurse's tits. The army ought to do something to see that the cavalrymen keep their feet in condition. When this is over I'll write a memorandum to Gen Buford on the subject, that's what I'll do.

You'll *what?*

No. It's not so. Stop.

Castetter thought of The Feeling.

He shook his head and told himself no. He mumbled something.

Now don't do that, he said to himself. You think you have The Feeling but that isn't so. You can't go believing it. Use all your intelligence (you do have intelligence don't you?), use your learning, think of Cambridge Massachusetts and the things they told you there, the things you read, the entreaties and exhortations and

sweet hypotheses of intellect. You know there is no such thing as
The Feeling; rid your mind of such superstition. You are an edu-
cated and reasonable man. Use that reason.

But there it was. It was a thick thing, a lump of misery, and he
could not say no, desist, to it. Men talked about it around campfires; men quoted other men who had had it; they called it The
Feeling. Only it was not precisely that. Rather it was a knowledge.

When you have The Feeling, the men said, *that means you're
going to die.*

Going to die?

Me?

Yes. You.

No. It's absurd. I lived through this morning didn't I? There is
no such thing as The Feeling. You read about it in bad books, the
brave hero with premonitions of death. Such nonsense.

The nonsense made him tremble.

The Feeling had hit Castetter that morning, just after he had
plunged his bayonet deep into the young rebel's unresisting gut. It
was the real thing all right. It was as though some grinning obscenity were riding on his shoulder, but disappearing each time
he turned to look at it. A grinning obscenity, yes, a face wrinkled
and planed and drawn taut simultaneously, a face of decay, a
stinking face with foul breath.

Goddam you Castetter. Stop it!

Castetter looked around. The file was moving slowly. The men
stared dully at the road, at the dust rising from beneath their feet.
Sound boomed around them, but not loudly. They were on an
island washed and lapped at by sound; the war was near but not
with them. They had been in a woods and now they were out in
an open space with enormous fields. The air was full of dust.
Smoke drifted overhead and there was a slight burning smell. The

file moved slowly and nobody said anything. Fists of smoke from explosions bloomed behind the trees but the men could see no fighting.

"My daddy," Max Gwinn said from the litter.

"There, lieutenant," one of the litterbearers said.

"Daddy."

"Don't talk, Max," Castetter said.

"Can't see . . ."

Castetter took a deep breath.

Blood streaked Gwinn's face. It caked his mustache. "A dog. A little dog. I love my daddy."

"Max," Castetter said.

"Future. They said I had a future. I am a Republican. In the legislature. Future here? I remember. No. I just *might* see it that way if. Iffy diffy doodlebug. So dark."

"God damn you, Max," Castetter said.

"You hate me."

"No."

"You a writer?"

"Max. Don't."

"You a writer?"

"Kind of."

"Writer. Kind of," Gwinn said. His eyes were open now, with much blood and grayness in them. He smiled. "Too bad you don't draw. Then you could draw a picture of me. Picture of a scallywag. Call it *Portrait of a Scallywag*."

"You want us to put you down for a while?"

Gwinn closed his eyes. "Yes Daddy, I'll take care of him. All by myself. He won't be no bother. And I'll love him and love him and love him."

Then Gwinn coughed softly and died.

Castetter knew it immediately. He motioned to the men to

halt. He and the other litterbearers laid Gwinn at the side of the road. Castetter crossed Gwinn's hands on his chest. "Godalmighty," one of the men said, but no one else said anything.

They gathered around the body. Finally, after a very long time, Castetter said: "We better go. The rebels'll bury him."

There were no protests. The march, the slow march, was resumed.

Castetter rubbed the muscles in his sore arm and shoulder. No one looked back. The fists of smoke still bloomed in the sky.

Gwinn is dead.

He *was* kind of a scallywag.

Was that his moment of revelation? To discover it? What kind of a foul joke is that?

All those men in this company this morning and now only fourteen. Did the others die for the social structure? *Really?* Is it that important? Is the discipline of society and justice worth so many lives? Maybe Masterson was right. Masterson, you old dog you, you ran. You weren't a Maxwell Gwinn; you tried to rally nobody. You were a poor officer. Gwinn was a good officer. But at least I don't think you died accusing someone of calling you a scallywag. Oh you were a coward and you should have been sent home but maybe you had the right idea. You were no Alf J. Castetter considering the imponderables of things you do not have either the moral or intellectual capacity to discover. Oh stop this thinking. You are a superficial man; you always have been. And now you have The Feeling so what difference does anything make? The answer for Masterson was to run. He died in a fat flabby undignified way, but it had nothing to do directly with this war. Indirectly yes. If he hadn't run he probably wouldn't have been drunk; he wouldn't have drowned in a dribble. But at least he died away from the war. That makes a difference. Or I guess.

Gwinn you shouldn't have died.

I have The Feeling and because it is knowledge who will lead these men after I am dead?

You were a scallywag even in choosing your time to die. It was a scurvy maneuver.

I never liked you Gwinn.

. . . she was Charlotte Anne Barton and she was a true thing and I remember how her breasts weren't hardly developed at all and she certainly would have been laughed at in any good whorehouse . . .

All around them now were fields. But there was no movement anywhere, only the sounds and smoke in the distance to the west and the north. Then they came to the top of a hill and looked down and there was Gettysburg, its steeples and buildings. And about a hundred yards before them was a small white house. A girl (she was in a white dress) stood on the porch and waved at the men. Castetter squinted toward her. Her hair was darker, he could tell, but she was the same size and general build as Charlotte Anne. He snorted with amusement. Now don't go reincarnating something you rejected a long time ago, he told himself. He jingled the two coins in his pocket. The Feeling was very strong. Perhaps I should be desolate over Gwinn's death. No, you hypocrite. You never liked him. Anyway, you know the truth, and the truth is that you will soon go to wherever Gwinn went and that will be punishment enough.

He frowned. The girl's waving was frantic.

He looked over his shoulder and saw a Confederate cavalry force come charging over a hill.

Of course. She was in a higher place. She saw them. She was trying to warn us. Now wasn't that nice?

There it was: The Feeling. You did not deny The Feeling. And so Castetter was taken by a great joy. At least a hundred Confederate horsemen charged at Castetter and his fourteen men. The

Confederates were yelling that goddam yell. They swarmed over the men on the road. Castetter, shouting now in inarticulate triumph, ran forward in the swirling dust and fired his rifle blindly. Everywhere were yells and screams and shouts and shots and dust and smoke and snorts and whinnying noises. A rebel officer, swinging a sword, rode directly at Castetter. The sword laid open Castetter's cheek. Castetter, laughing, tasted the warmth of his own blood. He seized the rebel's stirrups and pulled him off his horse. The rebel fell in the dust but swiped at Castetter again. This time the sword nearly took off Castetter's left arm. Castetter shot the rebel in the groin, then fell on him and clubbed him to death, pounding his face into a flat mushy thing. Horses kicked at Castetter. Men stumbled into him. He rose from the dead rebel officer and looked around. His left arm hung from strings of tissue and bone. Somebody shot him in the small of the back. There was a stinging sensation in his kidneys. He staggered forward and then his left arm fell off. He saw the white house with the girl standing on the porch. Blood was in his eyes and he was laughing. He ran toward the house, fell, got up, ran some more. Blood spurted from his mouth and nose. He collapsed for the last time in the road in front of the house. He died in one white flashing explosion of pain.

♣ The afternoon of July 1, 1863 Gen Winfield (The Superb) Hancock gave a demonstration in proof of his nickname. All along the line, all along the crumbling inverted L running parallel with Willoughby's Run and east to Oak Hill, the Union forces—now under Hancock—withdrew, heading for Cemetery Ridge, that place Gen Reynolds had seen as such a good defensive position. Many units were cut off and destroyed by the whooping Confederates, and most of those that arrived at Cemetery Ridge were in bad shape, but Hancock was not dismayed. He grouped these torn legions into an effective force

again, lined them along the ridge in such splendid order that
the enemy was dismayed. Now here Stuart's cavalry could
have been used by the Southerners; it could have prodded and
scouted; it undoubtedly would have brought back reports of
the defenders' huge weaknesses. But Stuart and his men were
far away, off on their raiding expedition near Harrisburg. So
the invaders hesitated after their initial victory. They did not
know exactly how strong the defenders WERE. Hancock's bluff
worked. And late that afternoon he began to receive help. The
main body of the Army of the Potomac began pouring in to fill
the defenses. Thus, in the cloud and web and confusion of
Hancock's bluff, the Southerners' advantage disappeared. They
had Gettysburg, but that was no advantage. There weren't
even any shoes there. The Army of the Potomac, that heavy
massive force, dug itself in on Cemtery Ridge. This was no
skirmish now; it would be a big fight.   ♣

CPL LEW MABRY walked whistling along an empty
road. Here and there lay dead horses and men. Most of the men
were Union soldiers. It was too early yet for them to stink.

The sun lay heavy and red in the west. Some of the afternoon's
heat had vanished.

His pack (all his loot was inside it, all the loot from all the
times he had rifled dead men's pockets) was heavy on his back.
The straps dug into his shoulders. Today had been a good day,
maybe the best. He pulled at the straps and heard the loot tinkle
and clank. He grinned and kept whistling. He was a good whistler.
The tones rose shrilly and clearly, accurately. A man who made
his living with dogs just naturally was a good whistler.

He had been wandering around the countryside all day. He was
a straggler, knew it and didn't care. He had made no effort to find
his platoon.

He had studied the faces of dead men. Most of them looked

stupid. He had seen them in all shapes and postures. The weight on his back was evidence of his journeying. Now, walking along this here road, there weren't so many dead men. Oh there were some, but not like back at that old railroad cut. There had been a lot of dead men back there. Glory an a blessin.

Glory glory glory!

Wouldn't bother me none if they all was dead. The Yanks I mean. Maybe some Virginians too.

The sound of the fighting was to the east now, far and indistinct. That was just fine as far as Mabry was concerned. He'd done enough fighting for the day. He'd killed that Yank captain and he'd been in that fighting at that little stream hadn't he? A man can't go too far on his luck, Mabry believed. There's just so much luck in any one day. After you've used it, the best thing to do is to stop. Go off someplace. Be by yourself. Loot dead men or do something else that is quiet and keeps you out of trouble.

The road passed through woods and fields. He kept whistling. He scarcely glanced at the dead men. He was tired of dead men. Enough was enough for one day. The sounds of combat were light. The fight's passed through this place for good, he told himself.

Presently he came to a large tree, an oak, very leafy. He sat down in its shade and eased the straps of his pack. There were more tinkles and clanks.

He stopped whistling. "Ahhh," he said. He stretched, then leaned back against the tree. He closed his eyes and thought of his wealth. A soft grin spread. His young face gleamed with contentment.

(Money: He'd never had *nothin* like all this money. Them watches too. Rings. Gold pictureframes. Worth a lot. Yas sir. Back home his only means of making a living had been running down niggers. Five dollars a nigger. Mabry and his wife Louella lived in a cabin in the swamps about six miles outside Charleston. Mabry was fifteen and Louella thirteen when they were married. Louella was skinny and she wasn't what you'd call pretty or smart, but by God she did like she was told and she didn't give a man an argument. She never said much; she spread her legs when told, and she sure as hell didn't complain. Good thing for her too. Mabry didn't believe in letting no woman shrew at him. They had two children, Lewis Junior and Vern. Scummy little bums now, watching them grow—but back before they'd been born Mabry had been proud. He had watched Louella's belly get puffy and he had handled himself and had thought of it, this thing they had done to produce another thing, and he had been proud all right, but then the boys had come squishing and covered with slipperiness and Mabry's feelings of pride had gone away. He had felt nothing. Maybe bored. They sure weren't much those two. Skinny, always running at the nose. But Lew Mabry never was bored for long. If his children were a disappointment to him, his work was not. He had a true and profound love for his work. The prospect of tracking down some nigger always made him sweat with joy. Somebody would come riding up to the cabin and tell Mabry of Soandso's buck coachman or fieldhand who'd run off and Louella would come to the door and watch Mabry, clutched with happiness, get the dogs and set out after them. Mabry, riding with the dogs, the sniffing and dancing and yipping dogs, was good at his work. He always thought one step ahead of the nigs. And, no matter how many of them were caught, the nigs always thought the swamp was their best route of escape. But oh no. Oh no sir. Not as long as Lew Mabry was around. He always caught them nigs. Maybe it took two or three days, but he always caught them. And he always let his dogs nip them a little. It was only fair, he thought. The dogs would yap and snap at the nig and the nig would plead and fall to his knees and weep and roll his buggy big eyes and Lou would sit on his horse and laugh and laugh, eyes narrow and mouth wide with amusement. After a time Lew would tie the nig to the horse and drag him back to wherever he came from. Lew then would go to the rear of the planter's house and take off his hat and receive the five dollars—in coin, gold. Lew and his like were never allowed even on the front porch. They took care of their business at the rear of the house. This was the way things always had been; Lew resented it but did not defy it. Five dollars was five dollars. (The planters' voices were soft and courtly; they always thanked Lew very politely but saw to it that they never had any physical contact with him, such as shaking his hand; they would drop the five gold coins into his palm; once Lew overheard old LeRoy Smart, reputed to be one of the ten richest men in the state, tell his wife he'd sooner trust a nigger than trash).)

I'm agoin to change that by God.

His smile widened. He thought of riches and honors. A man can come around to the front door when he got money. He don't have to take nothin from no man on this earth.

(And no man on this earth knew how much Lew Mabry hated the LeRoy Smarts and the Virginians and all those men who had such a pride that pushed you down like you wasn't nothing at all. All his life he had stood at the back of their homes with his hat in his hands and he had accepted it but he had hated it; he had hated the highanmighties, all of them. He remembered Andrew W. Pallee, who owned a big place in Charleston and another big place in the country. Pallee was tall and thin and spoke with that soft gentleness all of them had; he never raised his voice; he dressed with elegance and wore all kinds of fancy doodads. But he was no sissy. Everybody knew that. Maybe he wore doodads on his clothes and all that, but he was a hell of a good man with a gun and had won about a dozen duels. In South Carolina when you fought a duel you killed the other feller, you did not let him crawl away, and so Pallee's achievements were impressive. And a man just naturally did the things Pallee told him to do. He never threatened you. But it was the way he said things—with no passion, with thinlipped easy command—that told you who you were, and what you were, and what you were expected to do. Pallee was young; his wife was beautiful; he had those two big houses and three hundred niggers and a set of fine matched bay geldings and three thousand acres of plantation—and Jesus Christ how Lew Mabry hated him. *That sonofabitch has everythin,* Lew told Louella one night. *He can do anythin he wants. Anythin at all. He has all that land an all them niggers an every night he gets in bed with that goodlookin woman an does whatever he wants with her. An look at me. Go on. Look at me. What do I got. I got YOU, that's what I got. Now you tell me. You think that's FAIR?* Louella wept at this and Mabry told her to stop before he gave her a good one on the head.)

Highanmighties! Well by God I'll show them yas sir.

(Andrew W. Pallee was killed leading a charge at Second Manassas. This delighted Mabry, who was serving in Pallee's company. Mabry had hidden in some high grass during the charge. Earlier that day he had had a hand in a peppery little fight around a barn (they finally had driven the Yanks away), and so he had decided not to participate in the charge. His luck, he guessed, was gone for that day. He was right. Most of the company, including Pallee, was destroyed. And Mabry, who stayed behind not because he was afraid but because he had a certain measured knowledge of his daily quota of luck, was delighted by Pallee's death. But then he thought about it. Pallee had been a strong and powerful man and he had been chopped down. *What's that mean for me?*

Mabry asked himself. There was no answer. No answer existed. Only precautions existed. So Mabry took all possible precautions. He was no coward, but he fought only when the odds were favorable or when someone was watching him and he couldn't get out of it. Second Manassas, Sharpsburg, Fredericksburg, Chancellorsville—he had been through them all, but always he had remained on the edges, fighting in small fights that his side was sure to win, staying away from wherever the *big* fighting was. He was oh so careful. He even watched his own men, those goddam Virginians in his platoon. He knew they hated him because he had been made corporal because he had known Pallee and had caught niggers for him—and because he never gave in to them, and because he had a fine talent for avoiding disaster. He could understand these hatreds, but there was another hatred he could not fathom. They despised him because he looted corpses. Why? Was they afraid of dead men? Didn't they have the stomach for such work? A man has the gumption to go out and get something for himself and he is despised. That didn't make no sense. It wasn't like he was *stealing* the watches and money and rings and pictureframes. No. After all, what did them dead men care?)

Ah, they just can't stand to see a man get ahead when that man ain't a Virginian.

Mabry yawned and opened his eyes. He undid the straps of his pack, then lay down flat with the pack cradled in his arms. He rolled himself into a little ball and fell asleep right away.

♣   In the first shadows of twilight the Confederates sent forth several small attacking expeditions against Cemetery Ridge. These were repulsed easily. The Army of the Potomac was there now in strength. And all night long reinforcements would sweep in to aid the defense. Meade congratulated Hancock. The Confederates marched through Gettysburg and set themselves up in positions opposite Cemetery Ridge. The two armies faced each other across a shallow valley. Campfires burned all night long. Both sides were busy getting ready. It was a good night for sleeping, but no one had much of a chance. ♣

WHEN PVT RUFUS PATTERSON awoke late that afternoon there were no men around him except dead men.

He sat up and put his hands over his face. It was streaked with dirt caked in dried sweat. He sucked deep in his throat, cleared it and spat.

He looked around. The dead men, lying flabbed and red and boneless, were everywhere. They were in many positions. He even saw one sitting up on his knees with his head forward between his knees. A small fire crackled in a tree down by the little stream they'd tried to cross this morning.

He thought of what had happened this morning. He thought of Pete Bell. He gave a little cry. He remembered now. He remembered Pete. He didn't want to, but he remembered. He blinked and shook his head. He looked up through the leaves of the tree he was sitting beneath. The sky was clouding now with twilight, a soft drifting wispy grayness. The sun was a red ball in the west. Its light slitted through the trees.

Why'd he look up?

He knew better.

It's not like he was stupid.

Rufus wept.

He sat and wept for some time, thinking: What'll I do now? I had old Pete with me an everythin was all right. I was scared. I'm scared now. But then when I was scared I had Pete.

Why'd he look up?

I got to have somebody to take care of me, don't I?

Jesus what's a war do to a man that it makes him look up an

get himself killed when he know he shouldn't ought to look up
because some Yank'll, blaff, kill him?

(Pete, he remembered, used to talk with Rufus about girls.
Pete was a married man, had been for quite a time, but he still
liked a good piece of flesh. *I'll admit it, boy,* he'd said one night,
laughing quietly. *I like the gals an the day I stop liking them you
can go on an shoot me an I won't fuss. Not a bit. A real man, he
don't ever change.* Pete never volunteered a whole lot, but the
things he did say always seemed to make good sense . . .)

Now there ain't no Pete.

He wept more loudly.

He rolled over and closed his eyes and scratched his fingers
through the earth and felt the earth on his face and felt his tears
streak the earth on his face. He lay thus for some time. Finally he
gave a great shuddering sigh, rolled over, got up, wiped his hands
on his breeches, wiped his eyes with his fists and swiped at the
dirt on his face. He picked up his rifle from the ground (he had
dragged it with him back to this tree after Pete's death; he did not
know why) and walked to the place where Pete lay. He took off
his forage cap and stared down at his dead friend. Pete's lack of a
face did not make him sick now. He heard soft booming sounds
off to the east. He slung his rifle over his shoulder and walked
across the short grassy space to the little stream. Several dead men
moved gently in the water. One of these dead men was only the
bottom half of a dead man.

Rufus waded across the stream and climbed a mudbank. Now
the dead were Union dead. He smiled. He passed through the
Union dead and then was on a road. He walked east. A sutler's
wagon came along the road. The sutler offered Rufus some corn
whisky. Rufus took it, drank deeply, handed the jug back to the
man with thanks. The sutler told Rufus how the South had carried
the day. The sutler was very drunk. He'd been meeting strag-

glers all along this road, he told Rufus. Hundreds of men had become lost from their companies, he said. Sometimes entire platoons and even companies had lost their way, he added. But today there had been a *great* victory, the sutler said, waving the jug and belching loudly. That's fine, Rufus said, and asked for directions to where the army was camped. Just follow this here road, the sutler told him. Rufus thanked him and walked on. All he wanted now was to find his company and go out and kill Yanks. Kill Yanks. Kill Yanks. There was no Pete Bell now. Just me, he told himself. His face was grim. He was quite frightened. He found his company at nine that night. His sleep was profound and dreamless. He knew he needed his strength. All of it. There were Yanks out there to be killed tomorrow.

3

THE SECOND DAY

♣ They worked all night. Both sides. ♣

SGT LEON MARSHALL STRONG cursed and mumbled and gasped. He tripped over things he could not see. He groped and staggered in darkness. Each time he tripped, the other men would curse him and tell him to keep moving, fatty; you're holding up the file.

Sgt Strong followed the man in front of him, who was just the vaguest blur. Trees were thick here, blotting the moonlight. Sgt Strong staggered forward as best he could, but these men, these clods, these uneducated simpleminded ruffians, kept cursing him and laughing at him.

I spit on the army, Sgt Strong said to himself. I spit spit spit.

The clear night air was filled with the sound of marching men, that great composite stew of a sound that included feet scruffing through dust, wheezes, laughter, groans, arguments, moans, obscenities, commands shouted by impatient officers, shrieks from the victims of goosings and the clanks and rattles of equipment. This was all very new to Sgt Strong. He'd never had to undergo anything like this before and he couldn't understand why it was happening to him now. The straps of his pack dug into his shoulders.

His rifle was too heavy and he wanted to throw it in the dust. In all his life Strong never had heard a shot fired in anger. He had been a member of the Army of the Potomac two years now, but still his quiet record was unbroken. The army, he said to himself with deep contempt, doesn't know what it's doing.

(Sgt Strong was not a combat soldier. He had his function, but it was not combat. He knew he had carried out his function with high excellence and this made his present indignity even more unbearable. Why in the name of God was he out here? Had there been something the matter with his work? He worked this thought around in his mind. He lifted the thought and peered beneath it. He examined all its faces as a housewife examines fruit in a grocery store. He prodded the thought and pinched it—and finally, after determining it to be invalid, discarded it. No. There hadn't been anything the matter with his work. Sgt Strong was payroll bookkeeper for the III Corps. For two years he had done a superior job. Col Billington had complimented him often. So why then was he with these clods and oafs and ruffians? Didn't the III Corps realize how scarce good finance clerks were? What if I die tomorrow? Sgt Strong asked himself. O ho, wouldn't they be sorry then! Death? Dying? My God, don't even think such a thing. But yesterday Gen Sickles, who commanded the III Corps, had put out a general order that all men would be in combat this time. That included cooks and orderlies and supply men. It meant everybody. It meant even excellent finance clerks. For two years Sgt Strong had been safely in the rear, out of the sight and sound of combat perhaps, but fulfilling his appointed function, doing his job, a humble laborer in the vineyard of war perhaps, but one who had his place in the scheme of things and filled that place with honor. It had been good work, work that always had gratified Sgt Strong. Back home in Columbus Ohio he had been a bank teller. A good bank teller too. He was fortytwo, short, plump, with three chins and small soft hands. His legs were slightly bowed. His most remarkable feature was his mouth. It was very small, poutish, a priss of a mouth. He had been married sixteen years and had sired five children—all girls. His wife's name was Harriet and she was loud and affectionate and laughed all the time and Strong hated her and she was just as fat as he. Five girls yipping and giggling in the house (enough, certainly, to drive any reasonable man from the limits of sanity, to make his very blood steam and simmer with the hot desire for simply five minutes of complete silence, yet Strong had the prissy courage to withstand these attacks on his reason and thus only was annoyed, not maddened, by them), five noisy girls in the house and their only effect on Harriet was one of love and laughter. Has the woman no sensitivity? Strong would ask himself, and for this reason he hated her. Each night, even in this war, Harriet and the girls kept him awake, running bleating and tittering through his consciousness. But there was relief in one respect. At least he didn't have to see them. When the source of a noise is not seen, Strong believed, then the noise itself is less loud. Or so it seemed to him. This frenetic cacophony of his home life had ruined for him whatever satisfactions there were in the Pleasures of the Hearth and so he had been an excellent bank teller indeed. He never once considered leaving his wife and daughters (he was a Baptist) and so he centered his life on his work at the bank. Thus he developed a passion for simple mathematics, the small neatnesses and exactitudes required of a bank teller. He had no interest in or understanding of mathematics' higher spheres, trigonometry, calculus and the like, but within his chosen field, within his little flyspeckings, he was diligent and efficient. And this had carried over into the war. He had enlisted immediately, in April of '61, and his talents soon brought him the position of Chief Finance Clerk of the III Corps of the Army of the Potomac. It was the same kind of work that he had done in Columbus, only there was no Harriet in the Army of the Potomac, there were no five shrieking daughters. This overjoyed Leon Marshall Strong, as did his rank of sergeant. A sergeant in the army was more respected than a common teller in a bank. This gratified him. Not that he exerted any unnecessary authority. He did not. It was simply that he enjoyed having it, whether it ever was used or not. And he had his Reports and his Ledgers and his Procedures and his fine neat Compilations. The campaigns of Fredericksburg and Chancellorsville were to Strong simply matters of revising company payrolls, deleting the dead and wounded, adding the replacements, matters of Adjustments and scratchingly involved work with Ledgers and Computations—making sure, in the final step, that all figures balanced. Then yesterday he had been given a rifle and told to join in the march. March? March? Yes, to war. War? What, Sgt Strong wanted to know, is logical about that? Have I not fulfilled my duties well? Oh yes. Very well. But that makes no difference now. You must march and tomorrow you will fight. And so Sgt Strong now hated the army very deeply. It was blind and it was stupid and it had no gratitude for those who had done their work well. He *spit* on it.)

Breathing hurt him now. It was as though someone were scraping a heavy knife across his chest. But although he stumbled, although several times he fell down, he did not give out.

His tiny priss of a mouth was shaped now in a gasping o. He wanted to weep or make a speech or anything, so long as it called attention to the injustice being done him, but he did nothing except stagger forward in this clear darkness. He would *not* collapse. He would *not*. Oh that was what the army wanted all right, but he would *not*.

There was no justice in anything now. Not even his three stripes meant anything. He was in the infantry now, and a captain had told him (nastily, as though there had been something wrong in doing a job well for two years, with never a complaint, not one): *Sergeant, this here's the infantry. You're just a goddam replacement. They tell me you're a finance clerk. Great God in Heaven, a FINANCE CLERK. What'll they send us next? Midwives and Sundayschool teachers?* The captain had informed Strong that he was a sergeant in stripes only now. He would take orders from his squad leader, just like any other poor private. Strong's squad leader was a tall deepvoiced fellow from Indiana, a Cpl Ferris. A stupid Indiana hayseed!

Where is the justice? Strong wondered. Pain and exhaustion and shortness of breath hit him in waves. All up and down the line of march the men were quieter now. They had been marching the better part of the night. The stars were out but nobody looked up at them.

So Strong would take orders from a corporal. A sergeant taking orders from a corporal. Now wasn't that the limit?

His tiny mouth puffed in and out. He had heard stories about men who ran away and hid. He never for a moment considered this. He was a Baptist.

The road climbed. Officers rode past the marchers and shouted at them to hurry. "Gimme that there horse! I'll hurry!" one man yelled. No one laughed. The night framed the moon in a starry tatter and there on that road the enormous column (Sgt Leon Marshall Strong, the martyred laborer in the vineyard of this war, included) slowly moved toward Gettysburg. The sound of marching was heavy and uneven but it never relented. Some men spat and some gossiped quietly and some exchanged ribaldries and some smoked cob pipes and some drank whisky obtained only God knew where and they all were tired but they marched, uphill mostly (you always marched up a hill, never down it) and the word was that the rebels were waiting in force at this place called

Gettysburg. This was the III Corps of the Army of the Potomac, moving toward Cemetery Ridge.

There never had been a longer night for Sgt Leon Marshall Strong. First there was pain and then there was exhaustion and then there was a blend of both and then there was a numbness. Each step was more of a floating movement. His eyes bugged with the effort to keep going. He bared his teeth, kept swallowing and trying to catch his breath. His armpits had sweated so heavily that the hair there was stuck to his skin as if with glue. Thus to move his arms too far was very painful. His shoulders and arms and neck throbbed. He had a headache. But the effort to keep going was so great that these pains and distresses were not really noticed very much. These men marching with him were all strangers. At this time the day before he had been asleep, safe in his comfortable tent. Now look. He was out in the middle of nowhere with clods and hayseeds and oafs and ruffians. Was there no justice at all?

But finally—at four in the morning, just as Strong was about to swoon, to abandon his struggle to keep going, a struggle he couldn't even understand—the marchers arrived at Cemetery Ridge. They were greeted by the sound of industrious digging. Campfires speckled the ridge, throwing their shadows on hundreds of men digging earthworks.

But Strong did not see the earthworks. He saw nothing. He only had heard the order to halt. He did. Then he threw his rifle to the ground, ripped off his pack, fell in a heap and went to sleep immediately. Several men laughed and then, quite suddenly, someone kicked him in the side.

Strong grabbed his side and sat up. He rubbed his eyes. "No," he said.

"No man loafs in my squad," someone said. "You get up or I kick you again. I ain't no feller for jokes."

"Can't . . ." Strong mumbled.

The Indiana hayseed, Cpl Ferris, was the man who had kicked Strong. He kicked him again. Strong yelped.

"Goddam clerk," one of the men said.

"Please . . ." Strong said, putting his hands over his head.

Ferris grabbed Strong and pulled him to his feet. Ferris was six and a half feet tall. Light from the fires flashed across his face. "Now we know you're just a clerk," Ferris said, glowering down at̄ Strong, working tobacco in his jaws, "and we know you're a sergeant. But in this outfit you're just a goddam soldier and you're going to do like everybody else."

"You tell him, Ferris," someone said.

Strong blinked. "I got a right—"

"You got no rights only them rights I tell you about," Ferris said amiably, the words thick behind his tobacco. "I ain't a hard man to get along with. I know you're tired. But so's everybody else. Just as tired as you. But we was told to dig these here earthworks and that's what we're going to do."

"I—"

"No sass, mister. You mind me, you fat sonofabitch."

Strong's small mouth trembled. He felt the tears.

Ferris pushed Strong away, then reached down, picked up a shovel and tossed it to him. "You go with them men and you dig," he said.

"This way, fatty," another man said, snickering. Several men prodded and pushed Strong to where a company of Indiana volunteers was at work on earthworks. There was a steady clatter and scrape of shovels. Someone came out of the darkness and told Strong and his companions where to dig. The other men ragged Strong as he dug. He wept, but made no sounds.

♣ July 2, 1863 was the day of the fish hook; it was the day the fish hook sustained the first of two attacks. Dawn lay in a lazy haze over Cemetery Ridge, and below its damp grayness two armies faced each other and waited for this skirmish, now a battle, to resume. It would be centered on this thing they called the fish hook—an inverted letter J this time that had been built by the Army of the Potomac. It began at Culp's Hill, which was east and slightly south of Gettysburg. The line of the fish hook ran north and then west and south in a great arc, joining Cemetery Ridge at the cemetery and heading due south along the ridge to the Round Tops. Eighty thousand Union troops defended the fish hook. Facing them were seventyfive thousand Confederates, holding positions to the west and north. The Southerners actually lay north of the Union forces, which of course was the reverse of what the war's directional pattern previously had been. The generals must have found this curious. It is doubtful, however, if the men in the line gave a whoop. ♣

WHEATFIELD spent the night at Walter Johnson's house. (After the rebels' departure yesterday Wheatfield had considered going on, but he had been pretty tired and had accepted the old man's invitation to stay. Anyway, Caleb had been in bad shape, worse shape than Wheatfield had imagined. *Your friend,* Walter Johnson had said, pointing at Caleb, who lay unconscious in a big old bed in an upstairs room, *he ain't in no condition to move.* There had been no arguing with the old man about that. Wheatfield had dragged Caleb from the cellar and he and the old man had removed Caleb's boots. Caleb's right foot was twisted off to one side. A piece of bone stuck out. Wheatfield and the old man had sucked in their breath very quickly. *Lord God,* the old man had said. Then they had carried Caleb upstairs and Wheatfield had decided to stay.)

Wheatfield knew his friend wasn't about to be going anywhere for quite some time. He cleaned the place where the bone stuck from Caleb's foot and wrapped it in a strip of sheeting. He didn't know what else to do. He asked Walter Johnson about a doctor.

They were in the kitchen again. Walter Johnson had made coffee. They sat drinking it from huge cups. "Closest doctor's in Gettysburg," the old man said.

"How far's Gettysburg from here?"

"Twelve mile."

"The rebels got Gettysburg?"

Walter Johnson shrugged. "I don't know. I guess so. You know as much about that as me."

"Well, I—"

"That's all right boy. You friend he ain't going to die. I can take care of him until the doctor can come out. Them rebs ain't going to stay in Gettysburg forever."

"I want to get back to my outfit. It's somewhere around Gettysburg I expect."

"Yep. I expect it is," the old man said. "You hear the sounds?"

"Sounds?"

"Listen . . ."

Wheatfield listened. He cupped a hand over an ear.

He heard. Light puffing sounds.

"How long that been going on?"

"Since the rebs was here," the old man said. "There sure must be some kind of a fight going on in Gettysburg."

"I got to get back."

"Tomorrow."

Wheatfield rubbed the sore calves of his legs.

"You're tired," the old man said. "You ain't going to walk no twelve mile today. You'll give out before you get five mile."

Wheatfield nodded. There was no arguing with that. He knew

how tired he was. "All right. Tomorrow," he said. He sipped at his coffee.

At nightfall the old man sent Wheatfield down cellar to fetch a ham. This time Wheatfield used a lantern. He found a big fat ham. They fried great slices of the ham in a castiron skillet (the snappings and the poppings and the smell—ahhh, they were good) and washed them down with more huge cups of coffee. The old man told Wheatfield of the War of Eighteen and Twelve; he talked of old Andy Jackson, who was as fierce as a wild hog; he talked until nearly midnight, when Wheatfield stretched and yawned and said he guessed it was about time to go to bed.

"You don't have to hit me on the head," the old man said. "I guess I can take a hint. Come on."

He led Wheatfield upstairs and opened the door to a rear bedroom. "This is my oldest son's room. Him and his wife, this here's where they do all that kidmaking. Watch the bed. It squeaks like a sonofabitch. Ah huh huh ah. Don't go thinking about no girls, you know what I mean?"

Wheatfield laughed with no enthuiasm. "I know what you mean," he said.

"I just bet," the old man said. "Goodnight."

"Goodnight."

Walter Johnson stumped away. Wheatfield fell on the bed without turning down the spread. He fell asleep right away. He dreamed of his horse Gingerbread and he dreamed of his girl Jane and he dreamed of Caleb's foot and all the dreams were mixed together and Gingerbread was home in Illinois with him and he and Gingerbread were in the barn and Jane came into the barn and Wheatfield chased her around the barn and she kept giggling and saying No Whit now you STOP that! and then Jane tripped and fell and Wheatfield went to her and she was screaming and a bone was sticking out of her foot, which was off to one side, and when Wheatfield awoke at six in the morning he was not particularly rested.

He sat up, groaned and rubbed his eyes. He pinched the bridge of his nose, sighed, rubbed his arms and legs to ease the stiffness. After a time he went into the room where Caleb lay.

Caleb sat propped up. He was drinking coffee. "Hey, boy," he said.

Wheatfield grinned and pulled a chair to the bed. He sat down heavily. He still was sleepy, but he knew he had to be on his way so he rubbed his hands together briskly and massaged his arms. "Waking myself up," he said. "How about you? How you doing?"

"I'm alive. Hurts, but I'm alive. Sure did break it, didn't I?"

"Yep. You carried on real sick."

Caleb nodded. "I guess I did. I remember staggering along that road. You was holding me up. I remember that. But I don't know, everything sort of got away from me. Next thing I knew this old man—what's his name? Walter Johnson?—this old man comes in and gives me a cup of coffee."

They heard the old man clumping around downstairs.

"That's some old man," Wheatfield said. "He talked my ear off yesterday."

"Yep. Me too. This morning."

They both laughed.

"I guess you better stay here for a while."

Caleb smiled. "You think I'm going dancing?"

"He said he'd take care of you."

"Sure. Probably make me deaf."

"I'm going this morning."

"How's that?" Caleb said, blinking.

"I'm going."

"Where?"

"Back."

"Gettysburg?"

"Yep."

"Why?"

"Got to."

"Got to?"

"That's what I set out to do," Wheatfield said.

"You out of your head? You're a lot safer here than you will be at Gettysburg."

"I know. But there ain't nothing wrong with me."

Caleb frowned. "Hey, boy—what do you mean by that?"

"I don't mean nothing by it. You, you can't go on. Nobody'll ever hold that against you. It wasn't your fault you broke your foot. But me—there ain't nothing wrong with me."

"You want to be a hero?"

"No. Oh I can't tell you why. All I know is I got to go back."

Caleb shook his head wonderingly but didn't say anything.

Wheatfield grinned. "Aw—who you trying to fool? If you was all right you'd be going with me and you know it."

Caleb scratched his scraggly beard. His eyes were narrow. "How old are you?"

"Twentytwo," Wheatfield lied. He always lied about his age. He didn't like it that people should think of him as young.

"Twentytwo," Caleb said, chuckling. "Huh. Twentytwo. How come you know so much?"

"I guess I'm just smart," Wheatfield said solemnly.

Caleb whooped. Wheatfield rose and shook his hand.

"Watch out for them paths of sin," Wheatfield said.

"Yea, boy," Caleb said. "Amen."

"—and don't go to no dances."

"Don't worry," Caleb said. He squeezed Wheatfield's hand. "Good luck. Take care of yourself."

"Sure will. And you take care of yourself."

Wheatfield went to the door, waved once, then went downstairs. The old man was in the kitchen. He gave Wheatfield a cup of coffee and some ham from last night. "Much obliged," Wheatfield said. He sat down and began to eat.

"You still going back?" Walter Johnson wanted to know. He brought a cup of coffee to the table and sat down.

Wheatfield nodded over his food.

"Road's full of rebs," Walter Johnson said.

"I'll keep off it."

"I hope you make her."

"I'll make her."

"Why you so set on going?"

"I been asked that question once already today."

"Well?"

"I don't know," Wheatfield said. "All I know is I got to."

"Oh," the old man said. "Well, I hope you make her. I hope you don't lose no leg. You don't ever know how good a leg is until you don't have it. No sir. Fiftyone years I been going around on this wooden leg. Made it myself. It's good enough I guess, but there been lot of times I wished I'd of had a good one. I've always been kind of a goatish one I guess you'd say and I remember this time when I was about oh forty or so. There was this girl name of Barbara Jordan and one day I was over at her daddy's place helping get his hay crop in. He'd been sick. Anyhow, she was kind of a fat girl, but she was pretty and she had nice big bubs. Wellsir, I came across her in the barn. She wasn't no more than about seventeen but there'd been talk about her, you know the kind of talk that gets around. And all she did was smile at me a little and then she said Come on Gimpy, catch me! but by God I couldn't catch her. No sir. She led me a merry chase all right. And all the time she was laughing to beat hell. I could of had her

too I bet—but I just couldn't catch up. Oh she led me a merry
chase she did . . ."

Wheatfield was startled. He thought of the dream he had had
last night about Jane.

Walter Johnson went on: "Yes sir, that was one day I sure did
have the need of two good legs. I was a goatish one all right. And
when I had two legs the girls they liked me all right too. Down in
New Orleans I knew a little octaroon girl named Corinne LaBiche.
I used to laugh and call her La Bitch and she loved it. She had
the biggest and brownest eyes I ever saw. She was one of them
niggers who spoke French, you know, the kind I was telling you
about. She was only sixteen and every night we'd go down by the
river and oh ho! everything was dandy. I tell you. Say, you ever
seen the Mississippi River, all that mud and sand and all?"

"I live near it."

"That's right. You're from Missouri ain't you?"

"Illinois."

"Hum. Illinois. I got kin living in Illinois. Chicago."

"I know," Wheatfield said.

The old man finished his coffee. He smacked his lips. "Yes sir,
I guess I told them rebs. I guess I showed them I wasn't scared."

"I guess you did," Wheatfield said, scraping the last of his ham
off his plate. "I owe you a debt."

"You don't owe me nothing, boy," the old man said, smiling.
"Don't you see? I *did* something. I'm an old man, sure—but by
God I *did* something. That's the best thing that can happen to
an old man. You don't owe me a goddam thing."

Wheatfield pushed his plate back and stood up. "Guess I'll be
on my way."

The old man walked with him to the kitchen door. They shook
hands. The old man said he'd have a doctor for Caleb just as soon
as the fighting died down. Wheatfield thanked him for his hos-

pitality. God bless the Republic, the old man said. Wheatfield
went out the back door, across the barnyard, then headed east
through a thick woods. He did not look back at the old man, who
stood at the door and watched him for some time. The morning
sun warmed the back of Wheatfield's neck. The terrain was
smooth and not hard to cross. He kept his eye on the road.

He thought of Caleb. He thought of the old man. He grinned.
He looked up at the sun and pursed his lips. Be a scorcher I bet,
he thought. He put his hands in his pockets and trudged along at
a good clip. Of course he knew why he had to get back to his outfit, but to have explained the reasons would have sounded too
much like bragging. Every time you opened your mouth to talk
of Duty the words sounded funny and people thought you were
bragging. I got to go back, he told himself. I don't give a damn
what. I got to go back. It's good for a man to be able to face himself: me, I got to go back.

He thought of Gingerbread and Jane and Caleb and the old
man and the rebels and Duty and he walked briskly and birds sang
in the trees and he looked around at the farmland and it sure was
good, a lot better than in the part of Illinois he came from.

♣   There were amusing things too. One was a sign, an old
sign splintered and cracked. It was posted in the cemetery
where Union troops now lay behind earthworks. This sign
warned the reader against discharging firearms within the
cemetery grounds. Violators would be prosecuted, it said. Ah,
how the men laughed. They dug earthworks among the tomb-
stones and in so doing found skulls and bits of bones. Laughing and whooping, they played catch with the skulls, and now
and then a man fired his rifle in the air just because of the
sign. But most of the men lay waiting quietly for the Confederates to attack. It was morning now. They figured they wouldn't
have to wait long.   ♣

YESTERDAY, some time in the afternoon, when Leora
had been able no longer to lie trembling in bed with her mother
and brother, she had arisen and gone downstairs and had a glass
of milk and then gone back out on the porch.

She had seen those Union boys, who she guessed didn't know
they were behind the rebels' lines, come slowly up the road. And
the rebel cavalry—she had seen *it* too and had tried to yell a
warning to the Union boys, but they hadn't paid any attention.
Not one of them saw the rebels until—well, until there wasn't
anything they could do about it. They couldn't even run. The
fight was brief and loud. There were screaming sounds and
groaning sounds and whinnying sounds and snorting sounds and
whooping sounds and thumping sounds and cracking sounds and a
whole lot of dust and she couldn't see what was happening too
well and then that man, that poor *poor* man, came running
toward her. He had only one arm. He ran toward her and fell down
and got up and ran some more and got to a place just in front of
the house and fell down and didn't get up because he was dead.
She knew that. She closed her eyes and heard the sounds of combat out there and saw the man running in her mind's eye and oh
God she *hurt* . . .

(He had run as she imagined a scarecrow would run, his one
arm flapping and flailing, his head loose and heavy off to one side,
his knees and legs soft—staggering, falling, getting up, with dust
and smoke and noise all around him, and with everything so *hot*.)

Leora watched him and then ran inside to Mamma and Johnny.
She did not look outside the rest of the day.

But today, this morning, she did. She did not know why. She
went to the front door and took a deep breath, opened the door
and walked out onto the porch. The poor man still lay out there.
Other dead men lay up the road where the little skirmish had
been fought. "Ah," she said aloud. She stared out there for some

time. Confederate soldiers went past and waved and hollered and whistled at her, but she paid no attention to them. She stared at the dead man in the road and thought of how he had run so flopping and loose.

The sounds of fighting came from the east now, but they weren't as loud yet as they had been yesterday. The sun was high in the sky again today. Leora felt herself sweating again. She went back inside the house.

Mamma was up and around today. She wasn't crying anymore. Her eyes were red and occasionally she sniffled but she didn't cry. She hardly spoke, however. Four of her good plates had fallen from a shelf yesterday and had shattered on the kitchen floor. The trembling of the house from the cannons had done it, Leora guessed. She watched Mamma silently sweep up the pieces of china. Then Mamma started breakfast.

Leora wandered through the house. She touched pieces of furniture, running her fingers along their surfaces, and for a time went to her room and lay silently hugging her pillow and not thinking anything.

Johnny was quiet today too. He didn't say anything about wanting to go outside. He also wandered silently through the house.

There was a thickness in the air that Leora never had felt before. It was as though she were about to smell something. She sat up in bed and sniffed experimentally, but there was nothing. She went back downstairs to the kitchen and sat watching her mother prepare breakfast. They didn't say anything to each other. Mamma's fat face was red. She puffed as she moved around the kitchen.

Leora listened to the sounds coming from the east. All night long the Confederates had marched past the house, men shouting and singing and laughing and whooping. Leora had lain in her bed with her eyes wide open staring up at the ceiling and had heard the jubilant rebels and she had rubbed her lips with her tongue and had wanted to cry out but hadn't. In school for the last two years now Miss Grumpacker (the boys called her Miss Humpbacker) had told them that the Confederates were traitors, that the United States now was in a mortal struggle for the cause of freedom and that a victory for the Confederacy would mean the death of freedom. Until the beginning of the war Miss Grumpacker had been a cheery plump woman, easy with the children. But it was different now. She was grim; every day there was a lecture on the war and what the war meant. *This war is the most monstrous thing you'll ever live through*, she told them. *You look outside and it's Pennsylvania and it's good country and you like it. The war? What's the war? It's something down in Virginia. It doesn't mean anything to any of you does it? Things are quiet and peaceful in Pennsylvania so what does it matter about some fighting in Virginia. Well now, all of you, I want you to listen to this and remember it: When a man—a Union man, a man who is fighting for honor and justice and decency—when a man dies in Virginia fighting those traitors and their dreadful slavery (an abomination on the laws of Man and the Word of God), when that man dies he is dying for YOU; he is dying so YOU in Pennsylvania will be able to look outside and see nothing except peace and light and bounty.* There was nothing pleasant or cheery about Miss Grumpacker when she gave these talks. Her plump face always was stern. Her voice turned cold and low and level. And the children always were embarrassed. Sometimes there would be soft giggles. Nobody could understand what had changed Miss Grumpacker. Leora had been glad for the summertime. Going to school had been getting to be awful. Every day there was a sourness in the room and every day Miss Grumpacker would deliver a little lecture on the war. And nobody really had paid any attention. Leora thought of this now. She thought of Gettysburg: the war right here, with us. She thought of the things Miss Grumpacker had said: now there's a fight here and men aren't dying in Virginia they're dying here. This is nice country. We live quiet here. Why don't they go back down to Virginia to fight their old war? We don't want any war here.

I thought I was going to be some kind of a heroine.

That poor man. Running so. Where?

I want my daddy.

Breakfast was a silent meal. Leora kept getting up and going to the window and looking out. The sounds from the east still were low. She wondered if maybe both sides were going to go someplace else to fight their battle. She thought of the young cavalry officer who'd told her to go inside yesterday. He'd been sweating so. Goodness.

Mamma hadn't looked outside yet. All day yesterday she'd stayed inside her room and always had kept her back to the windows. But today at least she hadn't wept and carried on.

Leora didn't eat very much. A tear fell, blop, on her plate.

Mamma saw this. "Now," she said thickly.

Johnny looked up from his food.

"The poor man," Leora said.

Johnny's face was bleak and lost. He glanced back and forth from Leora to his mother. He sniffled.

"Now," Mamma said again.

"We lost," Leora said.

"Not yet," Mamma said, sighing. Leora never had seen her like this. Usually she wept and wept.

Mamma went on. "If we'd have lost, then we wouldn't be hearing any fighting—"

"I'm afraid," Johnny said, looking quickly down at his plate.

"Be quiet," Leora told him.

"We're all afraid," Mamma said.

They heard Confederates marching past on the road outside. The Confederates were singing. Leora used her skirt to rub the sweat off her hands.

"Eat," Mamma said. She chewed some bacon. The children picked at their food. "We have to stay here. We know that. We might as well make the best of it. Now everybody eat."

"I'm not hungry!" Leora burst out.

"Eat," Mamma said.

Johnny was crying now.

"John Bagley," Mamma said to him.

Johnny wiped his eyes and subsided.

"We want your father to come home and find us safe," Mamma said.

"Daddy!" Johnny wailed.

"You shhh," Leora told him. Her head hurt.

They managed to eat a little. Leora helped her mother clear the table. They did the dishes, then all three of them sat down around the table and were silent. Gradually, as the morning passed, the rumbling sounds from the east became louder. They smelled burning things, but this was not the thickness Leora had been sniffing for earlier. The room became hot. The parlor was cooler, but they did not think about going into it. Mamma sat with her hands folded on the table and her face was expressionless. She breathed very slowly, ponderously. Johnny worried the saliva in his mouth. Leora motioned to him to be quiet. Her head hurt and hurt.

Shortly after noon they heard the sound of whistling. They had not moved from the kitchen. The sound of whistling came from out in front of the house. It was a shrill and clear sound, accurate. It carried over the rumbling sounds from the east. It became louder and louder, as though whoever was out there was coming toward the house. Leora, sweaty and itchy all over now, went to look.

♣   Robert E. Lee, faced with the entire Army of the Potomac aligned along the enormous fish hook, had rather a simple plan of attack. It was simple and it was obvious, but Lee had seventyfive thousand men available to execute it and he had no reason to believe it would fail. What he had in mind was to catch the Army of the Potomac in the jaws of a great vise and either (a) force it from the high ground along the fish hook, or (b) wipe it out. Either eventuality would be a Confederate victory. Here is how he proposed to do it: first, have Ewell's men attack Culp's Hill at the extreme northeast end of the fish hook, which was the Union right flank. At the same time, have Longstreet's men to the south roll back the Union left at the Round Tops. Thus both ends of the fish hook would be broken and Ewell would meet Longstreet behind the Union lines, effecting an encircling movement—provided, of course, the federals had not chosen retreat to encirclement. Either way, however, the Confederacy would achieve a splendid triumph. But the Confederacy achieved no splendid triumph. The reasons lay in ineptitude, poor timing, good luck that quite unexpectedly became bad, underestimation of the enemy—and that one greatest catalyst of any battle: the men who fight it and the men who lead them. Nothing quite went off the way it had been planned; nothing quite went off as QUICKLY as it had been planned; simplicity became confusion—and the enemy, Meade's eighty thousand men, in the final analysis stood fast. They stood fast through one of the most grotesque blunders in military history. They stood fast through a monstrously fierce attack and saw the grotesque blunder turned into a piece of luck, a stroke of fortune that came about simply because the Southerners (taken completely by surprise) were stricken aghast by the blunder, did not follow it up quickly enough and thus saw an advantage turn into misfortune. And, also because of this blunder, a high wall was erected across the road of Lee's pincers movement. How could a mistake by the enemy

have ruined the Confederates' plan? Lee decided that Ewell's
venture against Culp's Hill would come first, thus perhaps de-
ceiving Meade into believing that the bulk of the Confederate
offensive lay in that direction. Then, with Meade diverted,
Longstreet's men would attack the Round Tops, which were defended by the III Corps of the Army of the Potomac under Gen
Daniel Edgar Sickles—a preening ambitious jackanapes who
now marches to stage center in the drama played in those
green Pennsylvania hills that summer day of July 2, 1863. He
supplants John F. Reynolds (carried off dead) and Winfield
Scott Hancock (who will, however, reappear). His time there
will be brief, but his words and thoughts and actions will be
important. It is the supreme moment in the life of a man whose
life possessed all kinds of moments. "One might as well try to
spoil a rotten egg as to damage Dan's character," one contem-
porary said of Sickles. There was more truth than invective in
this. Dan Sickles, murderer, scalawag, finagler, brave man,
lover, blunderer, had little reason in his life and no discipline
at all but ah, lord, the excitement! He believed not at all in
moderation or the joys of contemplation. He was a man of action and of stubbornness and of schemes and of passion. Passion, in point of fact, brought him his first notoriety. In 1859,
while in Washington serving as a member of the House of Rep-
resentatives, Dan Sickles shot and killed one Philip Barton Key
in broad daylight on a public street. Key, son of the man who
wrote the national anthem of the United States, had been having an affair with Sickles' wife. Key is said to have screamed
for mercy. Sickles (a crony of President Buchanan) was let off
by the courts but was ostracized by Washington—not because
he had murdered Key (death was the risk seducers had to run
in those days) but because he did a completely unexpected
thing: he forgave his wife. Forgiving husbands were dropped
from society in that time, and so Sickles (vain and ambitious
and aggressive) suffered setback after setback. Then came the

war and Sickles recouped. Through a series of adroit schemes and untiring political maneuvers he rose to general in the Army of the Potomac and took command of its III Corps. He cut quite a figure on a horse (some accounts say he was handsome, but his pictures do not show this; photographs reveal a thin face, thick mustaches, an arrogant the-hell-with-you manner) and his men loved him; he was no coward. It was this man who led the troops defending the vital left flank at the Round Tops, and it was this man who was responsible for the grotesque blunder that left the Confederates so astonished, that put into motion the series of events that would decide whether the battle would be a victory or a defeat or what. To understand the blunder one first must understand Dan Sickles—and especially his hatred of his superior, George Gordon Meade. Sickles was a good friend of Joe Hooker, the ex-commander of the Army of the Potomac; the two men were fond of each other and were fond of drinking and whoring together. When Hooker resigned, Sickles was convinced the reason lay in some treachery by Meade. Nothing would make Sickles change his mind. He stormed and fumed. He resolved to "get" Meade, who became his superior and thus, by oath, the man discipline demanded he obey in all things. Sickles disobeyed Meade the very first time an order was passed down. The very first time. Winfield Scott Hancock's men of the II Corps were north of Sickles, and Sickles' orders from Meade that July 2 were to defend the Round Tops, hold Cemetery Ridge and maintain contact with the II Corps and the I Corps. Gen Abner Doubleday, the man responsible for baseball, had succeeded the fallen Reynolds as I Corps commander. This idea of contact between Sickles' corps and the others was of extreme importance to the defense. If the defenders were split, disaster might follow. That was why the high ground of the ridge had been chosen in the first place. Meade arrived on the field that morning, congratulated Hancock on the previous day's good work in putting up

such an excellent bluff, then announced to his staff that the fish
hook seemed like the best place in the world to wait for the
rebels and hack them to pieces. The terrain was woodsy and
rocky; an attacker would have a difficult time there indeed. So
the line of defense was established—with Dan Sickles' III Corps
anchored on the left, in the Round Tops, at the extreme southern end of the line. Therefore, contact with Hancock was imperative, else the III Corps would be cut off from the rest of the
army and the left flank bent back. But Dan Sickles evidently
did not realize this. He was up early in the morning and toured
the sector his corps had been assigned to defend. He did not
like what he saw. His loathing of Meade must have deepened.
Either Meade did not know the seriousness of the situation or
else he had deliberately put the III Corps in a vulnerable position, Dan Sickles reasoned. Part of the terrain here is shallow,
Sickles told himself. It will be difficult to defend. He became
angry. He rode to a high spot and surveyed the ground. Yes,
part of the line dipped. It certainly was NOT, in Sickles' opinion, a good defensive position. Where were Meade's brains?
Did he have any? Dan Sickles looked around. He looked across
the field toward where the Confederates were. A peach orchard and a wheat field lay between the two armies. Somehow
Sickles thought the peach orchard would be easier to defend
than the line on Cemetery Ridge. His reasons for this opinion
are vague. At any rate, he rode to Meade's headquarters and
is said to have asked for permission to move forward. The road
south to Emmittsburg is straddled by the peach orchard,
Sickles pointed out. It would do well to have that road in Federal hands, he added. He then asked for permission to deploy
his corps as he saw fit. Meade's reply was: "Certainly, within
the limits of the general instructions I have given to you."
Which meant, of course, that Sickles should maintain his position on Cemetery Ridge. Sickles argued hotly; he asked Meade
to come see the situation for himself. Can't spare the time,

Meade told him. A staff officer, one Gen Hunt, rode back with Sickles instead. Gen Hunt looked at the terrain, heard Sickles' arguments. Sickles asked him if he would authorize the move in Meade's name. Hunt refused, then rode off on an inspection tour. At this point Sickles' actions become spiderwebbed with confusion and ambiguity. Sickles, interpreting Meade's remark, claimed it meant he should do as he thought best. But no matter. The point is: Sickles DID move his men forward to the peach orchard and what he thought was a tactical advantage. And so, in occupying the peach orchard, Sickles' corps very effectively cut itself off from the rest of the Army of the Potomac. It formed an enormous sideways letter V pointing right at the Confederates and splendidly ideal for encirclement. ♣

CPL LEW MABRY whistled gaily as he searched the corpse of a Yank lieutenant.

This here lieutenant had only one arm. He sure had been chewed up. Blood, brown and scabby, was smeared all over him, Mabry rolled him over on his back and went through his pockets. The pack was heavy on Mabry's back; it clanked with his movements. He pulled a book from one of the corpse's pockets. The title of this book was *Poetical Works of Thomas Gray*. He snorted and threw it away. He found two fivedollar gold pieces in another pocket. He grinned and put them in his own pocket. He prodded the corpse's midsection for a moneybelt. There was none. He straightened up.

He looked around. Smoke and thick sounds came from the east. He still hadn't found his platoon, but he was in no hurry. The sound of his whistling was very shrill. He looked toward a little white house that sat on a hill right near by. He remembered how hungry he was. His nap out in the woods yesterday had lasted all night. He guessed he sure had been tired. And now he sure was hungry. He'd eaten the last of his jam this morning. And anyway, a man needs more than jam to keep going. (That old Yank woman she didn't like me. Well, she ain't got nothin on me. I didn't like her either. Oh you Yanks many of you is goin to die an that's just fine oh I tell you yas . . .)

He walked toward the house. He carried his rifle casually at his side. He moved slowly. His pack was heavy.

Then the front door opened and a girl appeared on the porch. She was slim, with dark hair.

Mabry stopped whistling. He grinned at her and raised his cap.

"Go away!" she hollered.

Nice an soft I bet, Mabry said to himself. Nice an soft. He laughed aloud and continued walking toward the house. Now you know *that's* somethin I ain't thought about in . . .

"Go away!"

Mabry climbed the porch steps. The girl retreated. He made a wet sound with his lips. "I'm just hungry, mam," he said softly.

She ran inside and slammed the door. The latch clicked.

Mabry guffawed.

He pounded the door with the butt of his rifle. He heard someone scream. The wood in the door was hard, but Mabry was strong. Presently the paneling began to splinter. He jabbed a hole with his bayonet, then reached inside and undid the latch.

Laughing softly, thinking of what he had just seen there on the porch, he entered the house. The parlor was empty. So were a middle sittingroom and the kitchen. He looked out the back door but saw no one. The kitchen table was set for three. A pot was bubbling on the stove. He took the lid off the pot and smelled stew. "Ahhh," he said, breathing deeply. The juices in his stomach made loud noises. He ate some of the stew from the ladle. Potlicker ran down his chin and onto the floor but he did not care. The meat was juicy and tender, the vegetables firm. He gobbled down half a dozen ladles full, then decided to continue his search for whoever lived here. He especially wanted to see that girl again. He wandered back into the middle sittingroom and climbed a flight of stairs to the second floor. He kicked open the door to a bedroom. Nothing. Another door. Nothing. A third door. The girl stood in the middle of the room. A big fat woman was with her, and a skinny boy. They stood close together. The woman's arms were around the other two.

"Well now," Mabry said.

They were silent. The girl's eyes were wide. The boy shook.

Mabry stood grinning at the door. "Don't you folks *like* me?"

The girl opened her mouth, closed it.

Mabry looked the girl up and down. His eyes remained especially long on her breasts and thighs.

"Go . . ." the fat woman said.

Mabry took a step toward them. He smiled warmly. "Missus," he said, "you can go to hell."

The woman's mouth popped open. The girl made a squeaking sound. The boy trembled more violently. "You—you damned rebel," the woman said.

"That's right mam," Mabry said courteously. "An proud of it too. I don't know of nothin better than killin Yanks. I'm good at it too." He casually lifted his rifle to his shoulder and fired a shot through a mirror in a far wall. The mirror collapsed in cascading glass.

The sound was loud in that small room. The woman whooped with terror, then fainted into a fat mound on the floor. The girl also screamed, but did not faint. The boy wept. Mabry still grinned. The room was thick with the smell of burnt powder.

The girl bent over the woman. "Mamma . . . Mamma . . ." she said, stroking the woman's face.

Mabry reloaded his rifle and walked toward the girl.

"*Leora!*" the boy yelled, backing away, rubbing his eyes with his fists.

"There ain't nothin wrong with your mamma," Mabry said, grabbing the girl by the shoulder and squeezing it, hard.

The girl gave a little shriek. She straightened and pulled herself from his grip. Her eyes were bright with tears. She faced Mabry squarely, cleared her throat deeply and spat a thick gob in his face.

Mabry guffawed. "All hot ain't you?" he said, slapping her with all the power he could summon. The blow hit her full in the face and sent her staggering back, but this time she did not cry out. There was a huge red mark on her face.

The boy charged at Mabry and kicked him in the shins.

Mabry, who had been wiping the girl's spit from his face, yelped. "You little bastard!" he bellowed. He seized the boy, picked him up and threw him across the room. The boy landed sobbing on the bed.

Mabry went to the girl and took one of her hands and squeezed. The red mark drained from her face. She rolled her eyes with pain, but there was no outcry.

Mabry's grip tightened. She closed her eyes.

He put his face very close to hers. His voice was low. "Now—now you listen here to me," he told her. "I'm just a poor hungry soldierboy who's come here for somethin to eat. I aim to get somethin to eat. I ain't joshin you one bit. That little boy on that bed, you don't get me somethin to eat I kill him. I'll shoot him right in the face. Now missy, you better know I ain't joshin. You better know enough to go downstairs with me an cook me a nice big Yankee meal—without none of your Yankee sass."

The girl opened her eyes and nodded. Mabry gave her hand one last twist, then released it.

The girl glared at Mabry, then turned to the boy. She was rubbing her sore hand. "You watch Mamma," she told the boy.

The boy looked up at her and nodded. He couldn't say anything for his weeping.

"An sonny," Mabry said, "you just stay right here in this room with your mamma. You don't leave this room unless I say so. You leave this room I shoot your sister. I sure would hate to shoot your sister."

The boy nodded again and wailed more loudly.

"That's bein a good boy," Mabry said.

The girl looked down at her mother, who was groaning now and aimlessly moving her hands. The girl bent over her, helped her to her feet and took her to the bed. The woman made vague sounds in her throat. The girl got her stretched out on the bed next to the boy. "You mind her now," the girl said to the boy.

"Come awn," Mabry said.

He followed her from the room. The little boy was hugging his mother.

The girl carried herself very erect. Mabry grinned staring at her hips as he went downstairs after her. Her dress sure was tight and trim around her little butt. He appreciated it. He followed her into the kitchen.

She went to the stove and stirred the stew. She glanced at the floor where he had dripped potlicker. "Nice mess," she said coldly.

He sat down at the table and watched her movements. Her butt jiggled ever so slightly as she stirred the stew. She ladled some into a plate and brought it to him. She fetched a loaf of bread from a cupboard. She sliced the bread with a large knife. He watched the knife very closely.

She had nice titties too. Small, but he bet they was hard.

He ate quickly. He did not let her out of his sight. No sounds came from upstairs. She stood by the stove and watched him eat. There was no expression on her face.

He finished eating, belched and pushed back his plate. He

leaned back and eased the weight of his pack. He hadn't taken it off and he wasn't about to.

The girl made no move to clear the table.

"Now," Mabry said.

She stared at the floor.

"Ain't you goin to clear the table?"

Her body was rigid.

"Nothin to be scared of."

She looked straight at him. "You had your meal. Go now."

He grinned. "No hurry. Robert E. Lee he can fight you Yanks without me for a bit."

"You had your meal . . ."

"You done said that."

"I hope you die," she said levelly. She moved toward the door.

"Wup," Mabry said.

She stopped. "I'm going upstairs to my mother."

Mabry stood up. "No," he said. He took the two fivedollar goldpieces from his pocket and dropped them on the table.

She started to run. He caught her before she reached the door. He put his hands on her waist and turned her around. His hands went up to her breasts. "There ain't a one of you don't like it," he said, snickering.

She began to cry.

"Ten dollars," he said. "Lot of fun too." He kissed her and tried to force open her mouth. She ran her fingernails across his face. He punched her in the stomach, bending her double. He ripped off the top part of her dress. They sure did look hard all right. She screamed.

♣   So Dan Sickles moved his III Corps forward from its position on Cemetery Ridge, spreading it in the limp sideways letter V that pointed straight at the Confederates. This salient was spread thinly over nearly twice as long a line as he originally had been assigned to defend. Furthermore, there was no contact with Hancock's II Corps on the right. Dan Sickles' men were quite cleanly and completely isolated from the rest of the Army of the Potomac. Lee and his staff had no trouble detecting this movement (it all was quite out in the open) but for a time the Southerners could not act. Ewell, who was supposed to attack Culp's Hill on the north in the first phase of Lee's pincers plan, was having trouble getting his troops into position. Everything was going too slowly. It was well into the afternoon before there was any kind of concerted action. The plan was good, perhaps, but its execution was being conducted with not enough speed. Then, coming as a complete surprise to Lee (and Meade too, obviously) the Union III Corps positioned itself in the limp sideways letter V. Lee and his staff held a conference; they acted after much discussion. Longstreet was dubious, but finally, after one of his many arguments with Lee, he gathered together a massive weight of troops to attack the III Corps. ♣

WHEATFIELD heard the scream and it made the hairs rise on the back of his neck. He started running toward the neat little white house before he'd even heard the second one. He did not stop to think why. You just naturally run to see what's happening when a girl screams.

The screams (and sobs too, and many groans) came from the rear of the house. Wheatfield ran around to what he guessed was the kitchen. He wrenched open the door and lunged into the kitchen and saw the rebel soldier on the floor with a girl and the girl was naked above the waist and she was scratching the rebel soldier and she was screaming and sobbing and her skirts were pulled up and the rebel was laughing and so Wheatfield jumped on the rebel and the rebel cursed and rolled over and for a mo-

ment all three of them were a jumble of arms and legs and the
rebel tried to get his hands around Wheatfield's throat and the
girl rolled free and stood up and ran from the room and Wheatfield stuck a finger in the rebel's eye and the rebel shrieked and
the rebel then punched Wheatfield in the stomach and the breath
whooshed from Wheatfield's mouth and he gouged the rebel's
eye again and the rebel shrieked again and Wheatfield then
brought his knee up into the rebel's groin and the rebel rolled
free and stood up and Wheatfield stood up too and the rebel gave
a great hoarse cry and dived for Wheatfield's legs and knocked
him to the floor and they rolled over and over and upset the
kitchen table (dishes crashed to the floor) and the rebel took a
piece of china and tried to cut Wheatfield but Wheatfield rolled
away and stood up and the rebel stood up too and tried to grab
a rifle that was leaning against a wall but Wheatfield beat him to
it and seized the rifle and the rebel stopped, grinned, then
brayed deeply and ran to the back door and out into the yard and
Wheatfield followed him (raising the rifle, sighting it and firing,
but missing because his hands were shaking so) and chased him
out to the road and along the road for maybe twenty yards and
then fell and did not get up because his muscles couldn't quite
do it. The rebel disappeared down the road.

Wheatfield lay gasping in the dust. He closed his eyes to keep
out the glare of the sun. He breathed thickly, through his nose
mostly. His mouth hung open, but he couldn't seem to get any
breath from it.

My God . . .

Ohhh: I ever get back to my outfit I'm going to put in for a
transfer to the quartermasters or something.

That was one strong sonofabitch.

He lay still for some time. His throat and stomach hurt. He
rubbed his throat weakly.

Then he heard people running. He opened his eyes.

A woman and a boy were coming toward him. The woman was fat.

He propped himself on his elbows.

"Mister . . . mister . . ." the woman said. She bent over him. "You all right?"

He saw she was crying. He worked up a sort of grin. "Just laying here getting my breath," he said.

"Bless you. Oh bless you," the woman said, sniffling.

"You better—you better get inside," the boy said quickly.

"Uh," Wheatfield said.

"We'll help you," the woman said. "There're rebels all around."

They helped him to his feet. He lurched, nearly fell. They steered him to the house. "Whoo," he kept saying.

The girl was waiting for them in the kitchen. She was all covered up now. She had on a different dress. There was a scratch on her nose, but otherwise you'd never have known what had just happened. Her hair even was combed. She brought Wheatfield a chair. The woman and the boy put the table on its feet. Wheatfield leaned back in the chair and closed his eyes again. Afterimages danced. Flaming things, bright explosions, pinpoints. Then he felt a hand on his forehead. It was a warm hand.

He opened his eyes. The girl smiled down at him. He saw how pale her face was. She didn't say anything.

The woman and the boy stood behind her. They didn't say anything either.

Wheatfield blinked. "Feels good," he said.

The girl nodded. The movement of her hand across his forehead was slow.

The boy was grinning and fidgeting. "You," he said, hesitating, "you sure did—uh, you sure did give it to him!" His voice became louder as he went along.

Wheatfield shrugged.

"How did you get here?" the boy wanted to know.

"Now Johnny," the girl said. "Let him rest a minute."

"That was some fight," the boy said admiringly.

"Shhh," the woman said.

Wheatfield stared at the girl. "You was in it," he said. "You ought to go set down too."

The girl's smile vanished. Her face was tight. "No," she said. "I'm all right."

They stood awkwardly. Wheatfield tried to smile. He didn't know what to say either. That old reb had been trying to rape this girl. It wasn't something you wanted to talk about too much. She sure was a pretty girl. Real young too.

They brought him a cup of coffee, and gradually they all got to talking. He drank the coffee slowly; he told them of his escape, of Caleb, of the night he had spent at the old man's. And the woman agreed with him about Walter Johnson: there sure was one *peculiar* old man. Talked a person's leg off. Biggest windbag in Adams County—no one disputed that. They laughed when he recounted (censoring the dirty words) some of the things the old man had said. Even the girl laughed at the business about the old man's cousin who was named Fitch and not Johnson. She had been solemn up to that time, but Wheatfield couldn't understand why she was even in the kitchen at all. He thought girls went to bed or something when things happened to them like what almost had happened to her. She sure does stand up to things pretty good, he told himself. And he thought of that reb. There had been something familiar about that feller, but he couldn't place just *what*. He worried the thought, picked at it, tried to find the connection.

But—one thing for sure: this here girl sure was holding up good. Lot of backbone. And he liked people who had backbone.

"What's your name?" the boy asked him.

"Whitfield Johnson."

"Whitfield?" the boy said, giggling. "That sounds like Wheatfield."

Wheatfield grinned. "That's all right. Lots of folks call me that. I don't mind. There's a lot worse things to be called than Wheatfield."

"We're the Bagleys," the girl said. "This is my mother, my brother Johnny (he's twelve) and me. I'm Leora."

"How's that?"

She smiled. She was sitting across the table from him now. "L-E-O-R-A. It was my grandmother's name, my father's mother."

"You seen a lot of fighting?" the boy asked him. The boy's eyes were lively and bright.

"Some."

"We ain't never had a soldier here in our house," the boy said.

"He doesn't want to talk about fighting," the girl said.

The boy told Wheatfield about how the rebel had fired a shot upstairs in the bedroom. Right through the mirror—bang! "I kicked him though—and Leora she spit right in his face. He didn't—"

"Young man," the mother said threateningly. She smiled at Wheatfield. "Don't you pay any mind to him. We were frightened. All of us. We're glad you came along when you did. We're very grateful. You were very brave."

Wheatfield drank his coffee so he would have something to do.

"Did you leave his gun outside?" the woman wanted to know.

"In the road," Wheatfield said.

"I'm glad."

"Why?" the girl asked her.

"I don't want a gun in my house."

"Maybe we'll need it," the girl said.

"No. I don't want it."

"Mam, can I say something?" Wheatfield asked.

The mother nodded.

"It might be a good thing to keep a gun—until the fight's done anyway."

"No." Stubbornly shaking her head.

"I can show you folks how to fire it."

"She's right," the girl said, smiling at Wheatfield. "In the first place, it's not good to have a gun in a house—and anyway, we wouldn't do the right thing with it. We'd like as not kill each other."

"I could shoot it," the boy said eagerly.

"John Bagley," the mother said. "You open your mouth one more time you're going up to your room and you'll stay there a whole week. Now mind what I say."

The boy was silent. He went to a corner of the kitchen and sat down. He stared at his feet, but Wheatfield knew he was listening for all he was worth. It made Wheatfield think of Little Pitchers and Big Ears and all that.

Sounds, rumbling sounds, were growing in the east. Wheatfield glanced out a window and saw smoke rising.

"That's where I'm trying to get," he said.

"Not for a while," the woman said.

"Yes."

"Young man—you are in our house now. We are offering you our hospitality. You're a gentleman aren't you? In Pennsylvania a gentleman doesn't refuse an invitation—especially after he's done a family a good turn. There's no courtesy in you if you don't give people a chance to show they're grateful."

"We're beholden to you," the girl said. "It's not right that you should go off before we have a chance to do something for you."

"You got no call to be beholden."

"We're not going to make you break any oath," the woman said. "We just want you to stay for a little bit. We know you're a soldier. We know about your duty."

Color came into the girl's cheeks. It made her prettier. "Why," she said calmly, "why is there a duty? Mother, you wouldn't watch. I did. I saw them go by here yesterday. I saw those poor men get killed. Was it their duty to get killed? Why should they have to go out there and die? Duty—is it a big fat frilly word for the reason you die because there isn't any reason? What is—"

"Miss," Wheatfield said.

"Let me talk. I—"

"No!" Wheatfield shouted. He was angry with himself. He shouldn't have brought this up. Johnson who do you think you are? What do these folks care about what you got to do or think you got to do? See? Every time you open your mouth it comes out wrong. You sound like a hero. A hero. You can't even hint at Duty without sounding like a hero. Don't you know no better?

He held up an arm to keep the girl from talking. "Nobody—uh, nobody wants to die," he said, stumbling over the words. "You folks I guess you're mad because you didn't want no war and then we came along and the rebs they came along too—and now there you got out in front of your house dead men laying this way and that. Now do you think they wanted to come here and die? No! No man I know of wants to die anyplace—here or at home or any-place. We don't pick the place where we die. We come here and we fight because—uh, well, because—you know, it's hard to say just why. I don't know. I just kind of work it over in my mind. But in a fight a man he got to do things that ain't quite all the time just for himself. I—oh I don't know . . ."

"Go on," the girl said.

He stared into his coffeecup. "Well . . . oh, it's just that—well, just that when you're in an army and there is so many other fel-

lers the only way you can hope to get by is to do your duty. There
are so many fellers that oh I don't know you just got to put yourself second because then maybe you'll come out all right. You
try to do what's good for the army because then well maybe it'll
be good for you. It ain't being brave. That don't have nothing
to do with it. It ain't winning no medals and it ain't being slapped
on the back by no general. It's just that if you do what's right—
you call that doing your duty I guess—then maybe, if your side is
good enough, the war it'll end and you won't have to be scared
no more. We're all of us scared, Miss Bagley. Not a man who
ain't scared unless he's crazy. But we're here fighting this war and
we got to make the best of it and so we do our duty because well,
then maybe it'll end sooner. Lot of men die, sure. They come
and mess up your nice country around here. You can't see no
sense in it. Me, I can't see no sense in it either. But you got to
face the fact that the war it's with us. So then, uh, then you go
out and try to do what's best."

"That's why you have to get back?"

"I don't want to sound like no hero. I shouldn't of brought
this up."

The girl began to cry.

"Mister Johnson," the mother said, choking.

"I—" Wheatfield said helplessly. He reached across the table
and took one of the girl's hands. Oh Jesus Christ, he said to himself, no matter what I say it comes out all highblown and not the
way I want it. I oughta be shot goddamit for saying all this stuff.
THIS THING IT AIN'T HIGHBLOWN BUT HOW DO
YOU SAY IT?

He squeezed the girl's hand.

The noise was very very loud now in the east.

The girl looked up at Wheatfield. She wiped her eyes. "I'm—
I'm sorry," she said.

The smell of smoke was very thick.

The mother turned and faced the stove. Her shoulders shook.

"Please . . . please stay with us a little while," the girl said.

Wheatfield nodded his head yes.

He liked her. God damn. He liked her.

He let go of her hand and finished drinking his coffee. The girl watched every move he made. He deliberately tried not to look at her. He guessed she was the prettiest thing he'd ever seen. But he would be leaving in a little while, and so he did not want to look at her.

The mother turned from the stove. "Leora, you feel all right?"

"I'm fine," the girl said.

"You don't want to rest?"

"No. I'm all right. He didn't do anything."

The mother took a step back and bumped into the stove, knocking a skillet to the floor. It made a great clatter.

Wheatfield went to pick it up for her. As he did he saw two coins under the stove. He reached for them and brought them out. He straightened, and put the skillet on the stove. He held out the coins. "Look what I found," he said.

The girl stood up abruptly.

The mother stared at the coins in Wheatfield's hands. "Ten dollars—now how . . . ?"

"The reb," the girl said in a small voice.

Wheatfield quickly turned and dropped the coins on a sideboard.

The girl crossed the room to Wheatfield. "We—we want you to stay for supper. Please. I—well, I just want that you—"

"I'll stay," Wheatfield said. He took her hand again.

It was some supper.

Wheatfield took a nap on the parlor sofa while the woman and the girl bustled in the kitchen. He didn't sleep very well. The sound of the battle was too loud. The house kept shaking. He kept thinking: This ain't the craziest thing I don't know what is. Me, I'm a guest in a house that's in reb territory and out there they're making me a big feed and the guns is booming outside and it's like little kids having a teaparty in the middle of some kind of a big storm. And I'm laying on the parlor sofa right in the middle of a great big fight. Now don't that beat the dickens? He kept waking up to the blast of the guns. And the memory of that rebel picked at him. The girl awakened him for supper and he went into the kitchen and had chicken and boiled potatoes and carrots from the garden and some sausage and celery and applesauce and homemade bread all fluffy and fresh and warm and a steaming apple pie for dessert. Apple pie. Back home he'd had apple pie exactly three times in his life: his tenth birthday, the funeral of his granddad, when one was brought by a neighbor woman, and the day he enlisted in the army, when the women of Mattoon gave the departing boys a great feast.

As they ate, the noise outside made it almost impossible for them to talk. Just as he was finishing his pie the woman said something Wheatfield didn't catch.

"How's that?" he shouted.

"Shame!"

"Mam?"

"Shame shame shame SHAME!" Her face was red. She stood up. She was trembling.

"Mamma!" the girl hollered. Now the air was filled with great crashing and booming and grinding sounds. It was as though the battle were being fought right out in the yard.

"SHAME!" the mother shrieked. She fell to her knees. "O God! O God God God! I want my husband! Willard! Willard! I want him!"

The girl went to her mother. "Mamma!"

Explosions thundered to make the earth tremble. Smoke rolled in through the windows. The woman coughed.

The girl put her arms around the woman and helped her to her feet. They left the kitchen and went upstairs.

The boy ran to the window and looked out. He jumped up and down.

Wheatfield stood up too. He walked around the room. Those rumbling sounds, goddamit all anyway. Damn that girl. He liked her. He liked her a whole lot. Damn her. Get going, he told himself. Listen to all that out there. What are you doing here? You trying to hide?

No.

Well what *do* you call it?

I like her. It don't have nothing to do with me being scared.

How do you know you like her? You only just met her.

That don't matter.

Oh? It don't? Listen . . .

There was the sound of horses and shouts and marching men. More rebels tramped by out front. He didn't have to go look. He knew the sound.

He started for the door.

"You going?" the boy asked him.

He halted and shrugged. He smiled. The house shook from another explosion. "Your sister," he said, "I . . ." and his voice trailed away. He returned to the table and sat down again. He answered the boy's questions about how much fun it was to be in the army. He wished the girl would hurry and come back downstairs.

♣ At three o'clock that afternoon, when the Confederates finally got their attack under way, both the Round Tops (which Dan Sickles' III Corps had been ordered to defend) were de-

serted. Sickles' men were spread in their sideways V, a sprawling island of troops disconnected from the rest of the Army of
the Potomac. Gen McLaws' division of Longstreet's corps
opened the attack, hitting the forward point of the salient—
those federals who defended the peach orchard. Another division, under Gen Hood, sneaked off to the right. Its aim was to
flank the salient and climb the unprotected Round Tops. The
Confederate strategists finally were aware that capture of the
Round Tops probably would mean victory. Southern artillery,
placed atop these two hills, would be able to enfilade the entire Union defensive line along Cemetery Ridge. Thus, with this
plan (plus Ewell's attack to the north, at Culp's Hill, which finally was gaining some momentum), did the first real assault
against the fish hook begin. The sun pounded out of a sky
streaked with skinny powdered clouds. It was a dry day, with
a great deal of dust. It was a day to bake your skull, to freckle
your arms and turn them red. And the brightness and the heat
drained you as you moved forward; they made you value your
breath. There was noise and confusion and swirls of smoke and
dust and dirt; officers shouted and exhorted; artillery let loose
with their endless blasting sounds; you kept moving forward
but you couldn't see too well; the outlines of trees were clouded
and some of the trees were afire; you heard screams and
groans and gallopings and yells and footsteps crackling
through dry brush; you saw dead men spreadeagled this way
and that; you saw the wounded crawling to the rear; you kept
wiping grit from your eyes; you hoped you were still with your
company but you weren't sure because you couldn't see much;
sometimes you stumbled over dead horses and mules and
dead men too; trees splintered with great limbs crashing to the
ground; you fell to the ground and fired into the dusty haze
and everywhere riflefire went gik gik gik and there were whining sounds; men whooped past you into the haze and you got
up and whooped with them; somebody blew a bugle and its

pealing thinness soared high over the field in a frantic tinny tiny squeak; some colonel waved his sword and shouted something and pointed at the enemy; you wiped more grit from your eyes; now there was grit in your mouth too; you saw men clutch themselves and plop bloodily into the dust or perhaps not bloodily at all (somewhere behind you, perhaps on the side of a hill, cannoneers stood shirtless and sweating and black and rammed in the ramrods and then stood back and awaited the enormous roars and then did it all again); perhaps you noticed that this was a peach orchard and then again perhaps you did not; peach trees crashed to the ground all around you; you found the enemy and you threw yourself upon him and your bayonet turned incredibly red and then incredibly brown; you wrestled with a big bearded man; you slit his guts; you lay down behind one of the fallen peach trees and you fired gik gik gik at the dustobscured shapes out there that you guessed were the enemy; you ran toward the enemy again and bullets went piu, piu all around you and why you didn't die you didn't know (did you think of home and mother and meals big enough to choke you and the last girl who let you put your hand in her pants and the flag and parades and the doctrine of states' rights? what DID you think of? did you think of your own safety and nothing else? were you numb? were your glands secreting excessively? did you hate the enemy? granted you were afraid, HOW afraid were you? what were your conclusions on the perfectibility of man? on the immortality of man? did the noise annoy you? were you too dirty? did the dust and dirt and smoke and burning smells annoy you? were you too warm? did you itch? how much perspiration did you excrete? any illeffects on your bowels? could you swallow with proper regularity? did you have sufficient saliva? were you steadfast and brave? what was your theory of courage? were you selfless? how deep was your concept of honor? did you desire to throw up?). ♣

PVT RUFUS PATTERSON yelled and whooped and dodged and ran and crawled and stumbled forward and fired his rifle and swung his bayonet and he sure was tired but he figured he had to keep moving to keep alive.

Rufus and his company were right at the front of the advance. Miniéballs screamed all around them and dirt flew up, cutting at their faces, and the Yanks were putting up one hell of a fire. But most of the trees in this here orchard were down now and Rufus was glad. A fallen tree was good protection.

The Yanks were gathered in force about halfway through the orchard. They were behind fallen trees themselves; they were behind earthworks too. Their artillery was close, only about a hundred yards or so to the rear and vomiting up great hunks of anything metal, firing everything they had. All a piece of metal needed to do was fit in the muzzle. The air was one continual roar now, but Rufus and the others kept moving forward, darting, crawling, yelling, flopping on their bellies. The sun banged down on everything, cutting streakily through the dust and smoke, and Rufus grimaced, narrowing his eyes to keep out the dust. He kept firing. At anything that moved so long as it looked like a Yank. He was absolutely unafraid. He fired at fuzzy shadows; he sprinted from tree to tree; he yelled and even whistled; his mouth was tight and his heart whammed violently and he didn't even think of Pete Bell and he hated those Yanks, o how he hated them, and everybody was moving forward and not Abe Lincoln, not God, not any damn thing or army would stop them today. They sprinted and dodged and crawled and fired and fell dead and in their throats were snarling roars and yips and the sun banged down on them and the Yank fire was thick but they kept going forward, they kept going forward, and over the roars of the cannon and the cracklings of the rifles came their awful *yaaaaahhhhhoooo!* and they met the Yanks at the earthworks and behind the fallen trees and there was a tangled straining whooping scuffling melee and many men died and bayonets dripped redly and many Confederate men stormed upon the Yanks and stomped them and ran bayonets through them and shot them and knocked them back from the earthworks and the fallen trees, knocked them back, yielded briefly, knocked them back again. Rufus was absolutely unafraid. He was full of joy. Absolutely unafraid. Yes. He hated them: all he knew was that he hated them. He screamed and howled with rage and triumph and joy too. He hacked Yanks with his bayonet and jumped on them when they had fallen; he screamed and screamed and screamed; he beheaded one man with one great sideways swipe; he laughed and laughed and laughed; he spluttered and gasped and wiped the dust from his eyes and looked for more Yanks, more Yanks he could swipe at, and the Yanks finally went howling to the rear and Rufus and the others chased them, whapping them with the butts of their rifles, slicing them with their bayonets, never relenting, never giving them a chance to rally, chasing them, wave after wave and column after column, surging through the dust, grabbing, hacking, cursing, firing their rifles into the dust after the retreating Yanks, with screams and bleats and anguish all around them, but winning yes by God winning, with Pvt Rufus Patterson, the Virginia Virgin, there with them, Pvt Rufus Patterson right in there doing his part, killing Yanks yes by God killing Yanks, and some of the men even were singing yes by God singing, and it was as though all the air were sound and dirt and dust and smoke and heat, and Pvt Rufus Patterson ran forward forward forward, coughing and blaspheming through the thick sprays of dust and dirt and smoke, all the thick sprays, yelling and yelling and yelling yaaaahhhhooooo! and yip yip yippyyippy yip too, yelling high in his lungs, his lungs clogged with dust and the taste of burnt things, yelling and stumbling and flying to his feet and lurching on among all these men, these men who by God were winning, these milling men, these men all fuzzy and indistinct in the clouds of battle that rose from the ground, and there was a lot of confusion but they kept going forward, forward forward forward, and it didn't make a hell of a lot of difference if you were lost from your outfit because there always was another one running forward with you.

It took them less than half an hour to capture the peach orchard. The Yanks fled to the east.

Officers rode about and waved their swords and brought the attackers to a halt for regrouping. Reinforcements swept past, keeping the pressure on the retreating federals. About half of Rufus' company still was on its feet. Noise still swirled about these men, but they were dog beat; they didn't care. They gathered beneath a clump of trees that somehow (lord God only knew why) still stood. Capt Hawk, the company commander, came riding up to them and gave a cheer and told them they could rest a spell. Capt Hawk's face was very red and the men never had seen him happier. Usually he was a kind of quiet feller. Kept to himself. He galloped off for instructions and the men gratefully collapsed in the shade of the clump of trees. They waved tiredly at the reinforcements.

Rufus fell at the base of one of the trees. He closed his eyes and swallowed great heavy gulps of air, this warm air so thick with smoke and dust. His head buzzed. His chest strained with the effort to get back his wind.

All around him were shouts and gunfire and he heard the reinforcements run yelling forward. Bright things, little dots and streaks, jumped before his eyes. He kept gulping, breathing deeply. His heart whammed away.

Hate them.

I'm all right.

I proved it.

Why?

Hate them: that's why.

What about Pete?

There ain't no Pete.

I'm me; I got to get along by myself.

Scared?

No.

Not no more. Not never.

(Who you think you lyin to?)

The thing to do is be *hard*.

Pete's dead an he was hard.

Goes to show you what lookin up can do.

I'm me; I ain't scared.

(Who you think you lyin to?)

He opened his eyes and shook his head. A man named Thad Manwell lay next to him. "My Gawd," Manwell said.

Rufus stared at him. "What?"

Manwell had a flatplaned unremarkable face. It was the kind of face you had to look at twice to remember whose it was. "My Gawd," he said again, loudly. His voice was shrill.

"What you say? What you talkin about?"

Manwell squinted up at the sun. He was about Rufus' age, but shorter. His skin was very brown from the sun. "I'm tryin to figure somethin out," he said. Only his mouth and throat moved. He was flat on his back.

"What?" Rufus wanted to know.

"Why I'm always scared." Manwell's voice was not so shrill now.

Rufus didn't say anything, thinking: He been in the army as long as me. If he don't know why he scared an what he can do about it why do he talk about it?

"All the times," Manwell said.

"Huh? Speak up."

"Just now. I like to die just now." There was no expression on Manwell's unremarkable face.

"Pretty big fight," Rufus said.

"I don't mean that. I like to die, I mean, because I was so scared."

"Um."

Manwell rolled over and looked Rufus straight in the eye. "You scared too?" he wanted to know.

Rufus never answered the question. A cannonball screamed toward them. He rolled over flat on his stomach and buried his face in his arms. The cannonball crashed through the tree. Limbs splintered and fell. The men were showered with branches and leaves. "Yank sonsabitches!" Rufus yelled as he rolled over. He was covered with leaves. He sat up and began brushing them off. He glanced over at Manwell.

Manwell was pinned beneath a large branch. It lay across his stomach. He reached toward Rufus and made a choking sound.

"Hey. Lord. Hey," Rufus said. He crawled to Manwell.

Manwell's intestines and bowels had been gouged out. They lay, red and wet, exposed across his belly. His belly was white and soft.

"Now don't you move," Rufus told him.

Some other men saw what had happened. They went to Manwell and lifted the branch off him.

Manwell screamed.

The men stared at Manwell's belly.

Manwell reached up and shaded his eyes. The men stood in a circle around him. Other men ran past—forward, toward the Yanks. Flies buzzed in the heat and dust now. There still was a great deal of noise. Some of the trees had small fires high in their branches.

"I. Huh. Scared," Manwell said, turning his head to one side.

Rufus, who was in a sitting position now next to Manwell, looked up at the others. One of the men said something to him, but he didn't hear for the gunfire and explosions.

Manwell whispered something. He smelled of urine.

"You just lay easy," Rufus said.

Capt Hawk returned. He dismounted and walked to the men. He squatted beside Manwell.

"Boy," Capt Hawk said.

Manwell turned his head. Very slowly. He stared at Capt Hawk for a long time. His mouth was open and his tongue hung out.

Capt Hawk was short, bowlegged, with a wide heavy face and a high forehead. He was from North Carolina. Although most of the men in his company were Virginians, they liked him all right. He went where they went. That was enough to make them like him all right. Now he stood up and put his hands on his hips. He looked at Manwell and was silent.

Manwell motioned to Rufus to come closer. "Scared," he whispered.

Rufus looked up helplessly.

Men were yelling all around. It was one hell of a hot afternoon. Capt Hawk scruffed in the dirt with his boots. He looked up at the fires burning in the trees. There were shots and the sound of hooves. There were many explosions. No clouds were between the earth and the sky.

A trickle of saliva came from a corner of Manwell's mouth. Rufus tried to smile at him. Trying to smile, thinking: We ought to go away. Just move on out an let him die without all of us standin around like it was some kind of a show maybe.

Manwell screamed again.

He put his hands over the great bleeding hole in his belly. His hands weren't large enough. Redness seeped through his fingers. He twisted, kicked his legs in the air.

Capt Hawk turned his back.

Manwell thrashed and moaned. His head went from side to side, back and forth, from side to side. His eyes were wide open now, staring directly into the sun. He took one of Rufus' hands and pulled Rufus close to him again.

"Scared. Die. No," Manwell whispered.

Manwell's hand was warm. He breathed noisily into Rufus' ear.

Rufus closed his eyes to keep in the tears. He tried to pull away from Manwell, but Manwell's grip was strong. "I can't see nothin," Manwell whispered.

Rufus looked up at the others. "God. He says he can't see nothin."

One of the men spat and nodded his head.

Capt Hawk faced them again. "I wish," he said. "I wish once . . . I . . . Ahhh . . ."

Manwell's thrashings subsided. He pulled Rufus to him one more time. "I want please kiss oh I'm scared kiss please?" came from his lips. The words were all run together and Rufus barely could make them out.

Rufus kissed Manwell on the forehead. Manwell started to make a nodding movement, but died. His eyes remained open.

Capt Hawk bent over Manwell and closed his eyes. "I wish," Capt Hawk said, "that just once. Just once. Just once we could bury one of these fellers. I do. I do wish that."

Capt Hawk straightened and faced the men. "This here war," he said. He got on his horse and led them forward. The noise and the heat and the dust and the dirt and the smoke returned and Rufus was crying and they charged forward toward the Yanks again.

♣ Dan Sickles has the center of the stage now. No two ways about THAT. It had been his responsibility to protect the Round Tops. He had failed to do that. Furthermore, he had drawn out his III Corps into an indefensible position and the jubilant Confederates were whacking it to pieces. The peach orchard fell within half an hour despite a magnificent stand by Sickles' outnumbered men. Almost all of Longstreet's corps participated in the assault; it overwhelmed the III Corps and drove the federals across a wheat field. At the same time, Hood—a skinny pugnacious Texan, one of the finest officers on the field— moved his men smartly to the right in their flanking movement, then due east toward the Round Tops. They met with hardly any resistance at all. Sickles' men were being cut into bloody fragments by Longstreet's whooping Southerners; there would be no resistance from that quarter. And then, to compound the confusion (or was it an extraordinary piece of luck?), Dan Sickles was wounded. Badly too. He had been conducting himself with great gallantry, riding back and forth along the firing line, along the great limp sideways letter V that now was crumbling, when someone shot off his right leg. Smoking a cigar, waving cockily, grinning, he was carried off the field and never again saw action. He is carried off stage center and now his place is taken by a man with one of the most wildly improbable names in military history—a Union general who was called Gouverneur K. Warren. Who, save the student of this war, has ever heard of Gouverneur K. Warren? No one, of course. Yet Gouverneur K. Warren, he of the pretentious and evocative given name, is one of the Republic's supreme military heroes, a man whose mind and attitudes hardly constituted the stuff of heroism, yet a man who had more to do with the salvation of the Republic than many other men whose names still grope through the memories we have from textbooks. So clear the stage for Gouverneur K. Warren and his great deed. He was chief of engineers for Meade. His personality bore a great deal of resemblance to his chief's. He was obscure, rather conservative, a finicky bug for detail and administrative busywork—no doubt Meade, who came from the same tribe, admired him and trusted him. His heroism came about this way: Ewell's attack on Culp's Hill came first, as Lee had planned. Meade, busy with shoring up the defenses there, could not spare the time to investigate Sickles' dilemma at the peach orchard. So he sent Warren to look over the situation. Warren arrived at Sickles' front but could see nothing for smoke and dust. So he spurred his horse and galloped to the crest of Little Round Top. No troops were up there. A small signal detachment was working with its equipment, but no infantry units were in sight. Warren looked through his glasses toward the peach orchard and saw the attack by McLaws' men and other units of Longstreet's corps; he saw the III Corps (now commanded by Gen David B. Birney; by this time Dan Sickles had been rendered hors de combat and had been carried off waving and chomping hard on his cigar) fall back, its flanks bent; it was defending stiffly, but it needed reinforcements—and quickly. Warren noted this. He knew that two corps—the V under Gen George Sykes and the VI under crusty old John Sedgwick, one of the most beloved leaders in this war (he did not survive it)—were on their way. He prayed for them to hurry. He stared at the field, then frowned, put his glasses to his eyes again. What he saw certainly must have made his throat constrict. He probably looked again, blinking. Then he acted quickly and decisively. He had to: he had seen Hood's men climbing up the west side of Little Round Top; they had completely flanked the III Corps and were about to take possession of this undefended hill. Warren knew very well what that would mean: Confederate artillery would be able to enfilade the entire Union line. Warren acted. He rode hellbent for God and the Republic down the east side of Little Round Top and came across several units of Sykes' V Corps, just arriving on the field. He galloped like a madman and screamed at the first unit he saw, the 20th Maine Infantry, to climb that hill and defend it. The 20th Maine broke into a run (some men, in fact, didn't have time to load their rifles) and arrived at the crest just before Hood's Confederates, who had stopped halfway to rest. The 20th Maine was badly outnumbered, but it held, it held there among the rocks and tall trees, it held in a vicious handtohand melee, it pounded and pushed and yielded and advanced and tugged and wrestled; men screamed and hollered and kicked up dust, thick dust, but the 20th Maine held, and presently it was joined by other units from the V Corps. The Confederates sent reinforcements, but Warren (he of the preposterous given name) took personal command of the defenders and turned back thrust after thrust. He finally led a counterattack and pushed the Confederates back. The Confederates attacked again, but by this time Union troops were pouring up the side of Little Round Top, and it would be held. The superb Winfield Scott Hancock, blaspheming and yelling, rushed over from the II Corps' sector. He brought more reinforcements. And so the Southerners (they fought well too; all the heroism there was not Warren's and the V Corps') finally withdrew, slowly, with great reluctance. Hood, skinny Hood, the pugnacious Texan who had led the venture, lost an arm. His men were badly bruised; they had no choice but to retreat. Then reinforcements arrived to aid Birney's stricken III Corps. The advance of McLaws' division and other units from Longstreet's corps was halted. And, as all this was happening (the enchanted Warren, the blunting of the assault on the III Corps, all of it), the federals on Culp's Hill were beating back Ewell's attack. The whooping Confederates charged, and charged again, but Meade had seen to it that a huge artillery battery would be on the scene. Cannonballs smothered the attackers, smashing them, uprooting them, tearing them apart. And at the same time a steady rain of death poured forth from the Union infantry established behind the earthworks it had spent the previous night preparing. And so by evening both Confederate attacks were broken. The fish hook was stabilized; the Army of the Potomac (despite Sickles' error, in some ways because of it) had turned back the Southerners. There were great losses on both sides, but the federals had checked Lee's scheme. It was a clear defensive victory. The armies struggled well into the night and men kept dying, but the Confederates could gain no advantage. At about ten o'clock they quit for the night. And Gen George Gordon Meade, crabby as he was, must have permitted himself the luxury of at least one small smile. There is no record of this, however. ♣

SGT LEON MARSHALL STRONG sat in darkness crosslegged beneath a tree. Lights from campfires were reflected on his face. Parts of his face were black. Other parts were red and orange. His hands were over his ears. His shirt was torn, and his breeches were torn, and his face was cut and dirty. His chest and belly, flabby and pale, were exposed at several places.

This morning, when they had moved into the peach orchard, Cpl Ferris, the Indiana hayseed, had been disturbed. *We gonna walk right through the whole reb army?* Strong had heard Ferris ask a Capt Magill, the company commander. Strong did not hear Capt Magill's reply. These trenches and holes and earthworks and fortifications, representing all that work, all that digging and sweating, the soft wet blisters on Strong's hands—they were abandoned. The order came through: go forward. So forward they went, down the side of the ridge, across a wheat field and into somebody's old peach orchard. God in Heaven, Strong said to himself as he marched, what is this all about? They keep us up digging those earthworks and then—oh, the army. He dragged along with the others. None of them ragged him now. They all were too tired. They had had very little sleep. There was much loud grumbling. They marched along slowly. Most of the men were yawning and blinking. But Strong neither yawned nor blinked. There were rebel skirmishers out there, in front of them as they marched. Not many, and they did little firing—but Strong never had heard any shots fired in anger before. He gave a great yell the first time and fell to the ground. The others, tired as they were, guffawed loudly. Ferris went to Strong, grinned and helped him to his feet. *Don't get worked up sarge*, Ferris said. *Them's only skirmishers.* Strong did not reply. It was a hot morning, but he was shivering. He marched on; the others were silent again. Shots, vagrant shots, not loud at all, were loud to him, and each time he heard one he winced. But the march was uneventful. They arrived in the peach orchard without seeing one rebel. They sat around and ate; they were quiet; many men snoozed. Strong could eat nothing, neither could he sleep. He kept twitching each time one of those remote skirmisher pinging sounds carried to him. He lay back and tried to think of Harriet and the girls, but they were too loud; he saw them but he also *heard* them, and now—of all times—he wanted to hear nothing loud. He listened to the others talk—their small talk, desultory, about food, bravery, money, women. He tried to concentrate on the things they were saying, but he couldn't, and so his mind investigated the reasons, his methodical clerkish mind went to work: I never. Shocked? Why, I've never even said THAT WORD. Wonder what it would sound like. You press your teeth into your lower lip and then you blow the word out kind of. Fuhhh: like that. Hum. Every other word they say is THAT WORD. Ahhh, well now: be honest with yourself Strong. You like it too. You have five daughters don't you? Harriet likes it too. We never talk about it, but she does. I know it. Press your teeth into your lower lip. Hum. They can lie around and talk like this, but why not? They know what it's like.

I guess. Or is it different every time? Then if so, why don't they show fear? Do they have fear? Am I the only one who is afraid? What is it? Do they swallow their fear? Are they used to it? Do they just carry it around with them and take it for granted and go about their business recognizing it but trying to ignore it as best they can? That kind of talk: I never was in a situation for it. It's a hot day. I don't know why I can't sleep. Six goes into ninetytwo once carry the three, into thirtytwo five times carry the two; six into ninetytwo is fifteen and twosixths or onethird and all you have to do is press your teeth into your lower lip, and not too hard either, and say it: fuhhh. Softly he rubbed his blistered hands together. There was a large bulging egg of a blister on the palm of his right hand. He picked at it with a fingernail. It opened; some liquid flowed. There was very little pain. No one, well no one, he said to himself, there just wasn't the chance for this kind of talk back home; there was always your *position* to think about. These men are crude oafs—I should be shocked. I guess maybe I am. He sat bemused, staring at the open blister, not feeling its weak sting. His side hurt from Ferris' kick, but he did not feel that either. Maybe there won't be any fighting today, he thought, maybe both sides will call it off for one day. I think maybe if I have one more day it will be all right: this is somebody's old peach orchard and are you supposed to fight in a peach orchard? I thought fighting was done out in fields or somewhere. Two years in the army: never heard a shot. How many men can claim that? How many *want* to? Many, I expect. Many want to. I bet none of these men want to fight. He looked up at the sun. He was sweating heavily now. Nothing happened. The men all sat around; many still snoozed. They were behind a stone wall. Just beyond the wall was a road that led south. The men leaned on their rifles, or they snoozed, or they talked of food or bravery or money or women. Strong worked THAT WORD on his mouth, depressing his teeth into his lower lip, blowing through his teeth, softly. He did sums in his head; he did multiplication and division; flies buzzed around him; skirmishers' shots pinged occasionally; there were rumbling sounds to the north. But for quite a time nothing happened at the peach orchard. He was just dozing off when the rebels attacked, announcing their arrival with an enormous artillery barrage. Thousands of them, yelling and whooping that awful screaming challenge Strong never had heard before, came forward, running and crawling, and someone pushed Strong to the stone wall and the others crouched behind it and yelled obscenities at the rebels and let loose a stream of riflefire and Strong saw some of the rebels crumble and he stood up to watch, he stood up with his mouth open and watched the rebels crumble and shots whinged all around him but he simply stood there in profound numbness. He held his rifle at his side. *GET DOWN!* someone hollered. He did not hear. Then someone knocked him down. It was Cpl Ferris. Strong lay in the dust and stared blandly at Cpl Ferris, who was cursing him foully. Out beyond the wall the rebels were crawling forward now. Strong could hear their yells get louder. *GODDAM YOU!* Cpl Ferris screamed at him, grabbing him by the shirt and pulling him to the wall. Strong closed his eyes and hugged his rifle to his chest. Ferris slapped him. He opened his eyes. Ferris pointed at the rifle. *USE IT!* he yelled. Strong stared at his rifle. He smiled at Ferris and shook his head no. Ferris slapped him again. *You don't fire it, I KILL you!* Strong now was crying. Ferris pulled him around facing the enemy. Shells were landing behind them and now there was much smoke and dust in the air. Strong looked at his rifle. It was loaded. He remembered he had loaded it. *FIRE IT!* Ferris bellowed. Strong fired it. Straight up in the air. He coughed from all the dust. Ferris crawled very close to him and grabbed him by the neck. *I'm going to kill you in about one minute,* Ferris said. Then, finally,

Strong got an idea of what was happening. He rubbed his fists in his eyes and nodded. He bit a cartridge and reloaded (it was difficult for him; he hadn't had to fire a gun since he'd taken that two weeks' little bit of training just after joining up); he peeked over the edge of the wall. A big rebel was crawling right at him. He closed his eyes and fired. The rebel was only about eight or ten feet away. The shot blew off his head. Strong saw this and vomited. (He had opened his eyes slowly; for a moment he hadn't believed what he had seen.) Then Ferris slapped him on the back and crawled away. He looked around for Ferris. No Ferris. He bit another cartridge, reloaded his rifle and peeked over the wall again. He shot another rebel who had almost made the wall. This rebel screamed, fell forward across the wall, stared straight at Strong, then slipped back. Strong heard him moan but could not see him because the wall was between them. Strong was soggy with sweat now and he was unable to control the violence with which his hands were shaking, but he kept peeking over the wall and firing his rifle. The other men up and down the line were doing the same. But the rebels just kept coming. And yelling. Oh God that yelling, those high defiant screams. Wave after wave of rebels, column after column, and Strong fired his rifle, bit, loaded, fired again, bit, loaded, fired again, and the vomit's sour aftertaste was warm in his mouth with the taste of gunpowder and his hands kept shaking and now he felt a new thing and it was not fear and it was not notfear and he fired automatically, almost blindly, and he thought of nothing except biting, loading, firing, biting, loading, firing, biting, opening the breech, inserting the bullet, pulling the trigger, then doing it all again, then again, then again, and all around him were whinging sounds and booming sounds and yelling sounds and he felt no hysteria now; he felt nothing. He did not even have the time to feel his little discomforts, the tiny fretful bruises and aches and blisters he had acquired this morning.

He thought not at all of arithmetic. He thought not at all of the army's stupidity. He thought not at all of anything that had anything at all to do with flyspecking exactitudes. He simply fired his rifle and trembled and felt the vomit's sour aftertaste. They kept coming forward, those rebels, and all of it—the pounding, the roars and whingings and yellings, the explosions and the gritty screens of smoke and dust and dirt—would last forever: he knew it. He no longer wept. And the rebels, whooping and jumping and dying and shaking their fists, looming out of the smoke and sprinting toward the wall, kept coming forward coming forward forward forward. All the swirling thicknesses blotted out the sun. Strong coughed and wheezed and felt a close hot constriction in his lungs. A man crouched next to him looked over the wall, fired and then made a squeaking sound, seized his throat and fell back. He was dead. Strong stared at him blankly for a moment, then resumed firing. Finally the order came to fall back. Ferris crawled up and down the line and shouted the order. He slapped Strong on the back again as he went past. So these men, those who were left, withdrew from their stone wall. There weren't very many left. They ran hunched over, sometimes crouching behind fallen trees to take a few shots at the pursuing enemy. Strong's prissy mouth worked in and out with the effort to keep his breath coming. He ran, but he also crouched and fired with the others. And three times Ferris drew them into a line and they tried to make a real stand. But three times they were driven back. The rebels just kept coming. You couldn't hold them off. You just couldn't. Not today. They just kept coming at you and coming at you, yelling their terrible yells. Strong stumbled and fell many times; he crawled through brush and weeds; spiky growing things cut at his face; he ran (everything was blurred now); he dropped; he crawled again; he got up, sprinted, fell, lay panting, and all around him the others, those who were left, were doing the same: the earth heaved with roars and explosions; the men retreated; the whooping rebels pursued. The taste of vomit was gone from Strong's mouth now. It was very dry; it seemed to be lined with dirt and gunpowder. Officers galloped past him; he saw artillerymen dragging their guns back; he stood when the others stood and made a stand when they did; they crossed the wheat field again; he looked back and saw many trees afire; a thick black smoke came from them; he fell down once and ripped his shirt and breeches; his hands bled; rebel artillery shells threw up huge booming eruptions of dirt; once a clod hit him full in the face, cutting it; presently all things blended for him, all sounds and sights, and he didn't even notice the reinforcements streaming past him; he ran and crawled and his face bled and his hands bled and all things roared and shrieked. Finally Ferris came to him and tugged at his sleeve. Sarge, Ferris said. Strong (he was standing now, not crawling) blinked and looked around. He pursed his lips. They were in a wooded place, and now all these other men, these reinforcements, were moving quickly toward the front. No sense running no more, Ferris said. Make a stand, make another stand? Strong said. No need, Ferris said. What? Strong said. The rebs been stopped, Ferris said. I ran, Strong said. No. You did like you was told, Ferris said. Why'd they do this to a good clerk? Strong said weakly. You're a FIGHTING man now sarge, Ferris said, smiling. Ahhh, Strong said. You did real good, Ferris said. Strong shook his head, wiped some of the blood from his face. You was right up there with the rest of us. I kind of had an eye on you. You got no call to be ashamed, Ferris said. More reinforcements ran past them. A colonel rode past shouting something. The colonel had a sabre that thudded against his horse's flanks. Ferris patted Strong on the back. Strong wanted to hit Ferris. They returned to where the reinforcements had thrown up a new defensive line. Only nine men were left now in Ferris' platoon. They fought on that line until nightfall. They moved back to the ridge under cover of darkness. The other men now talked with Strong. He didn't hear the things they said.

Sgt Leon Marshall Strong sat in darkness crosslegged beneath a tree. Lights from campfires were reflected on his face. Parts of his face were black. Other parts were red and orange. His hands were over his ears. His shirt was torn, and his breeches were torn, and his face was cut and dirty. His chest and belly, flabby and pale, were exposed at several places. Thirteen goes into sixhundred and two, he said to himself, four times with eight left over; thirteen goes into eightytwo six times carry the four; thirteen goes into sixhundred and two fortysix and fourthirteenths times. I keep hearing so many things: maybe that's because I enjoyed it.

Ferris came and sat down beside him. "You tired?"

Strong took his hands away from his ears. "What?"

"I said you tired?"

Strong grinned hugely. "Mighty fucking tired," he said, enunciating that word clearly.

♣ Night, and early into the night there were explosions, flashing brightnesses. The valley between the two armies was speckled with fires. Then, at about ten o'clock, the generals nodded wearily: the fighting stopped and there was a great silence, silence in the peach orchard, silence in the wheat field, on the fish hook, on Seminary Ridge to the west, where the Confederates were encamped, silence on the scarred Emmittsburg Road, on Culp's Hill, on the Round Tops, in the cemetery where that morning men had played catch with skulls, where they had laughed so at the sign that forbade the discharging of firearms. And between the fish hook and Seminary Ridge the dead men lay stiffly. Tomorrow they would begin to bloat, then stink corruptly with a heavy thick sick sweetness, full of gas and wetness, nauseous, incomparable. But now the dead

men were stiff in all the agonized postures, the lazy relaxed
postures too, of death when it catches men not in proper bed-
fast dignity. A hand raised, hookshaped. A head. Half a head.
A foot. Two feet, legs, the lower half of a torso. A man sitting
against a tree. His canteen is on the ground beside him. He
wears sergeant's stripes. His head is missing from the forehead
up. An artilleryman draped over an uprooted cannon. Fires
high in the treetops, glow, pale glow, yellowish, flick, flicking
on craters and dead men and dead horses and mules and
even, now and then, the groaning abandoned wounded who
call out in tiny voices immediately enveloped by silence and
the night. Some medical orderlies, carrying white flags, move
out and prowl the field and find a few, a few, wounded men
who look as though they might survive the trip back to the
lines. Occasionally a wounded man screams, splitting back
the night. But mostly there is silence, silence and the night and
the glow, the pale yellow glow. And the dead men. The hand,
hookshaped. The sergeant whose head is missing from the
forehead up. The draped artilleryman. Men on their stomachs.
Men on their backs. Men sitting. Kneeling. An ear. A finger
with a Masonic ring. Catalogue all things. Very necessary. A
man with his hands over his face. He has no nose. His cranial
structure is shattered. Flies. O many flies. Ants too. Buzzing.
Washing their hands. Chewing. A regiment of ants marching
in and out of the mouth of a captain of artillery who lies
gaping, on his belly. His fingers made a wriggling pattern in
the dirt just before he expired. A hand, nails bitten to the quick.
Someone who was afraid? Here and there the stink of human
foulness. Others who were afraid? And on the two ridges are
pinpointed the campfires. Forty thousand men, dead and
wounded, were lost today by the two armies, but other men
still have their campfires. They sit around their campfires. They
think. They talk. They wonder what the generals have in store
for them tomorrow. The generals gather in farmhouses and

tents. They peruse maps. They argue. They plan. They count losses, estimate strength for this venture or that. Some are bemused. Perhaps these are thinking of the stiff dead men, of all the fingers, heads missing from the forehead up, Masonic rings, the flies oh the many flies. And the men, the survivors outside, ring their campfires with talk. Skirmishers ping away at vagrant movements and rustlings, but there is no what you would call REAL fighting now. The men ring their campfires with their slow talk; they lie by their guns and remember all the noise, all the screams and shouts and shots and explosions; they think of dust and smoke, all the thickness and grittiness and dryness; they remember all the men they saw die today, all the gallopings and rumblings and hurried little dartings, the lines advancing, merging, disappearing in the allpervading dust and smoke; they think of the advances and the retreats and the buglecalls and the detonations; they think of craters gouged out by exploding cannonballs; they remember ripped trees and falling limbs and they remember heat and they remember the yellow unhidden sun and they remember blood spurting from the place where a man's leg had been; they think of courage, preposterous courage, The Man Alone Against The Enemy, a thin girlish lieutenant loading and firing a cannon all by himself, a screaming little fellow, a Union man, loading and firing that thing all by himself, until finally the Confederates kill him and charge past him and leave him to curl in the dust; these men, these survivors, remember all these things and other things and sit talking about them or lie quietly with their guns at their sides and think of themselves and wonder if they will be alive at this time tomorrow and some of them feel themselves, run their hands over their remarkable bodies, squeeze themselves, prod themselves, stroke various members and organs and feel profound astonishment because they still are alive. For this thing, for this event, for this noise, for this exposure to hot screaming pain

and fear and death, these man have come from all over. More
than one hundred and fifty thousand men and boys and cowards and misfits and morons and heroes and evildoers and
leaders and followers and men who just plain don't give a
damn. And some have died but more have lived. Who picks
who dies and who lives? Some of the survivors (those who investigate themselves, the contours of their bodies and so on)
want to know—and then laugh at themselves for asking such
a question. You might as well ask how high is up.   ♣

L E O R A sat in the parlor with this boy, this boy whose
name was Wheatfield Johnson. She was in a rocker and he was on
the sofa.

(Mamma was upstairs asleep now. She had wept for the longest
time. Finally she had asked for Johnny and had made him crawl
in with her. Then she had gone to sleep. Johnny had been angry.
He had wanted to stay up and talk with Wheatfield, but Mamma
had insisted, sniffles and all. So he had crawled in reluctantly,
weeping himself, and Mamma had hugged him, and after a time
they both had fallen asleep.)

Now there was this Wheatfield . . .

Leora wanted to know him better. They'd been sitting together
in the parlor for some time. They hadn't said much.

Where do I start? she wondered. How? And what do I want to
say?

The rumblings and boomings had ended. She wasn't so frightened now. There was something about this Wheatfield, something about the way he sat there so quiet and everything, that
made her feel good.

She didn't even know how long he was going to stay.

She had put on a nice blue dress for him. She had spread the
skirt very carefully when she sat down. She hoped the effect was
nice. A boy likes a girl who is pretty.

She wanted him to like her. Wanted oh yes so very much.

Stay, she wanted to tell him. Stay stay stay.

Only one lamp was lit. It was on a table at the far side of the room and it flickered. Wheatfield was a halfblur over there on the sofa. He sat right on the edge.

The rocker creaked beneath Leora.

Wheatfield coughed softly. She saw his hand come up to cover his mouth.

Leora shifted her weight. Her skirt rustled. She crossed her ankles and there was a swish. That rebel, she thought, what he wanted; I know what it is; I felt it when he pressed up against me. This boy here I expect he knows what it is too because he's older than me and all. And she thought of when the rebel had ripped her dress and how this Wheatfield had come bursting in and had fought with the rebel (the rebel had been a whole lot bigger) and had driven the rebel away. Miss Grumpacker says it's not good to think things like this: there is Desire and then from Desire comes The Curse and it all was because Eve fell or something and what does that have to do with me? I didn't have anything to do with Eve falling. I'm not an old rib. I wish he'd say something. Go on Mister Wheatfield. Say something. Please don't sit there and look so tired. Do you want to go or do you want to stay or are you thinking about that duty you told me about this afternoon or what?

I wanted to be a heroine. I thought I knew so much. I wanted to be a heroine because I thought war was nice. But it isn't nice and I am afraid. But you are with me and I am not so afraid.

She studied him. His face was nothing special. There were a lot of boys right there in Gettysburg who were handsomer. He had brown eyes, she noticed, and wide cheeks, something of a small mouth, ears that stuck out a little too far. He was not too tall. He was certainly nothing extra—but that made no difference.

Rocking slowly, her ankles crossed in front of her, thinking: Maybe I am pretty? That rebel I think thought so. My poor dress. No man ever saw them before. Not even Daddy. Oh Daddy! Come home please. Come home because we love you and Mamma misses you and wept tonight for you; come home because I miss you and Johnny misses you too. After this boy leaves I will be afraid again. I will need you Daddy. Please come home. No man ever saw them before. Maybe I should have wept and taken to my bed. I guess maybe a lady would have. Does Mister Wheatfield think bad things about me because he saw them? Because he saw me when there wasn't anything covering the top of me?

Dress swishing softly with the movement of the rocker:

Does he think I'm brazen and didn't care that he saw them because I came right back out in the kitchen after the fight was over? How do you act like a lady and do the right thing? Those things he said today about what he had to do, what all the others out there have to do: maybe I shouldn't have cried. The crying gave away that I didn't understand before. Oh he must think I'm stupid.

"I—it's cool and nice in here isn't it?" she said.

"Yep."

"Kind of quiet too. Can't hear any cannons."

"Nope," he said. The word seemed to take a year to come out. He stretched his legs out in front of him, rested his arms on his knees and stared at the floor.

She laughed. It was bright and high. "You don't like to talk too much do you?"

"Nope," he said, slowly again. "Talked too much this afternoon."

"Nope," she said, just as slowly. "Nope. Yep. That's all you say."

"Yep."

She laughed again. "We're silly," she said.

"Uh. Why?"

"Sitting here like this."

"I guess you would say we're silly. There's a war right outside and we sit here talking about how nice and cool it is and about how all I say is yep and nope." He stood up.

"Don't be mad," she said, staring up at him. "Please talk to me. I'm just a girl. I'm afraid. Don't go away just yet."

"No. I—"

"I'll try to change it."

"Change what?"

"Whatever it is you don't like about me."

"I like you," he said.

"You don't act like you do."

"I like you fine."

"Then sit down."

"Um . . ."

"Sit down. They're not fighting now. You can go after a bit."

He sat down and didn't say anything.

She wanted to hit him or something. "You're awful tired," she told him.

He nodded.

"You don't like me," she said.

"Why you keep saying that?"

She'd never tried to steer a conversation like this before. "People if they like you," she said, smiling, "they usually show it."

"Oh," Wheatfield said.

She wanted to hold his hand or hug him now. His hand had been so nice and strong and warm this afternoon. She rubbed her palms together thoughtfully. Then: "It's some battle here isn't it?"

"I guess so."

"What I mean is—lot of men fighting?"

"Yep."

"Why?"

"Why what?"

"Why here?"

"No reason," he said. He stood up again.

"Now," she said. She leaned forward anxiously and her skirt rustled.

"I'm going for a walk. Just a walk. I'll be back."

She rose and went to him. "No. The rebels."

"It's dark. They won't see me. Anyway, I ain't going out on the road. Expect I'll go up that there hill behind the house. I ought to be able to get a view of where the fighting is."

"You have to know."

"Yep."

"I want to go with you."

"All right," he said.

She was surprised. She'd thought he would say no. She was standing very close to him now. She saw how wide were the pores on his face.

She blew out the lamp. She led Wheatfield through the kitchen and out the back door. There were no sounds in the house.

They walked up the hill. It was not very steep. Leora led the way, lifting her skirt before her. The night was very dark, thickly black, but it was cool. She enjoyed breathing deeply of the coolness. Wheatfield's hand was sweaty in hers. She enjoyed that too. She thought not of the war. She thought not of dead men. She thought not even of the dead man who lay in the road in front of her house. She thought not of the rebel who had tried to rape her. She was with him now; all the other things vanished. They walked slowly. Presently they came to the top of the hill and looked out across a valley.

"My God," Wheatfield said.

Leora squeezed his hand.

It could have been a revival meeting.

Leora had gone to a revival meeting once over by Lancaster. People had come from all over the Commonwealth and they had pitched tents on the side of a great hill. All night long their camp-fires had glowed and the people had sung. Leora had seen the hill first from the trainwindow. It had looked like fireflies.

But there were more fireflies here now. Thousands, she guessed. They were speckled along two ridges, tiny pinpoints of red and orange blinking and jumping. There was a dry snapping scattered sound of shots, aimless, nervous. She had heard that sound before when men had gone hunting. She looked at Wheatfield but it was too dark for her to make out the expression on his face.

"My God," he said again.

"Pretty," Leora said.

"Pretty. Yep. Lot of dead men down there. I bet they're pretty too."

"I'm sorry," she said. Her voice was small, contrite.

"I never seen it like this before."

"Here. All that noise and everything today. I'm sorry. It's not pretty."

"We didn't want to come here. It's not a thing where you want or don't want."

"Yes."

"Your hand's warm," Wheatfield said, staring at her now. She still couldn't make out the expression on his face.

She smiled and then he bent to her and kissed her. Nothing touched except their mouths. She tasted him. The backs of her legs trembled ever such a little bit. She kissed him back. She held his hand tightly. He put his free hand around her waist and drew her closer.

He was breathing thickly. He pulled back his head and pushed her off to arm's length, then: "How old are you?"

"Sixteen."

He shook his head and didn't say anything.

She moved toward him.

"No," he said.

"I love you," she said, and after it came out she was surprised. It had been so simple.

He kept shaking his head.

"Don't think about it," she said.

"You know what I'm thinking about?"

"The war."

"I got to think about it."

"No."

His hands were at his sides. He reached out with both arms and held her shoulders. She did not move. "You don't ought to talk that way," he said.

"I love you. How am I supposed to talk?"

"You're just a girl. You don't know anything."

She shook her head from side to side. "Maybe I do know something now. Maybe I've changed. Maybe all this has changed me. Who are you to tell?"

"No."

"You liked it when you kissed me."

"Never mind that."

"Maybe whatever it was that I was before is gone."

He took his hands from her shoulders and rubbed his eyes. "I don't know you. I never saw you before today."

"That doesn't matter. You know it doesn't matter. Maybe when things change they change all of a sudden."

"No. I just came along, that's all. This here battle, it brought me, and you're all worked up because of what happened today."

"Can't something make a person grow up?"

"How should I know?"

"If it's a real big thing?"

"You're talking dumb," he said.

"Maybe I am. Maybe I don't know anything. But the things I say, I mean them."

He made a clucking sound, and his thick breathing was very loud. Then he moved toward her and kissed her.

She wept, and he lightly touched his tongue to her cheeks where the wetness was. After a time they sat down on a large flat rock. Leora knew this rock well. Every so often, when she had things to *think* about, she would come up here and sit on this rock and be just as alone as a person could be. Now she and Wheatfield sat there and stared down at the jumbled pinpointed fires and they kissed each other and she lay her head against his shoulder and he ran his fingers through her hair and she heard again how thickly he was breathing, how slowly too, and she was breathing thickly too, and nothing like this, nothing nothing nothing, ever had happened to her before, and she kissed him and kissed him, she couldn't kiss him often enough, and she kept telling herself how grand it was that such a thing could happen even with all around them all the dying and everything, and she marveled at how nothing else mattered, not even the dying, and oh she loved him *so*, and she wanted to crawl inside his skin with him, and after a very long time he said to her (the words soft and slow like all his words):

"I. Well. Back home. I'm from down near Mattoon Illinois you know. My daddy he owns a farm. It, the country there I mean, it ain't much like this. He only got about eighty acres. Flat. I'll get it one of these days. I got a brother, but he don't take to farming. He's a fireman for the St Louis & Northeastern. I'll get that farm one of these days. I. I guess. Well. I like you a whole lot. I ain't never met no one like you. I shouldn't ought to talk. All the time when I talk. All the time it don't come out like I was meaning it to."

She didn't say anything.

She fell asleep hugging him. He carried her back to the house. She awakened as he climbed the steps at the back door. She kissed his wrist, the back of his hand. He set her down in the kitchen. She lit a lamp and stood back and looked at him and he smiled at her and she felt the tears on her cheeks and she went to him and squeezed him tightly and felt the hardness of him against her and whispered disconnected little words to him. O she *did* love him. She could not help wiggling against him and he kissed her ears and they went to a chair and she sat on his lap and he held her thus for most of the night. They fell asleep three times before she finally went upstairs to her bed. He slept on the sofa in the parlor.

4

THE THIRD DAY

♣ Morning comes gently. The hills are clouded, vague in outline. Dampness lies on them, soaks into the earth, feeds green things, gathers itself into narrow vagrant trickling streams down where the weeds and the grasses come from the earth. Bugs prowl busily. Little animals peep from their holes in the earth; after a time they venture out. Birds hop and sing and strut and preen. Dead men puff and stink. ♣

CPL LEW MABRY was so mad he hadn't been able to sleep all night.

It was early morning (the sun wasn't up yet) and he was lying in a field somewhere and he didn't even know where he was. He was hungry; he was tired too—but he was so mad (remembering that Yank who'd driven him away from the girl's house) that his anger kept defeating sleep. All night long he'd kept twisting and scrunching around. He had a great pride, did Cpl Lew Mabry, and sure enough didn't like thinking about a fight where he'd got beat. And by a Yank too. God *damn*. A Yank!

(He wondered if the Yank had recognized him. Mabry had recognized the Yank right away. It was the prisoner whose horse Mabry had taken. Now if that didn't beat all, Mabry didn't know what did. How'd that feller get away? Mabry wanted to know.

There was something mighty scary about it too. If you stopped to think of all the men who was in this here war, then thought about that one Yank coming back to beat you in a fight—that one Yank from all them men—well, it sure did beat all. But there was one thing anyway, and each time Mabry thought of it he felt a clutch of joy: that there Yank's horse was dead. Dead, by God. And Mabry had seen how much the Yank loved that horse. Gingerbread, he had called it. What kind of a name for a horse was that? Gingerbread. Godamighty. Mabry usually liked animals, and he'd felt kind of bad when he'd shot that horse. But now the hell with it. If he had that goddam nag with him now he'd shoot it and do it slow, real slow, one leg at a time maybe, and watch it bleed to death and laugh up a storm, laugh to split a gut.)

What I got to laugh about?

Goddam Yank.

Sure. Cuss him.

He beat you.

No! He pointed a gun at me.

It was your gun.

God damn!

He had run from that house, had heard the Yank's shot zing over his head and had skedaddled up the road as fast as he had been able, what with his heavy pack. He had passed through Gettysburg (all beshuttered and quiet; he saw no one except Confederate soldiers) and along a road that led south through a dozen camps. The camps were deserted except for cooks and orderlies and such. The troops were east where the fighting was. Mabry could hear it. He had no desire to go see it. Once he met a mounted officer and told him about the escaped Yank prisoner back behind the lines. The officer's face was streaming sweat. *What you doin back here you goddam straggler?* the officer wanted to know. Mabry said something about being lost. The officer pointed to where the sounds of battle were coming from. *Lost, my butt!* he shouted. He drew a pistol, pointed it at Mabry's head and ordered him to head east, to report to the nearest company commander. *You sonofabitch!* he bellowed. *I see you again I kill you!* Mabry took off east at a run. The officer kept yelling at him and waving the pistol. Mabry stopped running as soon as he was out of the officer's sight. He walked to the side of a hill and sat there for hours watching the battle. No one found him. When evening came he stayed away from the campfires. He wanted nothing to do with the army just yet: he knew the men didn't take kindly to stragglers. He guessed he would go back the next day, when there was a lot of fighting and confusion and he would be able to kind of melt in with the others. He wandered around in the darkness for some time. He considered going back to that girl's house, but he had been wandering around too much—he didn't know the way. Finally he went into this field, down into a narrow gully made by a little creek, lay down and tried to sleep. He couldn't. He kept thinking. Pride and anger were all mixed up. Them titties. Godamighty, it ain't right when a man gets all steamed up an then someone makes it so he can't. God if You was to put that Yank in my hands for five minutes, wellsir You'd have one good an dead Yank in Your kingdom real quick oh yas indeedy.

And the more Mabry thought about it the less he could sleep.

A man'd think that feller, that goddam officer, him an his pistol, would pay some mind when he's told about a prisoner who's runnin around loose. What kind of prisoner guards we got anyway?

Yanks an Virginians: a man can fill his life with hatin them. Hate all the highanmighties by God Mabry; don't you forget that.

Finally Mabry stood up. His pack clanked as he adjusted it. He was hungry. There was no light yet, but he figured it wouldn't be long. He walked across the field and came to a road. He turned left—no, right—no, left again. He pushed back his cap and scratched his head. Now by God which way? He looked up at the stars. He'd heard somewhere once how a man could tell which way to go by looking at the stars.

There were a lot of stars.

He frowned at them.

He bent over and picked up a clod of dirt. He stood sideways in the middle of the road and threw the clod straight up. It landed to his right. That was the direction he took.

He walked slowly. His pack was very heavy, just about as full as it could be. It weighted him down, pulled at his shoulders and back, but he didn't mind. No sir. Not at all. His future was in that there pack.

I gave her ten dollars.

Lord amighty.

The road climbed a low hill. Mabry came to the top and looked down and saw the outline of a farmhouse. "God damn," he said aloud. He headed for the farmhouse. He cut across a field.

The house was small, painted white. He saw no lights, no sign of life. Behind the house was an enormous red barn. It was decorated with funnylooking signs and such. He crossed the barnyard and headed for the house's rear entrance. He made little noise. There was too much darkness, and so he did not see the open cistern. He walked right into it. His pack took him straight to the bottom.

♣   Chance, as they say, is an imponderable. It spared the town of Gettysburg. The two great armies struggled there three days; one hundred and fifty thousand men pushed and wrestled and killed and maimed and destroyed—but Gettysburg, quiet Gettysburg, that neat little seminary town, felt very little. No buildings were destroyed; no shops were looted; there was relatively little fighting in the streets, and only one civilian, a girl named Jennie Wade, was killed. Jennie was twenty. She lived with her mother and sister in a house near the cemetery where the Union soldiers played catch with skulls. A stray sniper's bullet hit her as she was baking bread in the kitchen. It penetrated two doors. She had a heavy face and a wide mouth. She looks as though she probably had considerable strength of character. One imagines she did. After all, to stand in the kitchen and bake bread while bullets are whinging around you takes a certain amount of fortitude. An enterprising poet could find a great deal from her death. She had been engaged to a certain Cpl Skelly, a soldier in the Army of the Potomac. She did not know Skelly had been killed a few days earlier. But Jennie Wade was Gettysburg's only real tragedy. The farms outside the town were chewed up quite badly, but within Gettysburg itself there were few manifestations. The Confederates treated the inhabitants with courtesy. There was no rape or pillage. And, beyond this, there was the unalterable fact that Gettysburg was not important from a tactical point of view. It lay almost directly north of the fish hook, and as a consequence its only value to the Confederates was as a kind of base of operations. It was too close to the Union lines to be within artillery range. Thus both sides sent shells flying OVER Gettysburg. The Confederate batteries were to the north and west, the Union batteries to the east and south. This put the town in a kind of vacuum or pocket. It was ringed with artillery; it shook and reverberated with huge sounds, but it was no target. The cannonballs kept zinging OVER it. And the people there were properly thankful. They even went about their daily business with some regularity, although few stayed outdoors for any length of time. They hoped for the best; most of them hoped for a Union victory. And of course they were frightened. There were many rumors: the rebs were winning; the rebs were losing; Robert E. Lee was dead; Meade was severely wounded—ah, there were many many many rumors.

But actually, all anyone in Gettysburg knew for sure were two things: the weather sure was HOT; the noise sure was LOUD. ♣

GINGERBREAD!

Wheatfield awoke in one great burst, remembering right away where he had seen that rebel before. His eyes flicked open wide and he saw the rebel again and heard him say *This is a good old horse. Yep, sure is a good old horse.*

He sat up on the parlor sofa and rubbed his eyes. His back was sore and stiff.

Gingerbread . . .

Dead, dead.

My horse: dead.

No. Minute now. Maybe he ran away from the reb.

Ran away?

No. Dead.

Ah, God . . .

He stared at his feet. He made two very tight fists.

He sat thus for some time. The sun was up, but he heard no sounds in the house. Outside, out there in that hot brightness, there were rumblings and explosions, but they weren't as loud as they had been yesterday.

Then he thought of this girl Leora.

Love?

My horse is dead; I loved my horse.

What did I say to her last night? I guess I sure did talk. All day. Talk talk talk. Talk about Duty. It don't never come out right. What's talk?

She's sixteen.

Sixteen.

I sure am taking my time about getting back.

Talk!

Waste my time with talk. Ought to be getting back. Love, what's that?

I like to see that reb now I know who he *is*.

First Caleb and his foot, then that old man and his talk talk talk, now all this. What ails me?

I should of been back yesterday.

Nice girl, pretty, with nice long hair and I love her. Yes. No. *Yes*. All right, yes. But she's sixteen. Don't matter. Pretty. Don't matter. Love. Ah . . .

He unclenched his fists and stood up. There was a sound on the stairs. The girl came into the room. Her hair was combed and neat as anything. The sunlight showed up the freckles around her nose. She wore that blue dress from last night.

"Hello," she said shyly. She was so slender.

"Hello." His voice came out in a kind of croak.

"You—you sleep all right?"

"Yep."

She giggled. She ran to him and threw her arms around him. "You and your yeps and nopes," she said. She kissed him full on the mouth.

"Here now," he said, pulling away.

"You don't like it," she said, pouting.

"I didn't say that."

"My breath bad?"

"Nope."

"Ugly?"

"Nope."

"You think I'm ugly."

"All right. You say so. Ugliest girl I ever saw."

She giggled.

"Don't laugh. It's the truth," he said, shaking a finger at her.

She nodded meekly. She folded her hands in front of her and stared lugubriously at the floor.

"Girls these days are getting forwarder and forwarder. My daddy he told me that before I left. 'Son,' he said, 'a girl nowadays she won't let you kiss her. She'll kiss you first. You just got to suffer through it. There ain't no sense fighting it. That's the way they are these days.'" Then Wheatfield seized the girl and kissed her, very hard.

She gasped and trembled; she wiggled against him. They hugged each other tightly.

"There, by God," he finally said.

"Ohhh," she said. She pressed her face against his chest and closed her eyes. Her arms were tight around his waist. He kissed the top of her head and then gently stroked her hair, but the thing he kept thinking was: I got no right doing this. I got to go, that's what.

Finally she took his hand and led him into the kitchen. She told him to sit down. She went outside with a basin. He heard her pumping water. He went to the door and started to go outside to help her.

"You stay in there!" she hollered, looking up from the pump.

He hesitated, then went to a chair and sat down. The rebs, he thought, she don't want no rebs to see me. I'll try to go and she'll say no, no, the rebs'll see you. Well by God I got to go.

She brought the basin to him. He bent over it and washed his hands and face. She ruffled the hair on his neck.

The water felt good on his face. Nice and cool. She handed him a towel when he finally came up for air. He rubbed his face vigorously, smoothed back his hair and blinked up at her.

"I got to go. You know that. I told you why," he said.

"No."

"I'll come back."

"You'll die," she said.

"Don't say that."

"It's true. You got to go. You got to die too."

He stood up and put his hands on her shoulders. "You're sixteen."

"Isn't a girl who's sixteen supposed to say anything?"

"I don't mean it like that."

"Lot of girls get married when they're my age. Lot of girls. I know some."

He looked at his hands. He was still holding the towel. It hung down over her breast. "I—I like you better than any," he said.

"Then stay."

He shook his head no.

She was about to cry: he knew it.

He took his hands off her shoulders and tossed the towel on the table. He sat down again and stared away from her. "You want me to talk about love. Like last night," he said.

"Yes." Small voice.

He didn't dare look at her. "All right. I love you."

She made no move toward him. "You don't. If you did, you wouldn't go."

The rumbling outside was just the same—no louder yet.

"I don't—" Wheatfield began. He hesitated.

The girl walked around the table until she was facing him. She was very solemn. "You don't what?"

"I don't—I don't want to go," he said.

"Duty," she said.

He nodded. "You think it's stupid."

"It doesn't matter what I think."

"Well. Now. I."

She was very solemn. "Maybe I should stop aggravating you."

"No. You're not."

"I am too. If I wasn't, then you'd stay." Here she began to weep. She made no noise about it.

The mother and brother came into the room. The girl turned and hastily wiped at her eyes.

"Morning Mister Johnson," the mother said. Her eyes still were red but she was smiling.

Wheatfield nodded at her. At the boy too.

The mother bustled with a skillet and some eggs and bacon. The boy went to the table and sat down next to Wheatfield and asked him more questions. What did he like best, the infantry or the artillery or the cavalry or what? What did he think of Gen Meade? What about Hooker? Why wasn't Hooker in charge any more? What's your favorite kind of horse? (This brought a twinge.) How many rebs you killed? On and on.

"Oh Johnny, hush," the girl finally said.

"Leave the poor man be," the mother said.

The girl was standing at the window, staring up the hill where she and Wheatfield had gone last night. "Give him a lot to eat," she said to her mother. "Fatten him up so he can go out and die."

The mother dropped an egg, spatter, on the floor. "What did you say?"

"I said he's going."

"About dying I mean."

"Make him nice and fat for when he dies."

Wheatfield started to say something but the mother interrupted him. "Leora Bagley, you stop that," she said angrily.

"I'm hungry," the boy said.

The girl wheeled on him. "You snip!" she shouted.

"Leora . . ." Wheatfield said wretchedly.

The boy crouched back and put his hands over his head.

The mother pointed at the mess on the floor. "Leora, you clean this up. Now."

"Yes, Mamma," the girl said. She dampened a rag in the basin, got down on her hands and knees and wiped up the spattered egg.

The mother looked down at her. "What's the matter with you?"

Leora rubbed the floor vigorously. "Nothing," she said matter-offactly, "only that he's spoken for me." She rose, took the basin off the table and went out into the back yard with it. They heard her throw the water on the ground.

The mother stared at Wheatfield. "What?"

Wheatfield made a vague movement with his hands. "Well . . ."

"Well what?"

The girl came back into the kitchen. She put the basin on a cupboard shelf and hung up the rag. "I love him and he's going off to die."

The mother's face had no expression. Sweat now sat wetly on her upper lip. "Love him?" she said weakly.

The girl turned from the cupboard. "Yes. You might as well get used to it."

The boy took his hands away from his head.

The mother moved slowly. No one said anything. She set the breakfast down heavily on the table. The girl sat next to Wheatfield.

The mother picked at her eggs. "No," she finally said. "I say no."

"I can't help the way I feel," the girl said.

"No. A girl can't get married, or spoken for even, when she's only sixteen. She just doesn't grow up in one day."

The girl stared at her plate.

"The world ain't coming to an end," Wheatfield said.

"Who asked you?" the girl wanted to know.

He smiled. "Don't I have nothing to say about all this?"

The girl closed her eyes and shuddered.

"Why we making such a fuss?" Wheatfield asked.

"Spoken for . . ." the mother said numbly.

"No. Now—" Wheatfield began.

The girl opened her eyes. "No what?"

"We don't have to go running into something right away," Wheatfield said. "A man he can make too many mistakes as it is and he don't—"

"Mistakes?" She stared at him intently.

"No, no. Wait now. What I mean is: this probably ain't no mistake, but we ought to be sure—that's all. A mistake it stirs up too much of a fuss. We just want to be sure."

The boy scraped his plate.

"What did you two do last night?" the mother suddenly asked.

"We hugged and we kissed and we *talked*," the girl said.

"Mam," Wheatfield said to the mother, "we didn't do nothing wrong I swear." He stared down at his plate. "I know. It don't make no sense. First time knowing a girl and all. She's your girl and she's only sixteen and you keep thinking about that and I can't say as I blame you. But now hear me. I'd be obliged." He paused, thinking: Talk talk talk. Why don't you be quiet? and then: "I'm going away today but I'll be back and you'll see. There ain't nothing wrong with me. I ain't trying to take advantage of her or nothing like that."

"You," the girl said viciously.

"What'd I do?"

"Never I wanted anything like this and you have to go and say you're not sure."

Anger rose sourly in Wheatfield's throat. "I didn't say that!"

The boy went to the stove and took the rest of the bacon and eggs.

"Now children," the mother said. "You, Leora. You, Mister Johnson. All I want is for you to wait."

"Wait," the girl said. She began to cry.

"My God I can't marry you now!" Wheatfield burst out. "What do you want?"

". . . stay," the girl said, sniffling.

"No!"

Wheatfield stood up. "I thank you kindly," he said.

The girl reached up and took his hand. "Please . . ."

He shook his head no. He'd never wanted to stay in one place so much in all his life. Her hand was warm and wet. He released it and headed for the door.

"How you going to get back?" the girl wanted to know.

He paused at the door. "South I guess. Try to sneak around."

"In that?"

He turned. "In what?"

"Your uniform." Her voice was thick behind her tears.

He shrugged. "I'll try to keep out of sight."

"You'll be shot."

He turned to the door again.

"Wait a minute!" she cried. She ran from the room. When she returned she was carrying a long gray coat and a black hat. "Here," she said, holding them out to him.

"Too hot."

"Put them on. Maybe the rebs'll think you're a farmer."

"No."

She sniffled back her tears and the sound of her weeping. "You do as I say," she said coldly. "You do this one thing for me."

He nodded. She helped him into the coat. The hat was kind of a good fit. He cocked it to one side, knocked in the crown. He put his forage cap in a pocket of the coat.

‾ The mother and the boy came to them. "You look fine," the mother said, smiling.

The girl looked up at Wheatfield and tried to smile. She hugged him.

Wheatfield gave the girl a long kiss. Her hands rubbed the back of his neck. She whispered something he did not hear.

He held her at arm's length. "All right," he said.

"Wait a minute," she said. She went to the sideboard and took the two coins the rebel had left yesterday. She gave them to Wheatfield.

They were cool in his hand.

"They're mine," the girl said. "You keep them. You bring them back to me. You got to go, you say. All right. Now you got to come back. You have something that's mine."

"No."

"Yes. I say so."

He ran his fingers over the coins. "Keepsakes like?"

"Keepsakes like," she said.

"Um."

"Is that all—just um?" she said. She kissed him again, harder. He closed his eyes and tried to memorize everything about her face. Very solemnly he shook hands with the boy. The mother kissed him on the cheek and told him he was a fine man. He kissed the girl again, dropped the coins into a pocket of the coat and left. He looked back once and saw the girl crying. He waved. He guessed he sure did want to come back some day. He headed east, toward where the sound of the fighting came from, east and south too. He crossed fields and woods and several roads. Keepsakes like, he thought.

♣ A war is a succession of feints, stalemates, speculations, skirmishes, proddings and great boring waits—with few victories, few defeats. Three or four decisive actions may decide a war. One decisive action may decide a war. But sometimes it takes years for the combatants to agree on full commitment to a decisive action. That is why the struggle at Gettysburg was so important: both sides did commit themselves. Fully, and conversant with the consequences of defeat. There was no chance for either side to sneak away now for further maneuvering. The two great armies were at full strength; they faced each other squarely. There HAD to be a decision. And that decision would be drawn from either of these possibilities: victory for the South, which would mean the success of its invasion, probable capture of Washington, Harrisburg, Philadelphia and Baltimore, possible quick aid from Britain—and the added possibility that the North (the warweary North, torn by draft riots and Copperheadism and apathy and an enormous cynicism brought on by the Bull Run defeats and the Antietam stalemate and the Fredericksburg defeat and the Chancellorsville defeat) would seek to negotiate a peace that would recognize the sovereignty of the Confederacy; or victory for the North, which would mean the eventual, although slow, annihilation of the Southern armies—which had no reserves in arms or equipment or men, which was pouring everything it possessed into this invasion, which would lose everything if this one great gamble failed. Generals Lee and Meade were fully aware of all these possibilities. And they were fully aware of their own roles in this struggle: Lee was the aggressor, Meade the defender. It thus behooved Lee to make the first moves. Today, July 3, a day as hot as yesterday and the day before, again he would set a plan into motion. Two days ago his men had practically wiped out the enemy, but had been fooled finally by Hancock's superb bluff. Yesterday Lee's men had put into motion a good workable scheme, but it had fallen apart. Gouverneur K. Warren, Meade's fussbudgetish old woman of a chief of engineers, had been at the right place at the right time and had acted with bravery and intelligence. Despite the great attacks and brilliant planning, Lee's campaign had been a complete failure yesterday. Warren, the stiff defense of Culp's Hill, the rescue of what was left of the III Corps—the

federals had done impressively. Cemetery Ridge had held all
up and down the line. But today, the third day of the battle,
Lee would try again. He was a brainy old wizard and he had
great good resiliency. So did his army.   ♣

THEY SAT around their breakfast campfires, Pvt Rufus
Patterson and the other men left in his company, and they talked
of what had happened yesterday. Their voices were soft and quiet
and dry. They punctuated their words with chewing sounds, slop-
ping sounds.

Rufus sat alone at the edge of a ravine and did not join in.

". . . I get home, I ever get home," a fat bearded man was
saying, "I'm goin to lay me down in a goddam big fat bed and
there ain't goin to be no man, no man in this world, who's goin
to make me get up." He closed his eyes experimentally, then
blinked, sighed and filled his mouth with hardtack.

"Bed, hell," another man said. "I thought yesterday by God I
was goin to sleep in the Arms of Jesus till the Doomsday trump."

"Where'd them Yanks learn to fight so good?" someone wanted
to know.

A skinny towhead absently scratched his belly. He frowned
deeply. "I thought we had them licked," he said slowly.

"I never seen them fight like that," a middleaged man said.

"Maybe because they is on their own land," said the fat bearded
man.

The towhead picked his nose, drank some coffee. "That there
stone wall . . ."

"Man was a fool if he wasn't ascared," someone said.

"Wonder where Mabry went off to?" the fat bearded man,
whose name was Wynn, wanted to know.

Rufus threw his coffee over the edge of the ravine.

"Maybe he got shot," the towhead said, grinning.

"We ain't got that kind of luck."

"What you mean?"

"He'll come back. Fat an sassy an laughin."

"With that pack," the towhead said.

"With that pack. He sure do love that pack."

"Must weigh a hundred pound," the middleaged man said. He spat into the fire and there was a hissing sound.

Rufus thought of Mabry and how Mabry had twisted his wrist the other day: I bawled. God damn me, I bawled. I ain't goin to bawl no more.

"You know, that feller he don't look so mean," Wynn said.

"Got a face like a baby's ass," another man said. Laughter.

The towhead's name was Emery Franklin. He had a twin brother, Franklin Franklin, who'd been wounded the first day. "My brother—I expect he's back down in Virginia by now," Emery Franklin said.

"Spoilin all the girls," Wynn said.

"That's my brother," Emery Franklin said, grinning.

"Old Manwell he sure did get it," the middleaged man said.

"Ugh," Wynn said. "I ain't never seen a man near cut in two like that before."

The middleaged man turned to Rufus. "Hey Patterson you one lucky boy."

Rufus didn't say anything. He gathered some dirt in his fists and squeezed it.

This man's name was Incastle. He was small, wiry. "Damn near got you too that branch didn't it?"

"Talk about somethin else," Rufus said thickly.

Wynn laughed. "Hell! We all got to go sometime! Old Manwell he just went kind of funny that's all."

"Goddam you," Rufus said. He grabbed his rifle, stood up, pointed the rifle at Wynn.

"Hey now," Wynn said.

"You an your talk," Rufus told him.

Wynn smiled nervously. He slid back on his rear end. The other men were motionless. "Whup now boy," Wynn said. "I didn't mean nothin . . ."

Rufus aimed his gun at Wynn's head.

Wynn scrambled to his feet. He was drooling. "Was you in love with him? That why you kissed him?" he screamed. "You think you scare me with that thing? I'll—"

"Easy, Wynn," Incastle said. He got up, walked between Rufus and Wynn. "Put that thing down, Patterson," he said. "Wynn he didn't mean nothin."

"He don't scare me none!" Wynn yelled.

"You be quiet," Incastle said to Wynn.

"Incastle, you don't get out of the way I kill you too," Rufus said.

Incastle spread his hands. His tongue darted out to wet his lips. "Now why you all het up like this?"

"All the time," Rufus said, "all the time the fellers they die an this Wynn he thinks it's funny. Like Pete Bell. He was the best man in this platoon an that fat sonofabitch he sits there an talks all the time an I want you to tell me something: he think of anythin except his big fat butt?"

"Now a man can't—" Incastle began.

"A man *should*, goddamit," Rufus said. "Get out of the way."

"Nope."

"Incastle . . ."

"Nope." Incastle was sweating freely. His eyes were fastened on Rufus' gun. Wynn was backing away behind him.

Rufus burst into tears, lowered his rifle, turned and walked away.

The other men stared at each other. Incastle expelled a great deal of breath. Rufus stood by himself at the edge of the ravine. None of the men said anything, not even Wynn. Presently Capt Hawk came to them and ordered them to fall in, column of twos. They marched off down a road. Rufus took his place in line. He was next to Incastle. I'm crazy, Rufus thought, I'm crazy. I ain't got my good sense no more. Manwell, couldn't you of found some other tree you sonofabitch? The feet of the marchers made a steady cum gum cum gum and there was a lot of dust.

♣ Robert E. Lee (his men ah they cheered him wherever he went) devised a simpler plan of attack for the third day of this battle. No encirclements today, no elaborate pincers movements. Today there would be a direct frontal assault. No subtlety—but much power. And so the Confederate side of the field, the west side, came awash with great straining preparations this morning of July 3, 1863. There was intermittent skirmishing up and down the front, but no real fighting—not the kind there had been yesterday, not the kind there would be later today. Lee took a personal hand in the preparations, and his men, his tattered gray troops, ah they cheered him wherever he rode. The essence of his direct frontal assault plan was this: unleash a terrific cannonade, a monster roar of guns, directly at the Union center, thus slashing an opening for one crack Confederate division to make a breakthrough. Send that division marching straight across the field with flags flying and drums drumming and officers waving their swords, send it to demolish those bleeding federals who had managed to survive the cannonade. Why the center? Why not the flanks as yesterday? Because, Lee told his staff officers, the Union center undoubtedly was the weakest sector in its line today; its manpower was down; so many reinforcements had been sent to the flanks yesterday. Longstreet, never shy about arguing with his chief, could see no sense in this plan at all. What made Lee so sure the Union center was so weak? Couldn't it have been reinforced during the night? And was there any division on this earth capable of storming it? Lee had one answer to this question: the cannonade. This would be no ordinary artillery barrage. It would be the greatest sound of war ever unleashed on the North American continent. Every available piece of Confederate cannon would be brought into use—more than one hundred twenty pieces in all. Each gun would fire directly on the Union center. Then, after the artillery had done its work, the picked division would storm the ruined enemy. Fifteen thousand men would be in this division, fifteen thousand of the best men in the Army of Northern Virginia. This, plus a flank attack (or diversion) by Ewell's men at Culp's Hill, was the essence of Lee's plan. And so that morning the Confederate side of the field, the west side, came awash with great straining preparations.   ♣ 〜

LEORA BAGLEY said to her mother: "I know you've never heard of such a thing. Not me either."

"You're only sixteen."

"You've said that. Say something else. Please."

"What do you want me to say?"

"Tell me it's all right. Try to understand."

"I can't," the mother said.

Silence.

They were sitting in the kitchen. Johnny was with them. They hadn't let him go outside. He had been whining again, but now he was quiet; he stared out the window and listened to the sound of guns. It still wasn't as loud as it had been yesterday: a few scattered artillery blasts, some aimless crackling riflefire, but nothing to compare with yesterday. Last night, sitting with Wheatfield up on the hill, Leora had seen the campfires over by the cemetery—a good distance from her house, at least two miles. That was where most of the sounds were coming from now. The only other sounds were the rebels who marched along the road that passed her home. She thought of Wheatfield—out there someplace, wearing Daddy's coat and hat. She hoped the rebs wouldn't be able to tell he was a soldier. The coat was very long; it almost reached his shoes; his pants were such a dirty blue that she guessed they would pass for a farmer's. She hoped so. He had been so certain, so awful awful brave. (He's going to die. I'll never see him again. No. No. No. Why is it that yesterday there wasn't anything and then there was him but he had to go? I feel so funny, so empty. Him living, that's the most important thing ever for me. Ever. Without him, there isn't anything. Here I am without him and yesterday I was so scared and then he came along and he saw me like that but it didn't seem to matter; he didn't think nasty things for the seeing of me that way, and then he left He left He went away because he said *I GOT TO* because he said *I GOT TO*. Duty: doing what you think is right. Miss Grumpacker would tell me there's a lesson in that. What's the lesson? that I'm scared again? that because I saw him and he was my hero and saved me and then went away that now I'm lonely? No, no—it's different. I'm the one who's different. Ummmm, if they'd just go away. Daddy—you'll come back? My Daddy, I love my Daddy. Wheatfield now you too. Mamma says she doesn't know what to say to me because I tell her I love this boy, this Wheatfield who was so quiet and then had to go because of this thing he called Duty that he couldn't even explain to me so it all came out making sense. I guess now I do know. Goes with being different. O this house, here, this house, so clean and neat and everything and if I close my eyes, that's all, if I close my eyes and smell the air why there's not even that thick burnt smell in it any more and what's to tell me there's all this war and everything? Dead men out front? Close your eyes and push them away and think of Wheatfield and the way he saved you and when he told you he loved you and what more do you want; what other things are important? O my hero, I know you and I don't know you and I want to find all things about you and Miss Grumpacker would say I'm not a *lady* and I know I'm being stupid but I liked it when you kissed me and if that's bad well then it's bad but *is* it? Is there something crazy about me? Do I feel any different than other people have felt? Is it wrong that I didn't want you to go? Am I so bad? so that much different?)

They hadn't left the kitchen since Wheatfield's departure. There just wasn't anything to do. There were the rumbling sounds and the crackling sounds: you listened to them and you were helpless. You sat in the kitchen with your mother and your little brother and around you was this war and you saw it and heard it but really you didn't have anything to do with it. It was July and tomorrow, oh, goodness, tomorrow would be Independence Day, the Fourth of July, a holiday, goodness, and the weather was warm and you were in your nice neat house and so far you hadn't been harmed and your father was off fighting somewhere and just what were you supposed to do? just what?

Nothing.

You sat.

You thought of Wheatfield and your father.

You thought maybe of Miss Grumpacker and her daily speeches about monstrous things.

Just what else was there?

You are silent. Mamma is silent. Johnny is silent.

Might as well be dead for all you can do.

You stare at Mamma perhaps and Mamma stares at Johnny perhaps and Johnny stares out the window perhaps.

Mattoon Illinois. I wish I had an atlas so I could see where Mattoon Illinois is. Flat, he said the country is. All right. It'll be something different. I like you the best, he said. I love you, he said. He said it to me and he said it to me today and I heard him and three hours ago he was here. You talk with someone and kiss him and then he just walks right out the door and there is such a good chance that he will be killed. That coat will hide him? Will it? O God hear me: oh please make it so he will come back. You know I pray to You every night without fail: I believe in You. Now do this thing for me oh please. Don't make it so that I'll be all the time empty.

The mother sighed. "It wonders me," she said.

"You're talking Dutchy," Johnny said.

"Oh. Wonders me. Yes."

"You always yell at me when I talk Dutchy."

"Maybe I shouldn't."

"What wonders you?" Leora wanted to know.

"I don't know just exactly. All *this*, I guess."

"Those dead men?"

"Part them. Part all the noise. I don't know."

"What happens to you when you're dead?" Johnny wanted to know.

"God takes you," the mother said. "You live for always."

"How can you live for always when you're dead?"

"It's different," the mother said.

"How?"

"Because Mamma says so," Leora told her brother.

"I don't—"

"Oh be quiet," Leora said.

"We ain't talking about you no more, so it's oh be quiet," he said, pouting.

"Johnny," the mother said.

"I just—"

"Be quiet be quiet be *quiet*," Leora said.

"Let me go outside I'll be quiet."

"No," Leora said. She turned to her mother. "Why don't you send him upstairs? He just blabbers and blabbers."

Johnny sniffled. "I ain't got nothing to do; I ain't done nothing. I ain't been bad."

"Both of you," the mother said. "Hush now. Leora, you think something's happened to you that's made you more important than anybody else. That's not so. Your little brother hasn't done anything. You're just the same Leora you always were."

"I'm in love," Leora said.

"That doesn't make any difference. You still have to give people consideration."

"Who gives me consideration? You won't even believe me!"

"I didn't say I didn't believe you. All I said was you should wait. Mister Johnson said the same thing. He'll come back and then maybe we'll know."

"We! What does it have to do with you?"

"A lot. You're my daughter."

"It's for me to know!"

The mother nodded. "All right then. When he comes back, you'll know for sure."

"I know now . . ."

"Don't fuss at me."

"Mamma!" Leora wailed. She ran to the mother and hugged her. She closed her eyes and pressed her face against the mother's fat neck. She wept loudly.

"There . . . there . . ." Mamma said, patting Leora's head.

Leora wept freely. It felt good. She hugged her mother very tightly. It was good to have somebody to hug. Loneliness, Leora knew now, was the worst thing of all. The most awful things could happen to you, but if you had someone who, someone like Wheatfield who . . .

"*HEY!*" someone hollered outside.

Leora disengaged herself from her mother and jumped back.

"*ANYBODY THERE?*"

They all ran to the window and looked out.

"Why, it's Otis Wamsley," the mother said.

"Hoo," Leora said, sighing. She wiped her eyes. She had had visions of another rebel invading the house.

Otis Wamsley, waving and grinning, came walking across the yard in all his unkempt splendor.

"Otis!" the mother shouted, opening the door.

"Hello, hello—everybody all right? Looks like you had a fight here. Yes sir. Everybody all right? Say, I see you're all here. Good," Otis Wamsley said as he climbed the back steps. His words pushed at each other in their haste to get out.

He was ushered inside and given a seat at the table. The three Bagleys gathered around him.

He took off his hat and fanned himself with it. His hair was uncut and uncombed. He was a small man, with quick nervous eyes. He ran a stable in town, made good money, never spent any. The only thing old Otis Wamsley ever had been known to spend was talk. "Passing through," he said. "Thought I'd stop by. Yes. Thought maybe you folks didn't know the news. Been meaning to go to Luke Brandt's place for weeks now but ain't had the time. Now though, with the fight here, I ain't got no business at my stable so I thought I'd go out and see that colt old Luke's mare she—"

"Otis. *What* news?"

He grinned. "You don't know," he said.

"No," the mother said patiently. Sometimes Otis was a caution, but you couldn't hurry him.

"Boom boom BOOM!" he said. "Oh let me tell you, you ought

to be glad you don't live in town. Boom, boom, BOOM! Them cannonballs I'm telling you, you ain't never heard nothing like—"

"We heard a lot out here too," Leora said.

Otis fanned himself with great vigor. He grinned at Leora, then winked. He giggled. "Young lady, you want to know something?"

Leora had to smile. "Oh no," she said. "Nothing at all. I'm just leaning over you like this because of your good looks and—"

"Now," the mother said.

Otis smiled at the mother. "I can take a joke mam," he said. "Yes mam. All my life there ain't been nobody said old Otis Wamsley he can't take a joke. Why there was one time when—"

"Otis," the mother said.

Johnny giggled.

"Um. Uh huh," Otis said, nodding. "Yep. I got news all right."

The mother stared at the ceiling.

"What?" Leora burst out.

"Willard Bagley," Otis said, "I've known him all my life. When he went off to join the militia I said to him I said: 'Willard, don't you worry about your wife and your little chicks; I'll look in on them; I'll see to it they come to no harm.' And you know, Willard Bagley was grateful, real grateful. He said to me he—"

"We're grateful too, Otis," the mother said.

Otis licked his lips. He put his hat on the table. "And I got good news."

"Really?" Leora said.

He nodded profoundly. "Um hum. I do. Yes. We're going to win, that's what."

The mother sat down.

"Oh, you don't believe me?" Otis said. "You think old Otis he's just talking like always."

"Well, how do you know anything?" Leora asked him.

"I saw," he said wisely.

"You saw what?"

"Never mind. You don't believe me. What difference it make what I saw . . ."

"Otis. Now Otis, don't you fool with us," the mother said.

"You want to laugh don't you?" Otis said, his eyes darting over them. He picked up his hat and fanned himself some more. "All right. All right. You just go on. You just go on and laugh. But tomorrow I know who's going to laugh—and it ain't going to be you." He scratched his head, grinned crookedly at them.

The mother sighed and sat down. "Otis," she said. "*Please*. My Willard, I want to know if he's coming back soon. If you have some news, please for Heaven's sake tell us what it is. Please— just get down *to* it."

"Now hold on," Otis said. "I was. I was just getting down to it. But I kind of got the idea your girl here she wanted to laugh. If she laughs then there ain't no sense me saying nothing because she wouldn't believe me."

"She won't laugh," the mother said tiredly.

"I promise," Leora said.

"All right," Otis said. He stopped fanning himself. His voice became low and confidential. "Now yesterday, you know, there was all that fighting; you heard the noise; you know they must of fought pretty hard now don't you?"

"Yes," Leora said.

"Um hum. Well, I saw that fighting. All of it. Every bit. Oh yes you can wager your life on that: I saw it all right. I wasn't scared. Not me. I walked south on the Emmittsburg Road and climbed a hill, you know, the one on that ridge that looks across east to Round Top, and I had me a real good view of what was going on. Oh, the rebs they was all around me and some of them hollered at me and called me names, but they didn't have the time to stop and do anything to me I guess, because wellsir, you

see, there was this big fight, oh the noise, the noise and the smoke
and all, and the two armies they was fighting right there on the
Round Tops. I couldn't hardly see them most of the time for
the smoke and dust and all. Our boys, you know, they got that
ridge that runs south from the cemetery to the Round Tops, you
know the one I mean? and they got this big long line that runs
the length of the ridge and well, now let me tell you: all day
long the rebs they hammered at this ridge and I sat there and
watched them and you want to know something? At sundown,
oh yes, now I ain't lying, they wasn't no farther along than they
had been in the morning. No sir, not one bit. Our boys, they
took everything them rebs had to give them and they didn't budge
one inch. Oh I tell you it was some sight! A man he don't expect
to see a sight like that but once in his life! Well now, what do
you think of that?"

"So how does that mean we're going to win?" Johnny asked him.

"My boy, my boy," Otis said, grinning his crooked grin, "I saw
them rebs come back. I saw them after our boys had whipped
them. They had all the starch took out of them. I never seen
nothing like it; it was a sight like the fight almost, only there was
no noise or nothing—only them men, all them rebs, pulling back.
And was they dragging. They was hit hard I tell you. Real hard.
Oh I expect they'll try again today—but you mark what old Otis
Wamsley he tells you: the Union will win. Sure as I'm sitting
here talking to you."

"I wish—" the mother began.

"Wish, nothing," Otis said. "You wishing don't have nothing
to do with it. Don't matter a bit what you wish for. What matters is what's happening out there. You got a lot of men, and
they're split up into two armies, and one army it's attacking the
other army, and the army that's defending it's in a real good

position, and the army that's attacking it's tired now real good and tired you mark what I say."

Leora sucked in her breath. *Wheatfield!* Ah, she wanted to cry. Maybe Otis was right. If the rebels were tired and battered, why then . . .

Otis kept talking. He gesticulated grandly, described charges and retreats and cannonades, gallopings and explosions, men dying, the rush of troops from this place to that—and gradually Leora came to believe him. She did not know why. Maybe because she wanted to. Maybe because if his words were the truth then there was a good chance of Wheatfield returning soon. And the mother came to believe Otis too. And Johnny. Otis' words tumbled on. The three Bagleys all sat around the table and listened to him. The sun was very warm outside. Otis kept fanning himself. There was sweat on his forehead; on and on tumbled the words: ". . . the noise. Oh I know you was here and the rebel cannon wasn't far away—it isn't far away now and if it lets go you'll hear it real good just like yesterday—but, like I was saying, the noise here it couldn't of been nothing like what it was where I was sitting and watching. Ah, let me tell you there was rumbling sounds and screaming way up high kind of sounds and sounds that was all thick and mumbly like and sounds that was sharp, crack, crack, like that, and after a while wellsir I put my hands over my ears and now I ain't a brave man, what you'd call a real brave man I mean who'd go up real close to see what it's like, and so I made sure that there hill I was on wasn't in anybody's line of fire and so you'd have to say I was pretty far back—but even from pretty far back, even from as far back as I was, them sounds, they near tore off the top of my head . . ."

On and on went Otis, alternately grinning at them and frowning and looking wise and profound and experienced in the ideas

and attitudes and intellectual concepts of war. And he fanned
himself with great vigor. His words, all the things he kept telling
them and telling them and telling them—finally they had their
effect. The Bagleys believed him. Leora picked up Johnny and
whirled him around the room and hugged him and Otis Wamsley
beamed. Then they asked Otis if he had anything to eat today.
He admitted he hadn't. Leora wasn't too sure about that; she
knew Otis' reputation as a skinflint and she also knew he wouldn't
be likely to turn down a free meal—but that made no difference at
all. She and her mother made him a huge plateful of bacon and
eggs and he was quite eloquent with his thanks. He ate with great
enthusiasm. He kept asking them did they believe him? and they
said yes, and they were telling the truth. The kitchen was light
and bright and full of sun and for the first time they noticed this.
They heard the rebels march by outside every so often, but they
were not disturbed. No fear now. Otis kept talking: ". . . sure,
they'll send up everything they got; that's what they're doing
now—but our boys on that ridge, they threw back the rebs yesterday when the rebs was stronger, a whole lot stronger I say, and so
if they could do it yesterday why they'll sure do it today; that's
only good sense. Old Lee he shot his bolt yesterday. Oh now that
don't mean he won't try today, but he just ain't got the men like
he had them yesterday. An army it's like a man; it gets tireder and
tireder. His army it's good and tired now yes sir I know that for
sure. I seen them rebs. I seen them last night and I seen them
today. Oh they're singing and yelling and all that, but a man can
yell and sing and still know he's tired; why, I expect a lot of them
got to yell and sing else they'd just fall over and go to sleep. I seen
them I seen them drag along. Yesterday. Today too. One night of
rest won't make a bit of difference. They was hurt too bad; they
used up too much. You mark these things I say. I know. I was
there by Jesus . . ."

He ate noisily, worrying his eggs, splitting them, pushing them around his plate, sopping them up with enormous hunks of bread. The three Bagleys grinned at each other and were silent. Leora wanted to jump up and down or sing or something but now, for some reason, funny it being so close after she had picked up Johnny and had whirled him around the room, she could do nothing except grin, grin a silly grin, and listen to everything, every word old Otis Wamsley said.

Otis Wamsley: mouth and jaws going, noise, sucking sounds and heavy swallowing sounds and words words words, and Leora grinned at him and Mamma grinned at him and Johnny grinned at him. "I know," Otis said. "I know about me. I know what people think. They think maybe I'm a little funny up in the head you know?" He tapped his head. "But that ain't so. Maybe I don't spend money like I don't know what it's worth, but Great God that don't mean I'm crazy. It just means I'm careful. I know it. You ain't telling me nothing when you tell me I got tight fists when it comes to a penny. I know it. And some folks they say I talk too much. Well, I'm a bachelor. No woman. No nobody. So I talk. All right. I'll say yes. I'll say I talk. All right. Again: what's so allfired wrong with that? You don't have to listen if you don't want to. I ain't pointing no gun at your head am I? If you don't like to listen to me then don't listen."

They told him they enjoyed listening to him. Mamma brought him some more bacon and eggs. Now Leora was only listening with half an ear. The news was good: that was all she needed to know. The news meant that maybe real soon she would be seeing Wheatfield and her father too. She thought of love; she thought of how it was to hold hands with a boy and hug him and kiss him. She thought of how nice it was to hear him say nice things to you. She thought of how your breath sort of caught at you when he said the nice things. Love: you read about it; people clutch

their breasts and declaim great speeches and write poems and
such; you read about it and, no, you just can't quite believe it.
Really, when you get right down to it, those people who clutch
their breasts and so on are kind of silly. And then it happens to
you. You meet one boy and he changes everything for you and
yes, you weep and you carry on when he tells you he has to go;
you never have wept so much; every other thing that happens
makes you miserable and empty—and you know you are as silly as
those people who clutch their breasts and declaim and such, maybe
even sillier because, after all, you are real and those declaiming
people are in books. Maybe you shouldn't have been so selfish.
Maybe you should have understood that to go back was the only
thing he could do because that was the kind of boy he was and
that if you love a boy then, then above all, you have no right to
try to change him; if you change him then the thing you love isn't
there any more. Otis Wamsley and Johnny talked on and on;
Leora let her mind run on and on, and Mamma, she guessed
Mamma was doing the same thing. Mamma had been funny. First
she had wept so that first day, then she had been all right and had
kept Leora and Johnny calm and then she had fainted and then
she had been all right again and then last night she had cried
Willard! and *shame shame SHAME!* and had gone to bed and
then this morning she had been first angry a little but more surprised and then she had been quiet and now she seemed happy
and was it the fighting that had made all these changes? Leora
guessed so. The fighting and the fact that Daddy wasn't home and
the fact that she had been told that her only daughter was spoken
for and the fact that a rebel had tried to attack her only daughter
and the fact that the noise, oh the noise, that the noise had been so
loud: all these facts, put together, and who can help but be confused? Me, Leora thought, am I confused? The heat maybe? All
the noise? Brain fever? Love? Not love but something I think is

love? NO! Not those things. I'm me but I'm different because now I love this boy Wheatfield and I don't know why but I don't think the why is worth trying to find out: when you love it's there, that's all; there isn't anything more you need to know. I guess. I hope. You'd think so anyway.

Finally, after an interminable account of how he had promised Luke Brandt he'd come out and look at Luke's new colt, Otis Wamsley took his leave of the Bagleys. He thanked them kindly for the nice meal. "Now don't you folks worry about a thing," he told them. "Tonight them rebs'll be on their way out of here. Willard Bagley he'll come home and it'll be just like nothing happened, and now blabber blabber, blabber, oh blabber, yes, and now I blabber blabber blabber, and don't you blabber because I blabber yes and thank you blabber it was nice and neighblabberly of blabber . . ." and so on, out the door and into the yard, shouting and gesticulating. The Bagleys screamed out their laughter as soon as he was a safe distance away. Confederate troops marched past outside.

♣   The bombardment began on a signal from two cannon at one o'clock that afternoon. The field had been quiet, full of suspense and watchfulness. Then, breaking the stillness: a roar, followed by silence, reverberation, echo, pause, then: another roar, silence, reverberation, echo, pause, then: the beginning of the great cataclysmic cannonade. It was the ultimate distillation of what it was for two armies to fight; it was the gross bonesplitting roaring essence of combat. So dig yourself deeply into the ground, bubber. Pull the ground over your head. This is the first step of Lee's plan; all his one hundred twenty pieces of artillery are being used against you; here come the enormous balls of ruin and death. Swallow your tongue from the sound of it; there never has been anything to approach this sound. One hundred twenty cannons, all training their muzzles

on one segment of the Union line, blasted and blasted and
blasted and the federals groped and screamed and ran and
their line was hit and hit and hit and some of these men were
torn into vagrant red strips of skin and sinew and bone and
the shells screamed and whistled and flashed and there was
the bloom of explosions, smoke, the smell of burning things;
trees were split and sent crashing; the sun vanished behind
all the smoke and the rising dust; men whooped with pain as
they were hit by flying fragments of iron; earthworks crumbled
beneath the power of the fire; explosions sent men flying
through the air, screaming, kicking their legs; bleeding horses
ran aimlessly, trampling men who could not get out of the way
fast enough. And, on the other side of the field, the Confederate gunners put to their task with enthusiasm; they blasted
away and blasted away until to touch a gun meant perhaps
burning your fingers through to gristle and bone. The guns
first made a huge explosive rhythm, then blended into one
enormous undiminishing steadiness, with all the great sounds
combined now into one greater sound, the greatest sound of
them all, the loudest men ever had heard. This was, as Lee had
informed the dubious Longstreet, no ordinary bombardment; it
was indeed the essence of combat, of hate, of the desire for
victory; no army ever had had to undergo such a bombardment; no army would be able to withstand it. Lee and his staff
sat on their horses and watched it (the horses bucked and
whinnied nervously from all the noise; these were good horses,
horses accustomed to the sounds of war, but they never had
heard such a loudness as THIS; it frightened them a great
deal), and the men of the Army of Northern Virginia watched
it too. Or what they could see. The Union lines were almost
obliterated by smoke and dust. The fifteen thousand men in a
division commanded by Gen George Pickett had a special interest in the barrage: they were just about the elite of the
Army of Northern Virginia (few doubted this), and they had

been chosen to storm the Union center after this greatest of all barrages had done its work. It was their responsibility, in conjunction with Ewell's new attack (or diversion) against Culp's Hill, to smash the enemy and send him fleeing. Most of Pickett's men were Virginians. Now, as the monstrous bombardment went on and on, they gathered in ranks; officers dressed their lines; buglers and drummers and guidon bearers moved to forward positions—and all these men watched the smoke and dust and explosions rise from the federal lines. Some cheered and whistled and yipped. Others stood quietly, shaking their heads. Some put their rifles between their knees and held their hands over their ears. They waited. They watched. The guns kept blasting and blasting and blasting. There was hardly any Union fire at all. Pickett's Virginians squinted toward the enemy's works—exactly nine-tenths of a mile to the east—and some of these men joked and some of them fidgeted and some of them were motionless and behind them the one hundred twenty pieces of artillery roared endlessly, SOUND stop SOUND, reverberation on reverberation on reverberation, the sweating dirty cannoneers cheering gaily, cursing gaily, load, FIRE, load, FIRE, load, FIRE, blast upon blast upon blast, guns rocking and bucking, and what army could withstand all this? Pickett's Virginians awaited their call; they stood in ranks, fifteen thousand of them, and they saw the fires and they saw the smoke, the thick white smoke, the billowing smoke all aswirl from the detonations: all coming from the Union lines there, just yonder, less than a mile away, on Cemetery Ridge. ♣

WHEATFIELD'S OVERCOAT was awful hot on him, but he guessed he'd keep it on. This way he could walk in the open some. He looked like a farmer all right. I expect the rebs'll be too busy today to pay much attention to one farmer, he told himself, adding: I sure do hope so. Keepsakes like. I got me a couple of keepsakes like. I got to go back there sometime. Well, I don't care: no sir: that's all right too. I like her; there ain't no running and hiding from that.

Sounds of combat were louder now. He had been following them. He had skirted the edge of the town and now was heading south. He saw smoke off to the east. He was on a narrow road that was climbing into some hills. His idea was to head straight south for a good piece, then cut east and north: in other words, to go around the fighting and wind up on his own side of the field. He figured the walking would take him a good part of the day. The sun was hot and bright. He sweated inside his overcoat. Now and then he would go off the road, cut across a field, stopping now and then to pick up a piece of the thick earth and cluck his tongue with appreciation. Except for the noise and the smoke coming from the east, a man was hard put to tell that a war was going on here. He thought of what Leora had asked him: *Why here?* That was a good question. He looked around as he walked. The fields were green and this earth, this thick earth he bent to pick up in his fingers, it lay nice and healthy. It's not right that the battle should be fought in such a place. You should rip and tear in a place where it don't make no matter. Just a little bit ago he had passed about a hundred yards away from a big battery of Confederate artillery. Them guns, he thought, today they'll rip and tear and these folks who live here, what's anything about *them* have to do with it? They was living, going along like always I guess, and then we come here and the rebs come here and now everything's rip, tear, boom boom boom. Look here at all these fields, these woods and all—they're real good. Fat. Good land. Man can make a good living. Then these two armies they come along and . . .

Hell's fire, I lost my horse here.

Good old horse he said.

He laughed too; I remember how he laughed.

Well anyway, I gave it to him pretty good I guess back there at Leora's.

She sure does like to talk about love.

I got me my keepsakes.

Real fine keepsakes.

There was a thin daub of cirrus clouds strung across the sky. Wheatfield, black hat pushed to the back of his head, walked slowly. His blisters still hurt. He watched the smoke and sound rise in the east. His hands were wet with sweat; so was his face. He'd never had to walk so much before; the cavalry had made that part of being in the army unnecessary—and so now he was tired. He felt dirty too. He jingled the coins in the pocket of the coat. He walked on the road and across fields and through woods. The wind made vague snicking sounds in the trees, but there really wasn't too much of a wind. Sunlight filtered through the trees. Birds were noisy and busy. Once he saw a pheasant. It rose majestically, flapped redly, then disappeared into the sky. He'd never seen any pheasants before the war. The first time he'd seen one had been down in Virginia, just before the big fight at Fredericksburg. Lt Castetter had led about a dozen men out on a patrol early one morning and there the pheasant had been—big, red, flapping. Lt Castetter had told Wheatfield what it was. Wheatfield liked Lt Castetter: quiet feller, no worry to have along with you; he ain't likely to send you off on some fool thing. And he don't get scared. A lot of officers got scared. That Masterson, that friend of his, he gets scared. That must of been something at Chancellorsville when Masterson turned and ran. Must of been something. Now there's a funny thing: me, I could of run any time and well, there wouldn't of been much of a fuss. I'm just me. I ain't no officer. Some men say they wish they was officers. Not me. I'm lucky. I can run by God and it's just an old private running. No one gives a damn if one old private he runs away. But an officer, if *he* gets scared, wellsir that's a different thing by a whole lot.

So many things a man has to think about.

The older I get, the more things.

I wish I could sort of get things in order.

One thing at a time. Nice and neat.

But how's a man to do it when they're so many?

I don't make no claim to being much of a thinking man, but by God there are some things I'd like to figure out. Sure. I know. A thinking man he would laugh at me for asking some of these things I ask, but why ain't a man got a right to know? Why ain't a man got a right to know why there's all this dying? Why'd my horse die? (He's dead; I know that for sure; I ain't going to fool myself.) Why am I out here in this place where I ain't ever been before walking along some road I ain't ever seen before, going to some fight I don't have to go to where I might get killed? I ain't no hero. I know that. I ain't no thinking man either. I wish I was either one or the other. That way, either I'd be brave and not think why, or else I'd think why and maybe be brave and then again maybe not. At least I'd *have* something. What've I got now? Nothing, goddamit. Nothing but a lot of questions. All these things that been happening to me: my horse, that reb (meeting him twice I mean), coming across this Leora Bagley, my talk and her talk about love and all that—what's the reason for all these things? A thinking man, maybe he wouldn't ask. Maybe a thinking man knows there ain't no answers. Jesus. Is it the war doing this to me, all this funny thinking I mean?

Funny thinking all right.

He kicked up little puffs of dust. They settled slowly behind him.

The road was narrow and winding; it climbed, dropped, climbed again. He walked slowly. He saw a company of rebel infantry come marching up the road. He did not dodge or hide. He had been in full sight of quite a few rebels today, and they hadn't bothered him. Anyway, he was too tired to run every time he saw them. The company of rebels marched past him. He stood at the edge of the road and watched them. His hands were deep in the pockets of his coat. Some of the rebels yelled at him. Some laughed and yipped. He said nothing to them. "Come on an join up!" one man hollered at him. "Get in on the winnin side!" shouted another. They marched raggedly. He saw how thin they were. They looked tired. Their uniforms were torn. Some of them were barefoot. Wheatfield watched them with great interest. (These the fellers we're fighting; they sure do look poorly; ah, now don't go feeling sorry for them; if they knew who you was they'd kill you sure.)

"Hey Yank!" one of them, a fat bearded man, yelled. "You live around here?"

Wheatfield nodded.

"How you like the war?" the fat bearded man said, coming abreast of him.

Wheatfield shrugged and took a step back.

The rebel stopped. "Nicelookin coat you got there."

Wheatfield tightened his fists.

The rebel spat a brown glob into the dust. "I like it too. You know bub, I—"

A mounted officer galloped up them. "Wynn! You get your ass back in ranks!"

"Aw, Cap. I—"

"WYNN!" the officer bellowed.

"Yessir," the rebel said. He returned to ranks and marched off with the others. The captain didn't say anything to Wheatfield. He galloped away. The horse kicked up a lot of dust; Wheatfield sneezed from it.

He wiped at his nose with his sleeve and watched the rebels march off down the road. Slowly he unclenched his fists. He let out a high squeaking gasp. He started to take his hands from his pockets. His hands were trembling too much. He left them in there.

He watched the rebels. He saw them turn east, spread out and head across a field. Going out to set up flank picket, he supposed. Most of the fighting sounds were coming from the northeast. This must be just about the end of the reb line, he told himself. Maybe now if I go straight east (real careful, I mean), maybe now I can get across. Our fellers might be real close by. Good chance anyway. My God, that reb. Now don't think about that. Think about getting back: that's your reason for being out here.

The rebels disappeared into a clump of trees. He looked around and saw no one. He left the road and headed east too—a good distance south of where the rebels had gone. And he kept veering south. He knew they would fan out. He sure didn't want to be meeting that fat bearded feller again.

He crossed what he guessed was a pasture. The grass and weeds and low plants were green, here and there brown; the ground lay thickly beneath his feet. He could feel the thickness of it. He kept looking around. He didn't see anyone. His heart was beating very heavily from what had just happened. He came to a tree and leaned against it. He sat down to rest. The coins jingled as he lowered himself. He took them from the pocket and stared at them. They were pretty shiny. He wondered where a rebel had got them. Probably stole them; he looks like the kind who would steal. He was a mean one all right, and to think I met him twice. Hum. Goes to show you. I just guess it goes to show you—that's all. Hoo. That reb. Close? Oh I tell you yes. My coat—he wanted my coat. Such a hot day too. I guess they just want to take anything they can get. I saw Virginia. I know why. Jesus. How long they expect to keep on? Hoo-ooo! I mean to tell you that was close.

He relaxed against the tree and closed his eyes. He reached up, took off the hat, scratched his head. He thought of Leora standing in the parlor, standing there so scrubbed and combed and pretty. He jingled the coins in the hand that wasn't scratching.

The air was heavy and hot. It was heat like the heat back home on his father's farm. He thought of his home, the flat farmland, so straight and hard and unwrinkled; he thought of his home and the outbuildings all stark and tumbly and gray and thin against the flatness. He had always lived there—until the war, that is, when the man rode around the country signing up volunteers. Wheatfield's father did not object. He was stocky with a thick red face and enormous hands. *I know. I know. You got to*, he said when Wheatfield told him. That was all he said. Wheatfield's mother cried a little, but not a whole lot. His older brother—the fireman for the St Louis & Northeastern—already had joined up and was serving with Thomas in Tennessee. The morning Wheatfield rode to Mattoon to leave, his mother packed him four nice big chicken sandwiches, all white meat on thick warm fresh bread, and she stood in the barnyard and kept waving and throwing him kisses and he kept looking back and his father (who was driving him to Mattoon in the buckboard wagon they used for transportation) kept flicking old Hannibal's rump with his whip and old Hannibal kept going glik glok gok glik, glik glok gok glik, unevenly, for indeed Hannibal was old, and the women of Mattoon fixed all the volunteers a nice meal and his father saw him off at the depot and his father kept waving too and he ate the chicken sandwiches in the train and it took Wheatfield and a dozen others to St Louis, where they were given uniforms and guns, and after his initial drilling Wheatfield, a farm boy who knew horses pretty good, was shifted to the cavalry and Gingerbread became his horse and he came to love Gingerbread and then Gingerbread was taken away from him by that snickering rebel and, well, he didn't have much of a doubt now that Gingerbread was dead.

"Goddamit all anyway," he said aloud. He opened his eyes and looked down at his keepsakes. (She says I got to bring them back. I know that. She didn't have to give me no two coins, especially the two she got from the reb. Now I got to keep them. Carry them around with me so I think of her. She expect me to forget her right away? What kind of a feller she think I am? Hum. Now I got to keep them. Hum. Wellsir, now let's see . . .)

He put the hat back on his head, pounded it down hard. Then he took the shoe off his right foot. He put the coins in the shoe, then put the shoe back on. The coins were cold for a moment against his foot. (There. Now by God I guess I won't lose them.)

Be about your business, boy, he said to himself. He stood up. He was just entering a woods when the barrage began.

He stopped and looked around. It seemed to be coming from all over. The earth shook beneath him. He squinted to the north. The sun was very bright. The barrage was coming from the rebel side of the field. He'd never heard one like it. The earth shook more and more. Smoke and dust rose from where he guessed the Union position was. He looked around for some high ground. He wanted to be able to see what was happening. There was no sense going on until he knew which way was the safest. (This thing it might change everything. Lord knows what them rebs are up to.) He saw a wooded hill to the east and set off toward it. The sound of the barrage kept getting louder. He couldn't understand this— how can the loudest get louder? But it did. He had heard an awful lot of sounds (the sound of Antietam had been the loudest he'd thought he'd ever hear), but none of them were anything compared with this. Smoke was rolling toward him now. It rustled thickly through the treetops. He stumbled through brush and weeds; now he very much wanted to see what was happening. He

hurried up the hill. He saw no one. The smell of burnt powder
came to him in great waves. Trees were thick here. A rabbit skit-
tered across his path. The heat was heavier now. The smoke and
burnt smell seemed to be having something to do with it. His
breath came in gasps—he was running now. He did not stop to ask
himself why. There was no one around him, yet he was running.
It was very important that he see what was happening. The sound
did not relent now. Smoke was filtering down through the trees.
He coughed several times. Finally he came to the top of the hill.
He ran out into a clearing, darted across to the far edge. He looked
to the north.

He put his hands on his hips and breathed deeply.

There were two ridges, with farmland and a road in between.

He stood on one of those ridges, the rebels' ridge, the one to the
left. The other ridge, the one where he guessed his army was, lay
beneath enormous swirls of smoke. The steady unrelenting sound
came from the Confederate batteries. He could make them out
very clearly. They were draped west and south of the little town.
They seemed to be concentrating their fire on one section of the
Union line. He saw what looked to be thousands of rebels massed
about oh a mile from the Union line. They sure were gathering
for an attack all right. There were fires on the Union side, explosions too, geysers of dirt. And he couldn't see that the Union men
were returning any of the fire. He gave a sort of groan. Loud came
the sounds from the rebels' ridge and he stood and could not move
and watched the smoke swirl and the dirt swirl and the rebels
gather for their attack and he just could not move from where he
was standing (a man, he said to himself, all in a rush and roar of
thinking that for a split of an instant came through the enormous
sound, a man he don't never expect to see something like this)
and he watched and smelled the smoke and felt it in his eyes and
in his mouth and he spat several times and then he saw some

Union cannon begin to fire (but it was firing a lot less) and he had no idea how long he stood there and the sun now had him soaked in sweat and he wanted to take off this damn coat but he guessed he shouldn't because it had been *her* idea and a good one too, he knew, and he scratched himself and wiped the sweat from his face and rubbed his toes against the coins in his shoe and the sound, the endless sound, made his head hurt and this sound went on and on and the smoke kept rolling over him and he stood there the good part of an hour (although he didn't know it, didn't care, was rendered immobile by what he saw) and then, on what he knew must have been a signal, the great monster roar of sound ceased and the massed troops moved out. He gasped, felt something clutch at him: those rebels were moving straight across the field—*marching*, by God, dressed in ranks. He held his breath, watched them wheel out and head straight for the Union lines. Mounted officers specked the field; he watched them gallop back and forth. Gradually the smoke lifted from the Union lines, and then cannon began to fire and there was the crackle of shots and the great advancing mass moved forward more quickly now and isolated clouds of smoke grew in the ranks and on the rebels went and then again the smoke descended and he heard the crackling sounds roar and cannon on both sides joined in and this was as much as he could stand. He ran forward. He looked around in front of him and saw no one and so he ran forward (he had to get back now; it wasn't right just to stand and watch; it wasn't even so bad if you turned and ran, just so long as you did *something*) and so now Wheatfield wanted to get back to his side of the field and there was nothing else he wanted and he stumbled down the hill and this thing, this *I-got-to-go-back*, was all thick and hard inside him and he kept looking around and he saw no one and he ran across a field and thus across another road and then across another field and across another wooded place and lope, lope, lope he

went and he wanted to get back (this was what he had done all
the other things for and right or wrong it couldn't be explained:
did the thinking men see it this way?), he wanted to get back
more than anything else and the coins rubbed against his foot as
he ran and the sounds were loud in the north but he was almost
back now, almost back now by God, and he wondered just exactly
how far away that rebel flank guard was and he kept running, lope,
lope, lope, easily now and the joy clutched him because he was
about to finish what he had set out to do (despite Caleb hurting
himself, despite the old man, despite Leora even and her love,
despite the rebels, despite all the things that had come up to delay
him, all the things that had thrust themselves between him and
something he had to accomplish even though he did not know
why) and he was halfway between the two ridges now and he
looked back and saw no sign of the rebel flank guard and he
guessed maybe it was silly to run like this because all a man had
to do was wait until dark and then he would be able to get across
safely but he did not want to wait until dark; he wanted to get
back now, and so he ran and several times he nearly tripped over
roots and things but he kept his balance, flailing with his arms
going in circles and in clutching motions, and he was very tired
but he was happy knowing he was fulfilling that thing he had set
himself to do (to finish something is a good thing) and the earth
was rich beneath him and forward, forward he went and he barely
heard the sound of the battle now because he was feeling so good
and all around him were these fine fat fields and the big trees and
the rolling land and the warmth and then someone shot him
through the left eye and he fell down dead.

♣ Union artillery joined in the cannonade after a time and
the noise, this monstrous eruption of sound, became so loud
that artillerymen later testified they were unable to hear the

sound of their own guns, and Cemetery Ridge vanished in
smoke and dust and dirt beneath an acrid cloak of burning
smells and Pickett's Virginians watched and wondered if the
Yanks had been destroyed and on the Union side of the field
men were disintegrated by the screaming flying iron and the
smoke and the dust lay close to the earth and men sometimes
could see only the feet of other men and ah God how the air
was filled with fragments and cannon was destroyed and
wagons were destroyed and piles of equipment were destroyed and riderless horses ran neighing shrilly and the Union
artillery, those pieces that could be manned, returned some of
the Confederates' fire (but not too vigorously; the generals
knew there would be an attack and they wanted to save am-
munition) and there were flashes and detonations and fires and
crashings and men could not see where they were and staggered and groped and became lost from their units and even
in the rear, where the cooks and orderlies and quartermaster
men and drivers were, the Confederate fire found its way and
that day there were many terrified noncombatants who fled
east and south and the earth kept trembling, trembling, and
there were whining sounds and booms and screams and neigh-
ings, dust whirling in huge pools that covered entire regi-
ments, setting the troops to coughing and staggering and rubbing their eyes, and sometimes the fires cut through the smoke
and dust and the Confederates saw and cheered and their
gunners kept at it—load, FIRE, load, FIRE, load, FIRE—and
some men crouched and held their hands over their ears and
wudged up their eyes real tight so they would not have to see
and so the dust and smoke would not get in their eyes and
some men—mostly Union men—hugged the earth and felt the
earth shake beneath them and lay perfectly still and moved
only when the earth moved and Pickett's Virginians (aug-
mented by men from Heth's division and other units) stood and
watched for an hour as the great hot iron balls whirled over

their heads and landed among the federals there on Cemetery Ridge and then an order came through from Lee and the monstrous eruption lessened, and lessened, and lessened, and these Virginians squinted forward and gradually the sunlight knifed through the acrid cloak and the field lay quiet, so very quiet there for an instant, so very green and brown and raw and scarred and corrupted, so very torn and split, and Pickett's Virginians shifted their weight from this leg to the other leg and back again and some men spat and there were jokes and goosings and from the north came the sound of riflefire and cannons (strong and loud, yes, but nothing compared with what had happened here in front of these Virginians) as Ewell's men again moved against Culp's Hill and the sun glinted against the bayonets on the guns of Pickett's Virginians and both sides for a time were so quiet and if you were a Virginian that day you scratched yourself and sucked in your breath and let it out very slowly and there was a tightness in your loins and then the order came: go forward, and forward you went, you and all those other Virginians (Pickett went to Longstreet and asked for the order to go forward; Longstreet, still dubious, felt such an emotion that he could not speak and so Pickett rode away, rode to the front of his men and pointed east to Cemetery Ridge, just across the field there only nine-tenths of a mile away), and the Virginians wheeled out on the field, rank after rank, rifles at port arms, drums drumming, bugles blowing, banners catching at the dusty breeze, officers (holding their swords high) riding slowly back and forth, and the Union troops on Cemetery Ridge scurried into their positions and then watched the advance and were silent from the sight they were seeing, and ah by God now, as these Virginians came marching out of their positions, rank after rank of them, was the time of all the times that have meant courage and performing an act of duty and these advancing men spread out across the field and dressed up their lines and

slowly came across the earth so raw and scarred and corrupted and the valley between the two ridges was filled with
them and did some West Pointer here think of parades? and
the Union men watched silently and cheers from the other
Confederates rolled across the valley and the Union cannoneers readied their guns and then there were some snapping
sounds and the first federal rifles now were firing and these
snapping sounds grew and then no longer were snapping
sounds at all and closer the marching Confederates came,
closer, steadily, at a pace that was neither hurried nor slow,
and then all up and down the line the Union men, kneeling
behind their earthworks, let loose blast after crackling blast
of riflefire (they had rallied quickly, these men of the Army of
the Potomac, regrouping in a mass of confused shouts and
stumblings, running to their positions as soon as the dust had
cleared sufficiently, holding their rifles, aiming them, waiting,
then letting loose blast after crackling blast); most of these
men were Hancock's veterans from the II Corps and their blaspheming leader himself rode sometimes in full view of the
enemy and yelled at his troop, to hold, boys, hold, and from
behind them now the Union artillery let loose a shattering
crash of fire and smoke puffed out where the Virginians were
advancing and gaps appeared in their ranks but they kept
coming, those Virginians (there is the dry textbook heroism
out there, the classic pictorial grand old valor, only now it is
compounded of heat and dryness and blast after crackling
blast and shattering crashes and explosions and men going
down in grotesque armflailing limpness; the dry old valor,
only now it is real and sometimes means pain and sometimes
means death), and their officers pointed forward and put their
hats on the tips of their swords and great craters appeared
in the corrupted earth and more and more Union men were
rushed into the defenses; they elbowed each other, knelt almost shouldertoshoulder and fired fired fired and the artillery

fired fired fired and the advancing Confederates fired fired fired and these Virginians now there were great losses but by God they kept coming forward and Winfield Scott Hancock, cussing with a stupendous Messianic fervor, rode back and forth and yelled steady, boys, steady, to the crouching defenders, and his boys were steady but still the Virginians advanced (pride and courage, belief: where is the cynic now?) and the cannonballs tore through them but still they advanced and some of them screamed their final terrible screams but still they advanced and disemboweled officers toppled off their horses but still these Virginians advanced (was this reflex? or was it pride and courage and belief and adherence to the act of duty?) and slowly they climbed the side of Cemetery Ridge and the federals fired at them absolutely pointblank but they did not stop (they wavered, yes, but they did not stop) and the air was a great thick thing poured full of sound and now the dust and smoke was heavy again (was, not were, for they were combined, a thing not dust, not smoke but rather some noxious blend) and now for each man who moved forward there was a man who fell and now it was white puffs and an arm upraised holding a banner and a chaotic ridiculous little buglesound and shrieks and blueness and grayness indistinct beneath the dust and the smoke and wild swinging movements and shouts and shouts and shouts, and now it was wrestlings and slashings and bullets going ping ping, piu, and peculiar whirring sounds and blood bubbling from dead men's mouths, and now it was all the noise, all the running and moving and wrestling and pounding and dying and courage and terror and panic to which men are able to lend themselves (the act of duty?) and the Confederates stormed forward, stormed forward with their blood running back behind them down the side of Cemetery Ridge and finally, ah finally, gasping, they stormed over the top, crawling, scrambling (not many, but some) and they fell upon the Union men and

slashed them and hacked them and pounded them and then
from their throats issued the great screaming yell, the fierce
piercing EEEEEYAAAAAHOOOOO! and they milled with the
federals and killed and were killed and ran and dodged and
staggered and crawled and grabbed and no man was with
any other man and now all men were lone things of hate and
fear scrabbling and killing and dying on an obscure ridge
there in the early afternoon of a warm July day in 1863 near
a small town in the southeast of the Commonwealth of Pennsylvania, where things are fresh and the earth is good, and
this now indeed was a lonely chaos and it was a blind thing
too (you didn't just exactly know where you were; you didn't
just exactly know where your companions were, or even if
there were any left) and for the Virginians as they stormed
forward (those who were left: not many, but some) now, right
at this instant (dust, smoke, screams, dying, all the dying,
sun so hot, the sound of horses and running men, the crawlings
and dartings, the sound of shots and shouts), now, right now,
those few Virginians, here, straining, gasping, hanging on,
whacking and slashing and pounding, pressing forward, feeling
the enemy brace, falling back, pressing forward again, milling
and swinging and hitting and kicking, hanging on in the dust,
on this dry ground, this ridge, at these works, here, now, directly within a specific time within a specific day within a
specific season and temperature within a specific year and
place, a place so green and now scarred and corrupt, a place
of fire and noise and trembling earth, here and now was the
farthest they penetrated, and it lasted hardly any time at all
and men fell in clusters to pay for this penetration that was
hardly any penetration at all, and then the movement stopped.
Winfield Scott Hancock, wounded now but not defeated and
knowing he was not defeated, blaspheming away with a great
high feverish intensity, deployed his troops and sent fresh men
back to recover those few yards (the Virginians never had

been more than a few yards within the Union line) and the fresh men did just that; they drove the Virginians back; they leaped upon the Virginians and chopped them down and whomped them and stomped them and there was no doubt now, no doubt at all: the Confederates' yell had vanished and the fresh Union troops moved upon them and the few Virginians who remained, those few staggering weak Virginians, turned and ran: some gave up; others shouted a shrill thin defiance and died where they stood and did not try not to die; and the area there at this thing that had been the high-water mark was speckled now with men running, men lying flat pumping blood into the brown earth and men surrendering and men pursuing and men standing and shouting their inarticulate defiance, that shrill sound of hate, and there was the noise too and of course the heat and the thickness from the dust and smoke and the shouts now came from the Union men and one man bellowed FREDERICKSBURG!, remembering Marye's Heights and the stone wall there, where the two armies' positions had been reversed, where Ambrose Burnside had come close to destroying the Army of the Potomac by sending it forward in one blind senseless charge after another, and this man remembered it and bellowed it out to the Virginians because the Virginians had failed and knew it (and perhaps some of them had known they could not succeed, had known this and had proceeded with the act of duty despite the knowledge: where is the cynic's answer?) and so those who were left on their feet turned and fled and the Union guns sent the miniéballs whizzing through them and men were split and torn and perforated by this furious fire and the wounded lay groaning, waving rags in surrender, waving white rags, rags of any color, waving anything to signal defeat, and the others fell back, ran, and behind the earthworks the federals shouted their triumph and raked the field with bullets and shot and cannonballs, and now only two thousand of the fifteen thousand Virginians were on their feet (three thousand were dead; the rest wounded or captured) and they turned and fired when they could, but mostly now they just ran, and the federals loosed one crushing blast after another into their fleeing ranks (running now, torn and defeated: where was the dry old valor? who remembered the paradeground order with which they had advanced? who thought of history and the lessons learned from history? was there anything in the world except bullets and explosions and death and pain and heat and dust and smoke and noise, the allencompassing monster roar of war?) and the federals jumped and cheered and clapped; the federals embraced each other and the guns boomed and the sun flicked through the swirling dust and the Virginians withdrew, leaving behind blood and pain and terror and death (accomplishing the act of duty, then yielding to defeat); the Virginians, those two thousand remaining from fifteen thousand, were scattered across the field, a man here, two men there, three or four someplace else, a riderless horse, and they fled through the explosions and the smoke and the federal fire; they returned to their lines; they had been defeated; the great gamble had not worked, and there are those who report Robert E. Lee wept, saying: "It's all my fault; it's all my fault," yet that day—and all days—the men cheered him: even from within the confines of agony. ♣

SGT LEON MARSHALL STRONG blinked and watched his victim fall.

There. First one today. Good.

He smiled.

He was lying on his stomach behind a fallen tree at the edge of a woods. Cpl Ferris and the rest of the squad were stretched out to his right for about thirty yards. There were only nine men on this patrol altogether.

He reloaded his rifle. There was a crackling sound in the weeds near him. Cpl Ferris crawled to him.

Cpl Ferris slapped Strong across the face.

Strong put his hands over his face and whimpered.

Ferris grabbed him by the collar. "You know what you did?"

"Uh . . . ?"

"Stop that goddam bawling."

Strong took his hands away from his face. "I just. He. Well, he was . . ."

"Attacking us? One man?"

"One man?"

"You see any others?" Ferris wanted to know.

Strong looked out across the field. He didn't see a soul. The field shimmered in the sunlight. The dead man was a gray lump.

"Well? You see any others?"

"No . . ."

"You know what you did?"

"What?"

"You fight one day," Ferris said thinly. "You fight one day and you think you know everything. Well I'll tell you something. I don't know who that man was you shot, but I bet he wasn't no reb. No reb in his right mind would of come running across that field like that. You. You know what I expect you did? I expect you shot some farmer. That's all. Just a goddam farmer. Maybe he was coming to tell us something . . ."

"Ah—"

"You keep still. There's something else I want to tell you. We're supposed to be scouts. You know what a scout is? He goes out and he finds out things. And he tries to keep out of sight. Capt Magill he got orders to take a look down here to see if maybe the rebs'll try to flank us. So he sends us out. I spelled all this out for you

before. I got to do it again. All right. I got to do it again. It don't
seem like you learn so quick . . ."

Strong clenched his teeth. His breath whistled out between
them. He kept blinking.

"Was you listening to me back there at the bivouac?" Ferris
went on. "The thing I kept saying was keep quiet; we don't want
to attract nobody's attention. So what do you do? You fire at the
first goddam man you see."

"He was in gray," Strong said.

"Looked like a coat to me. You want to find out for sure?"

"I—"

"You scared?"

Strong rubbed the heel of his right hand along the stock of his
rifle. He hated Ferris very much. "Was I scared yesterday?'

"Maybe you didn't know what you was."

"I fought just like everybody else."

"One day," Ferris said, "and you know everything."

Strong stood up. He sucked in his small prissy lips. His belly
hung down over his belt. He was breathing thickly. He nodded.
"All right. I'll go look. I did it. I'll go look."

"No."

"Why not? That's what you want isn't it?"

Ferris stood up too. Now he towered over Strong. "You go out
there and the rebs see you, that'd be all we'd need."

Strong lifted his rifle and pointed it at Ferris' belly. "You say
I don't know anything. I know that. But after yesterday not you
and not one man on this earth is going to tell me I'm scared."

Ferris took a step back. He grinned. "You trying to scare me?"

Strong shook his head no. His small tongue darted out over his
lips. "No. Not me. I don't scare you. I'm not trying to. But I'm
going to go out there and look. Maybe I made a mistake. And if
you try to stop me I'll kill you. I like killing. What did you call

me? A fat clerk? All right. Certainly. I was. I still am. But now I like to kill. I don't care." He nodded toward the north. "Listen. That's where they're dying. I wish I were there. But I'm here and I guess there's not much I can do about it. I saw someone I thought was a rebel. I killed him. Now you tell me I'm dumb. I thought the purpose of being here was to kill people. Yesterday it was fine, fine Strong, you're doing fine, keep killing away like that and you're a good soldier. That was yesterday. Today I'm dumb. Well to hell with you, Ferris. I'd kill you now just as soon as I'd look at you. I'm going out there and look and you aren't going to stop me."

Strong backed away from Ferris. Several other men stood up. Ferris motioned to them to stay where they were.

"Strong," Ferris said.

"No," Strong said. His voice was loud. He felt very calm.

"You ain't going to do no good," one of the men said.

"What do you expect from a fatass clerk?" Strong said, grinning. He backed out into the field, then turned and walked toward where the dead man lay. Great booming sounds came from the north. He saw smoke and huge rising pillars of dust and he smelled them too. (Not right. Know that. Then why? Think about it for the love of God. You didn't have the stomach for anything and now the more the better. How does that happen? Thirteen and thirtyfour is fortyseven times six is fortytwo carry the four is twentyfour carry the four up and add and fortyseven times six is twohundred and eightytwo. You like it. You like to kill them. Where has this been all your life? and now ah Jesus is it time for me to die? Have I fallen somehow? What did I do? Why think at all? Why try?) He wiped the sweat off his face. (I had no idea I was such a good shot. This is quite a distance. You just never finish knowing things I guess. Hum. Ha.) He glanced toward where the noise was coming from. The earth trembled just a bit.

He came to the dead man and bent down. He opened the dead man's coat. There was the blue uniform.

Part of the top of the dead man's head was gone. It wasn't a man; it was only a boy really.

The bombardment was very loud.

Strong looked up toward the smoke. He looked around. He saw no one. It is really quite loud, he said to himself, and yet here I am in the middle of this field and I see no one, nothing, only this.

Oh Ferris won't you be glad . . .

Blood ran down across the lower part of the dead boy's face. His mouth was opened wide and turned up in a smile. His left eye had been gouged out by the bullet but his right eye was open. His uniform had cavalry insignia, Strong noticed.

He straightened and turned to where Ferris and the others were. "All right Ferris!" he shouted. "You know everything!" He waved his arms and jumped up and down. "You happy? Aren't you glad to know? Hurrah for Ferris! He knows everything!"

Ferris appeared from behind a tree and began walking toward Strong.

"Hurrah for Ferris!" Strong yelled. "Oh there never has been a man like Ferris! All God's children make mistakes except Ferris!"

Ferris walked slowly. He kept looking around. The sun was very hot.

Strong began to laugh. He bent over the dead boy and closed the dead boy's one eye. "I'm responsible for you," he said. "Yes sir. You're mine now. You died for your country but you're mine now. Oh yes sir. I took you. I certainly did." Now he was crooning, chanting over the dead boy. He grabbed the dead boy under the arms and began dragging him toward Ferris. He dragged the dead boy through high weeds; these weeds crackled and snapped. "God," he said, weeping now, his head close to the dead boy's, his tears dropping on the dead boy's face, "I didn't know . . . I oh well you see I thought you were something you weren't now isn't that funny yes ha ha? I mean well I am new at this and I thought the thing you were supposed to do was kill a man when you saw him coming at you and ahh, Jesus, ahh I am new at this and ahh, did it take long? I mean: what did you feel?" and his voice was soft and confidential and then Ferris came up to him.

"Hold on," Ferris said.

Strong looked up at Ferris. "He's mine. I killed him didn't I?"

"Now you—" Ferris began. He was interrupted by a company of Confederates that came screaming down a hill to the west. He was shot through the chest. "Ehhh," he said, falling dead. Strong turned and was shot through the mouth. The rebels came whooping. Strong fell across the dead boy in the embrace of the act of love.

♣   "It's all my fault; it's all my fault," the weeping Lee said. He ordered no more attacks.   ♣

PVT RUFUS PATTERSON blinked and watched his victim fall and ran forward yelling with the others because these were the first Yanks they'd seen all day and there was a big fight there to the north and everybody kind of had felt left out.

Rufus ran through high weeds. The Yanks were firing from a woods yonder. He was panting. He stopped to reload, then ran on. There weren't many Yanks in the woods. Rufus' company stormed over them. They raised their arms and threw down their rifles. There were only seven of them. They were herded out into a field —that field where Rufus had killed himself a Yank.

Rufus prodded a thin Yank's behind with his bayonet. "Not so hard reb," the Yank complained.

"Come on," Rufus said, jabbing.

"Eeee," the Yank said. He put his hands over his buttocks.

The prisoners were lined up in a column near where three dead

Yanks lay. Capt Hawk came riding up. "That all? Just seven?" he asked a sergeant.

"Yep," the sergeant said. "Scouts."

Capt Hawk nodded and dismounted. He walked to the prisoner whom Rufus had jabbed in the behind. "Outfit?"

"Thirtythird Ohio," the prisoner said.

"What corps?"

"Third."

"Scouts?"

"Yep."

"Any others around?"

The prisoner shrugged. "Them generals they don't tell me."

"Um hum," Capt Hawk said. "Sergeant!"

The sergeant was a heavy fellow named Odlum. "Yessir?"

"Remember yesterday?"

"Sir?"

"You was standin there."

"Standin where sir?" Sgt Odlum wanted to know. He looked uncomfortable.

"When Manwell died. You remember what I said?"

Sgt Odlum scratched his head. "Uh. Well. No sir. I guess maybe I disremember."

Capt Hawk walked to where the three dead men lay. He prodded one of them, a fat sergeant (the one Rufus had killed), with the toe of a boot. "We're goin to bury these men," he said.

Rufus wanted to fall down and weep.

Capt Hawk stared at the dead men. "Hey now," he said. He bent down and pushed the fat sergeant's corpse aside. It had been draped over another man. "Well God damn me," Capt Hawk said.

The men crowded around.

This dead man was the feller they had seen back there on the road. Rufus remembered the gray coat.

Wynn (who had tried to take the coat away from this feller) elbowed past Rufus. "A spy," Wynn said.

One of the prisoners began to snicker.

Wynn turned on him. "What's so funny?"

The prisoner shook with laughter. "That shows what you know . . ."

"How's that?"

"That fat feller you just pushed off. *He* was the one who shot your goddam spy."

"What?" Capt Hawk said.

"That's right," the prisoner said. "Saw him coming across this field. Shot him just as nice as you please."

"That was the shot we heard," Rufus said.

Capt Hawk nodded.

"Well, I guess I get me my coat now," Wynn said. He bent over the corpse.

Rufus ran to him, grabbed him, knocked him down. "You leave that coat be!" he screamed.

Wynn shook his head woozily. He looked up at Rufus. "What you got against me boy?"

The laughing prisoner wiped his mouth with the back of a hand. "I guess that feller's a real tiger . . ."

"You keep still," Capt Hawk said.

"He sure does like to be mean. He kept jabbing me in the butt. And me a nice peaceful prisoner."

"I won't tell you again," Capt Hawk said to the prisoner. He walked to Rufus. "Patterson, you get back there with that prisoner. You *stay* there."

Wynn stood up. "Captain," he said, "this Patterson he got it in for me. I'd like to settle up with him right now." He moved toward Rufus.

"No," Capt Hawk said.

"Cap—"

"I said no. You fight the Yanks. You don't fight Patterson."

Rufus returned to the prisoner. Quickly the prisoner put his hands over his buttocks again.

Wynn glared at Rufus.

Sgt Odlum changed the subject. "You say you want to bury these men?" he asked the captain.

Capt Hawk nodded. "Have the prisoners do it. Detail Wynn an Patterson to stand guard."

"Wynn an Patterson?"

"You deaf?"

"No sir," Sgt Odlum said uncomfortably.

Capt Hawk walked to the prisoners. "You fellers want to bury them?"

"What choice we got?" one said.

"I'm leavin it up to you."

"We'll do it," said the prisoner who was holding his buttocks.

Capt Hawk nodded. He went to his horse and mounted it.

Wynn kicked at the dirt. "Goddam," he said.

Capt Hawk reined around. "What you say?"

"Nothin."

"You don't make trouble Wynn. I mean that now."

Wynn spread his arms. "What they goin to dig with?"

"We'll let them use bayonets," Rufus said.

Wynn turned on him. "Who asked you?"

A prisoner coughed back laughter.

"You got a gun," Capt Hawk said to Wynn. "Have them take turns with a bayonet. One of you watch the man with the bayonet. Other feller can watch the others. How long you been in the army?"

"What?"

"Say sir."

"What sir?"

"How long you been in the army?"

"Long as you."

"Then act like you was," Capt Hawk said. "Fall in Sons of the South!" he shouted to the others. The men gathered in ranks. Rufus kept his rifle trained on the prisoners. "We're goin back where we was posted," Capt Hawk said to Rufus. "You bring them back when you're done."

"Yes sir," Rufus said.

The men marched back toward where they had come from. Some of them glanced at the dead men as they went past. There was much dust and heat. Rufus and Wynn supervised the digging of a deep grave. One prisoner at a time used a bayonet. Some of the others used their boots. It took nearly two hours to dig a grave deep enough for three. Rufus and Wynn said nothing to each other. The ground was soft. Occasionally a prisoner would stop digging and watch Rufus and Wynn. Rufus knew the prisoners were waiting for a fight. Wynn glared at Rufus and spat in his direction several times. The three dead men went thlud into the grave. The prisoners used their hands to push dirt back into the grave. Nobody said anything. Rufus and Wynn gathered the prisoners into a column of twos and marched them to where the company was posted. Late that afternoon a courier came with a message for Capt Hawk. He read it and frowned. He ordered the company north. The men were tired. Feet flapped listlessly in the dust. Many men watched Rufus and Wynn. The prisoners marched along with them. Cum gum cum gum went the troops and the prisoners and after a time they passed a long column of wagons filled with screaming wounded men and Rufus was glad those three Yanks had been buried and that night Rufus and Wynn stood in front of a campfire and fought and after a long and exhausting bloody go at it Rufus finally beat Wynn and then

Rufus, bruised and cut and feeling many pains, lay down and said to himself: You kill them because you got to but you got to keep in your mind that they're men and that even if you *got* to kill a man that don't make him something you should leave *out* somewhere. I ain't thought of Elizabeth for two days. Ben Farrell neither. When this is over I ain't goin back to no drygoods store. I'm sick of all this. Elizabeth, you go on an do what you want. Me, I got trouble enough just bein a man. If they kill me, I hope by God somebody puts me in the ground an just don't leave me out somewhere.

♣ The next day, the Fourth of July, with evening and the first weak blowing little coolnesses, the Army of Northern Virginia began its withdrawal. The news spread quickly through the Union side of the field and there was some joy but mostly there was a kind of tired quiet acceptance, certainly not unhappy but then again not full of the wildest joy. The men of the Army of the Potomac had repulsed all Confederate attacks and had inflicted great losses, but they also had sustained great losses and as a result they were awful tired. Cum gum cum gum went Lee's army, back through Gettysburg, back to the west and eventually south again. Lee had failed to break the fish hook and with the disaster of Pickett's advance—well, that disaster had meant defeat. Any further attempts to break the fish hook would have meant ruin. Lee, weeping and taking the blame, all the blame, knew this and ordered the withdrawal. His men, his thin gray wiry yipping men, marched away silently, in grim heaviness, and most of these men were hungry and many of them were shoeless and of course they were tired; wounded men stumbled, hobbling painfully; horses snorted and heaved and sweated pulling cannon through the hills, and there was no singing now, no cheering, none of the high EEEEEYAAAAAHHOOO-ing; these men had lost; they knew it. They had not been wiped out, but they had lost and

Lee's gamble had been crushed there in the dust with Pickett's Virginians and the Confederacy would ebb from now on and perhaps some of these retreating men realized this. They moved away from Gettysburg (J. E. B. Stuart's cavalry, which had arrived yesterday, too late to be of any great tactical advantage, although it had fought well at Culp's Hill, guarded the rear—but the federals did not pursue); they moved away from Willoughby's Run and the railroad cut and Seminary Ridge and Cemetery Ridge and the Peach Orchard and the wheat field and Round Top and Little Round Top and the house where Jennie Wade had been killed; they abandoned their dead comrades who were bloating blackly and splitting open from their own sweet corrupted gases; they abandoned many wounded men who could not be moved; these wounded men screamed into the night and in some cases they were found and cared for by federal doctors but in many other cases they died, not easily. Meade, whose army was exhausted and badly bruised, did not pursue—despite strong pleadings from Lincoln. No, Meade wired Lincoln, the Confederates may be in bad shape but so are we. We have repulsed them but we are weary. So Meade permitted the Southerners to escape. What good general would not give his men a chance to catch their breath? Where is the general who will send them off in a wild pursuit after they have expended all their energy in a gallant and victorious action against a powerful enemy? Is it not better to permit your foe to fight again some other day than to jeopardize your own gains in the hope of wiping him out? George Gordon Meade said yes. He had led the Army of the Potomac to a decisive victory. He then considered all aspects of the situation and decided not to chase the enemy. He stuck to this decision. The Army of the Potomac had won no battles prior to this day and this victory had been achieved at a fearful cost. Was there any man who knew this better than Meade? And so he permitted his men to rest. The crabby old commander (not old at all; he was born in 1815 and thus was only fortyeight when the battle was fought, but considered old for his age because of his cautious attitudes), this illtempered George Gordon Meade, therefore ordered his troops to maintain their present positions. And went to bed knowing the Confederates would escape, knowing he would be roundly criticized—and also knowing his army had defeated the Army of Northern Virginia for the first time in its history. This gave him the courage to beat back the critics. Which he did. His name is an honored name. So the Confederates retreated and their feet went cum gum cum gum in an endless listless shuffle and the corpses split blackly and excreted the sweet corrupt gases and raised silent rigid arms to the night sky and the Confederates' wagons bounced and rolled and swayed and farmers stood in barnyards and silently watched them pass and the Southern officers rode with their backs perhaps not as straight as before and wounded men groaned as they hobbled along or bounced in litters and there was no music and many flags were dirty and many were streaked with a thinness of blood and many were lost and many had been captured and as the Confederates pulled away from the field there was a great rainstorm and there was a curious silence and the Union men looked out from their earthworks and smelled the deep incomparable smell of corpsebloat and medical men moved about searching for wounded and the medical men kept throwing up not through horror so much as through reflex. (There can be only so much horror. Then it ceases to have any meaning and you vomit because of physical, not horrified, lack of control over your digestive apparatus.) Here is the ear and the foot and the leg and the headless man and the gut and the armless and legless men and the heartless man and the man with nothing left except his torso and the man who is dead and yet does not seem to be dead because the observer can see no wound; here is the man who seems to be sleeping (a deep bayonet slash runs from his navel to his neck, yet his head is cradled in his arms in the manner of one who is taking a quick nap); here is the grinning man; here is the agonized man whose hands are rigid over his stomach, whose eyes are open in the final horrified blindness, with the pupils rolled up; here is the bloated man who died yesterday, whose skin is black, whose stink makes it immaterial whether or not you have a stomach for that sort of thing because after enough of it you will vomit as often as other men spit; here is a disemboweled horse and an overturned caisson and a pile of abandoned knapsacks and a pot halffilled with coffee that is cold; here is a stack of rifles belonging to God knows whom; here are craters and bayonets and torn flags and even by God several bugles and drums; here is a forage cap and a pair of trousers and a piece of paper with the cryptic phrase "The best thing you" written across it in a thin fastidious scroll; here is moonlight and bugs and peeping furry creatures and a constant buzz of huge rapacious flies glutting themselves on the sweet corruption. Here, then, are all the leavings, the compounded obscenities, the results of the dry old valor, the testaments to the act of duty. The night of July 4—when one side had won and one side had lost. Which was which? The victors were an exhausted raggletaggle mass. So were the defeated. Victorious dead men popped their gases; defeated dead men popped their gases. Rain fell on both armies. Was there any difference? The cynic trumpets no; he cites the absurdity of the act of duty; he cites the stinking absurdity of valor; he cites Pickett's Virginians and their great foolish courage, their idiotic parade-ground insistence on faith in an idea. Who can deny the cynic's validity? Who can deny that not even the Virginians thought of faith when they were being whacked to pieces? No one can. But still there must be something. There must be. That night the Confederates slept along the roads that led from Gettysburg and the federals slept on Cemetery Ridge and horses slept and mules slept and the great wagons were immobile against the face of the earth and the enormous cannons pointed silently and Gen Lee slept and Gen Meade slept and the corpses stank and the rain fell and tomorrow the sun would roll from Heaven's lap and bounce down across the chinks and valleys and round warm places of the Commonwealth of Pennsylvania and the burial details (holding handkerchiefs and rags over their faces) would get to work and nothing ever would be the same again. ♣

LEORA BAGLEY and her mother and her brother Johnny stood for hours on the front porch and watched the retreating Confederates pass. The dead man in the road had been pushed into a ditch so as not to impede the Confederates. The wind blew north and thus the Bagleys did not smell him.

The Bagleys stood silently. Leora felt awful good, but she just didn't feel like making any noise. She watched the rebels, their faces; she heard their slow steps, their groans and screams and mumblings; she watched horses strain in front of wagons and artillery pieces. She felt good, but she felt no loud joy. She thought of how these men had been yelling so only three days ago. Now there were no yells, only the slow surly composite sound of the retreat.

Otis Wamsley's military prognostications had been correct. There, out there on the road, was the proof.

They watched the retreat until darkness finally made it impossible for them to see anything. They went inside, back through the house to the kitchen. Outside, rain was beginning to fall.

"Well," Mamma said, sitting down heavily.

Leora took an apple from the sideboard. "Mumf," she said.

"Don't talk with your mouth full."

Leora swallowed. "Daddy'll be home soon I guess."

Mamma smiled and nodded.

Johnny took an apple too. "You think that feller'll come back?" he asked Leora.

"Yes," she said.

"He has your keepsakes," Mamma said, smiling.

"Don't make fun."

"He won't come back," Mamma said. "He's a soldier."

Leora stared at her but didn't say anything. Yesterday she would have said something. She would have been angry.

This time she took a big bite from her apple.

Later that night the rain and the wind rattled the windowpanes. A Union officer knocked at the back door and asked Mamma if she would permit the house to be used for the care of wounded men. Mamma said yes, gladly. The wounded men screamed and groaned and made wet sounds all night. Leora helped the doctors. She was calm and worked hard. The work made her not so empty. She wanted no one to know.

The next day her father returned. She told him about Wheatfield. He smiled and said he was looking forward to meeting the young man.

Date Due

MAY 2 0 '61			
MAY 2 0 '61			
APR 1 7 '69			
N 1			
OCT 2 7 70			
MAY 1 0 '89			
DE 20 '93			
DEC 1 6 02			
⑬	PRINTED	IN U. S. A.